U0004168

羅密歐與茱麗葉

Romeo and Juliet

中英雙語典藏版

威廉‧莎士比亞、蘭姆姊弟——著、改寫

張佩雯——譯 楊宛靜——繪

晨星出版

導讀

一起來讀莎士比亞

東海大學外文系副教授 蔡奇璋

「玫瑰就算不叫玫瑰，聞起來還是一樣芳香。」
「眞愛之途，永不平坦。」
「世界是個大舞台，所有的男男女女都是舞台上的演員。」
「愛情是盲目的……」

　　沒錯，這些我們在成長過程中讀到或聽過的名言，都是英國十六世紀戲劇大師威廉・莎士比亞所創造出來的。這位身世至今成謎的劇作家，在他五十二年的人生裡，留下了三十八部備受稱頌的劇本，以及多首膾炙人口的十四行詩；這些作品隨著英文逐漸成爲通用國際語言的潮流，慢慢地浸潤了全球各地讀者的心思，成了世人耳熟能詳的經典：不論是《哈姆雷特》、《羅密歐與茱麗葉》、《仲夏夜之夢》中跌宕起伏的劇情，還是諸如「我該將你比爲盛夏之日嗎」這般典麗優雅的詩句，都能一一乘著情感的翅膀，飛越國族與文化的藩籬，翩降於我們的腦裡、心裡棲息。

　　莎士比亞崇高地位的形塑過程，本身就是一則耐人尋味的傳奇。儘管當今有越來越多各界人士，對於莎翁究竟是何方神聖、其來頭之虛實眞假大大起疑，但此君做爲西洋文壇一方之霸的銳氣，卻絲毫不受其攖；舉凡歌德、席勒、雨果等名家，談起莎士比亞的文學成就來，個個都是讚賞有加。而在眾多如雷貫耳的美譽裡，約與莎翁同期的詩人兼戲劇家班・姜森 (Ben Jonson)，於其詩作《詠憶我所摯愛的文豪威廉・莎士比亞及其留予我輩之物》（*To the Memory of My Beloved Master William Shakespeare and What He Hath Left Us*）中，所寫下的歌頌詩行，最是令人印象深刻：

您是一座不朽的紀念塔，
只要您的著作流傳於世，
而我等有閱讀與讚美的才能，
您的精神將會永遠留存。

　　雖說文人相輕，但姜森在這首詩裡，絲毫不掩他個人對莎翁的拜羨，直接認定他是個不限於某一特定時代，而是人類千秋萬世皆可翹首仰望的巨匠；對莎翁的書寫功力，可說推崇備至。

　　儘管當莎士比亞埋頭書寫這些劇本時，其首要目標並非是要將之付印來賺取版稅，而是希望可以創作出讓演員在舞台上發光發熱、感動觀眾的好戲，但是因為他的文字功力實在了得，行筆之間充滿奇思妙想，且內蘊及意象又格外精闢，所以單從書面閱讀本身，便能汲獲大量的靈感與樂趣。有鑑於此，後世有些作家，便針對不同年齡層讀者的需求，著手將莎士比亞的劇本改寫成故事集；取其精華，捨其艱澀，期望能把莎翁透過文字所留給我們的智慧，介紹給不熟悉戲劇念白格式的群眾認識。其中，英式散文作家蘭姆姊弟專為年輕人而作的《莎士比亞故事集》，普遍被視為是這類翻創集冊裡的翹楚。

　　瑪莉 · 蘭姆和查爾斯 · 蘭姆二人，都有豐富的書寫經驗；他們藉由自身洗鍊的文筆，將一部又一部莎翁費心編製的劇本，翻轉成敘事流暢、清晰易懂的故事。有了姊弟倆化繁為簡、卻又保有莎翁原典那份慧點質地的再創，讀者既不必買票進劇場，更無需擔憂文學造詣欠佳，就能心無罣礙地領略《羅密歐與茱麗葉》、《仲夏夜之夢》等莎士比亞悲劇和喜劇的精髓，從中感受愛情的傷痛與愉悅，親情的羈絆與救贖，讓自己得以推開戲劇藝術殿堂的大門，一睹舞台人生和人生舞台相互鑑照而出的鏡像暨實像；而這也正是晨星出版社推出這本故事集的意義之所在。

作家生平解析

威廉·莎士比亞
(William Shakespeare)

　　威廉·莎士比亞為英國著名詩人、戲劇家。一五六四年四月出生於沃里克郡的史特拉福鎮。父親約翰·莎士比亞經營皮革製造及羊毛生意，一五六五年任鎮民政官，一五六八年被選為鎮長。

　　莎士比亞童年在史特拉福的學校學習古典文學及拉丁語，四歲開始就接觸戲劇。戲劇在十六世紀是大眾娛樂，史特拉福鎮經常有劇團來巡迴演出，莎士比亞常有機會觀賞戲劇，而且經常學著劇中的人物和情節演起戲來，這對於他日後在戲劇上的發展有重大的啟蒙作用。但不幸的是，父親經商失利，莎士比亞十四歲就離開學校，跟著父親學做皮革生意。十八歲時和比他年長八歲的安·哈瑟維結婚，不到二十一歲，已有了三個孩子。

　　莎士比亞在一五八六年左右前往倫敦發展，先在劇院門前替貴族顧客看馬，後逐漸成為劇院的雜役、演員、劇作家、股東。一五九四年莎士比亞加入「宮務大臣劇團」（Lord Chamberlain's Men），一五九七年在史特拉福購置了房產，一五九九年成為環球劇場擁有十分之一股份的股東，是當時最活躍的劇壇人物。一六一○年莎士比亞賣出了他的股份，返回故鄉，逐漸退出戲劇活動。一六一六年四月二十三日去世，享年五十二歲，葬於史特拉福的聖三一教堂。

　　莎士比亞是伊麗莎白時代最偉大的劇作家，他共寫了三十八部戲劇，大致可分為歷史劇、喜劇和悲劇三種，另外他還寫了兩首長詩、

一百五十四首十四行體詩。一般來說，莎士比亞的戲劇創作可分為三個時期：

早期（一五九〇～一六〇〇年）：以寫作歷史劇、喜劇為主。這時期所寫的歷史劇和喜劇都表現出明朗、樂觀的風格。歷史劇如《理查三世》、《亨利三世》等，譴責封建暴君，歌頌開明君主，表現了人文主義的反封建暴政和封建割據的開明政治理想。喜劇如《仲夏夜之夢》、《第十二夜》、《皆大歡喜》等，描寫溫柔美麗、堅毅勇敢的婦女，衝破重重封建阻攔，終於獲得愛情勝利，表現了歌頌自由愛情和反封建禁慾束縛的社會主張。就連這時期所寫的悲劇《羅密歐與茱麗葉》，也同樣具有不少明朗樂觀的因素。

中期（一六〇一～一六〇七年）：以寫作悲劇為主。莎士比亞所寫的悲劇重在揭露批判社會的種種罪惡和黑暗，代表作有《奧賽羅》、《李爾王》、《馬克白》、《哈姆雷特》等。這時期所寫的喜劇《終成眷屬》、《一報還一報》等也同樣具有悲劇色彩。

晚期（一六〇八～一六一二年）：莎士比亞深感人文主義理想的破滅，乃退居故鄉寫浪漫主義傳奇劇，創作風格也隨之表現為浪漫空幻，代表作有《辛白林》、《冬天的故事》、《暴風雨》等，這些作品多寫失散、團聚、誣陷、昭雪。儘管莎士比亞仍然堅持人文主義理想，對黑暗現實有所揭露，但矛盾的解決主要還是靠魔法、機緣巧合和偶然事件，並以宣揚寬恕、容忍、妥協、和解告終。

莎士比亞最偉大的天才表現是在他的悲劇上，他跟古希臘三大悲劇家艾思奇利斯（Aeschylus）、沙孚克里斯（Sophocles）、尤里匹蒂斯（Euripides）合稱為戲劇史上四大悲劇家。他的戲劇至今還在世界各地演出，馬克思稱他是「最偉大的戲劇天才」。

瑪麗·蘭姆
(Mary Lamb)

　　瑪麗·蘭姆爲英國作家，一七六四年生，最著名的作品是與弟弟查爾斯·蘭姆合寫的《莎士比亞故事集》（Tales from Shakespeare）。一生爲精神疾病所苦，三十一歲時不幸在發病當下誤殺母親，之後由弟弟查爾斯照顧，脫離終生被囚禁在精神病院的命運。

　　瑪麗喜愛閱讀，近乎癡迷，並且經常與弟弟二人和一群藝術家及作家來往，因此結交不少同好。一八○六年，其好友威廉·戈德溫（William Godwin）和他的第二任妻子瑪莉·戈德溫（Mary Godwin）一同邀請瑪麗改寫莎士比亞的戲劇作品，希望能將莎劇改寫成散文，以供孩童閱讀。於是瑪麗邀請弟弟合著《莎士比亞故事集》，由姊姊負責喜劇，弟弟負責悲劇的部分，他們盡可能保留莎士比亞的語言，並將莎劇化繁爲簡，使其好讀卻不失神髓，改編作品因此大受好評，風靡一時。

　　然而瑪麗晚年的精神狀態每況愈下，最終不得不住進精神病院，死於一八四七年。

查爾斯·蘭姆
(Charles Lamb)

　　查爾斯·蘭姆為英國詩人、小說家、評論家，一七七五年生，筆名伊利亞，以《莎士比亞故事集》和《伊利亞隨筆集》聞名。

　　一七七五年生於倫敦，七歲時入基督教公共學校就讀，與詩人柯爾律治成為終身朋友，一七八九年因家計窘迫中途退學。一七九二年在東印度公司當職員，直到一八二五年退休。查爾斯自家中發生憾事後，一肩扛下照顧姊姊的責任，並且斷絕與愛侶安·西蒙結婚的念頭，終生未娶。

　　其在工作之餘不忘寫作，一七九八年始出版詩劇與小說，但未能引起文壇的注目，直到一八○二年開始與姊姊合作，把莎士比亞戲劇改寫成少年讀物後聲名鵲起。一八二三年出版的個人著作《伊利亞隨筆集》則讓查爾斯達成自身文學方面的最高成就，並於一八三三年出版續集《伊利亞後期隨筆集》。

　　查爾斯退休後，由於姊姊病情惡化，兩人遂移居愛德蒙吞。他離開志同道合的友人，鬱鬱寡歡，日益藉酒澆愁，一八三四年因跌傷引起併發症逝世。

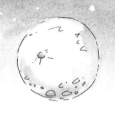

目錄

CONTENTS

I.

羅密歐與茱麗葉

　　富有的卡帕萊特家族和蒙特鳩家族是維洛那地區的兩個大家族。這兩個家族昔日曾發生過一場激烈的爭執因而產生嫌隙，雙方仇恨越結越深，甚至達到攸關性命的程度，就連遠親、擁護者和家僕都受到牽連：只要蒙特鳩家的僕人偶然碰到卡帕萊特家的僕人，或是卡帕萊特家的人恰巧遇到蒙特鳩家的人，他們就會互相叫囂，有時候還會鬧出見血的事情。這種碰面就吵架的情形時常發生，擾亂了維洛那原本快樂清靜的街巷。

　　有一晚，老卡帕萊特大人舉辦了一場盛大的晚宴，邀請了許多美麗的夫人和貴族。維洛那地區所有受人仰慕的仕女都到場參與盛會，這場宴會歡迎所有人蒞臨，除了蒙特鳩家的人。在這場宴會上，老蒙特鳩大人的兒子羅密歐愛慕的羅瑟琳也在場：雖然蒙特鳩家族的人於這場晚宴現身將會非常危險，但羅密歐的朋友班弗里還是慫恿這位年輕的公子戴上面具參加，讓他把羅瑟琳和維洛那出色的美女們比較一番，這樣一來，羅密歐就會明白他心目中的天

鵝只不過是一隻烏鴉罷了。

　　羅密歐不怎麼相信班弗里的話，但為了深愛的羅瑟琳，他還是去了。羅密歐是一個真摯多情的人，他為愛目不交睫，避開人群獨處，終日思念著羅瑟琳；可是羅瑟琳卻藐視羅密歐，從來不表示一丁點兒的禮貌或感情來回報他的愛。班弗里想讓他的朋友見識一下不同的女人和伴侶，好治療他的癡情。於是年輕的羅密歐、班弗里和他們的朋友莫枯修就戴著面具參加了卡帕萊特家的宴會。

　　老卡帕萊特大人上前迎接這群年輕人，告訴他們：這些仕女腳上沒有長雞眼，並且都想與他們共舞。這個老人心情相當輕鬆愉快，他說自己年輕的時候也曾戴著面具在姑娘的耳邊說情話呢！之後他們便在舞會上跳起舞來。

　　忽然間，羅密歐的目光被一位隨著音樂輕舞的美麗姑娘吸引。在那一刻，他覺得燈火似乎因她更加璀璨動人了，她的美貌就像黑人身上穿戴的貴重寶石，在夜晚時顯得特別光彩奪目。這樣的美實在是太珍貴了，簡直捨不得一碰！她身旁的女孩們完全比不上她的美貌和姿態，她就像一隻雪白的鴿子跟烏鴉結群一樣（他這樣說著）。羅密歐讚美她的時候，被一旁卡帕萊特大人的侄子提拔特聽見了，他認出羅密歐的聲音。提拔特脾氣暴躁且易怒，他可不能容忍蒙特鳩家的人戴著面具混進來，鄙視和嘲弄他們這個隆重的場合（他是這樣說的）。他異常憤怒，狂暴地叫囂著，想要痛毆年輕的羅密歐。但是他的伯父老卡帕萊

特大人卻不肯提拔特在這個場合傷害羅密歐，這是出於主人對賓客的尊重，而且羅密歐的言行舉止很有君子風度，全維洛那地區的人都誇讚他是位有品德、有教養的青年。提拔特當下被迫耐著性子，可他發誓有天一定要讓這個不請自來、卑劣的蒙特鳩人付出慘痛的代價。

跳完舞，羅密歐的目光仍緊追著那位姑娘不放。藉助面具的掩護，他的放肆才得以被輕易原諒。羅密歐鼓起勇氣，非常溫柔地握了一下她的手，稱呼她的手為聖壇，既然碰著它已是褻瀆，作為一個卑微的朝聖者，他想吻它一下，當作贖罪。

「好一個朝聖者。」女孩回說，「你朝拜得太殷勤、太隆重了吧！聖人有手，朝聖者可以撫觸它，但不許吻它。」

「聖人有嘴唇，朝聖者不是也有嘴唇嗎？」羅密歐說。

「是啊！」女孩說，「但是他們的嘴唇是用來祈禱的。」

「哦，那麼我親愛的聖人，」羅密歐說，「請妳聆聽我的祈禱，答應我，否則我會就此絕望。」

正當他們說著這些充滿隱喻的情話時，女孩的母親前來喚走她。在羅密歐的打聽下，得知這位令他為之傾慕的女孩原來是茱麗葉，是蒙特鳩家的大仇人卡帕萊特大人的女兒兼繼承人；羅密歐這才明白，自己已在不知不覺中將

他的心託付給他的仇人了。雖然這件事讓他非常苦惱，卻依然無法讓他放下這段愛情。片刻後，茱麗葉發現和她交談的男人是蒙特鳩家的羅密歐時也感到相當震驚，因為她對羅密歐的愛和他對她的愛同樣倉促且輕率。茱麗葉覺得這愛情來得太不可思議了，她必須去愛她的仇人，她的愛情必須寄託於他；然而考量到自己家族的話，她應該恨他。

午夜時分，羅密歐和他的同伴一起離開。可是不久他們就走散了，因為羅密歐早已把他的心留在剛才的屋子裡，所以獨自徘徊一會後，就從茱麗葉住房後面那座果園的圍牆跳了進去。他在那兒回味方才發生的愛戀，不久茱麗葉竟出現在他前方的窗臺上。她美麗的容貌就像東方初昇的朝陽那般耀眼；在羅密歐眼裡，果園上空黯淡的月光，在她這輪燦爛的旭日下顯得憔悴蒼白。茱麗葉用手托著臉頰，羅密歐恨不得自己是她手上的一隻手套，好撫摸

她光滑動人的面龐。茱麗葉誤以為此處只有她獨自一人，便深深地嘆了一口氣說：「可憐的我啊！」

羅密歐聽見她說話後為之狂喜，他以茱麗葉無法聽見的音量輕聲喃語：「啊，美麗的天使，再多說一點吧！妳出現在我視線上方，正如一位有翼天使從天而降，凡人只能昂首瞻仰。」

茱麗葉並未察覺此刻有人正偷聽她的喃喃自語，內心充斥著今晚的冒險奇遇帶來的刺激感，口中不禁呼喊著自己情人的名字（她不知道他在那裡）：「喔，羅密歐、羅密歐！你為什麼會是羅密歐呢？為了我，斷絕與你父親的關係、放棄你的姓氏吧！如果你不願意，那麼只要你發誓愛我，那一刻起，我就不再是卡帕萊特家的人了。」

羅密歐受到茱麗葉這番話的鼓舞，本想開口說話，可是他還想再聽她多說幾句。那位女孩仍舊熱烈地自言自語著（她以為是這樣），他責怪羅密歐不該叫羅密歐，不該是蒙特鳩家的人；她情願他喚

作別的名字，或者把那可恨且不屬於他的名字丟掉，他就能擁有她的一切。

聽到這樣的情話，羅密歐不禁搭聲說話，好像她剛才是直接對他說話似。他要茱麗葉稱他為「愛人」或是她喜歡的名字，如果她不喜歡羅密歐這個名字，那他從此不再是羅密歐。

茱麗葉聽到花園裡有男人說話的聲音，大為吃驚。起初她不知道是誰摸黑偷聽她的秘密。不過情人的耳朵都相當敏銳，當羅密歐再度開口，沒說幾句話她就認出他是羅密歐了。她警告他攀爬果園的圍牆進來是很危險的行為，萬一被她的家人發現，必定小命不保，因為他是蒙特鳩家的人。

「唉，」羅密歐嘆了一口氣接著說，「妳的目光比他們的二十把劍還要厲害。女孩，只要妳溫柔地望著我，我就會毅然決然地抵抗他們的恨意。如果得不到妳的愛，我寧可死在他們的仇恨之下，也不願延長這可恨的生命。」

「你是怎麼到這裡來的？」茱麗葉說，「是誰領你進來此地？」

「是愛情指引我進來的。」羅密歐答道，「我不會駕舟，可是哪怕妳遠在天外的海邊，我也會為尋妳這件珍寶冒險犯難。」

茱麗葉想到羅密歐不經意地得知她的愛意，臉上便羞得泛起一陣紅暈，不過夜色昏暗，所以羅密歐沒能看見。

她想收回方才情不自禁的那些情話，可是已經來不及了。
她想遵循大家閨秀們的慣例，以惡劣的態度跟情人保持距
離，並狠狠地拒絕求婚者；雖然她心裡很愛對方，但必須
裝作羞怯、冷淡，或者毫不在乎，這樣情人才會覺得她們
並非自己能輕易得手的人，因為越是求不得的東西，身價
就越高。可目前的情況不容許她以婉拒、拖延或是那些求
婚時經常使用的推託手腕了。因為她作夢也想不到羅密歐
竟會出現在她身旁，他已經親耳聽見她傾訴的愛意了。在
這特殊情況下，茱麗葉只好坦承他剛才聽到的都是真心
話，並且稱呼他為俊秀的蒙特鳩（愛情可以把一個刺耳的
姓變得甜蜜）。她請求他不要因為自己如此輕易地答應他
的求愛，就以為她輕佻或是不端莊，這都要怪今夜突如其
來的偶遇來得太不湊巧了（如果這是個偶遇的話），沒想
到會以這樣的方式暴露她的心思。她還說，以婦女必須遵
守的禮法來衡量，她的舉止也許不夠矜持端莊，可是比起
那些虛偽的端莊和矯柔造作的靦覥，這樣的她真實多了。

羅密歐對天發誓，他絕對不會就此認為高貴的她有一
絲一毫的不端莊，但茱麗葉馬上攔住他，求他不要發誓，
因為儘管她很喜歡羅密歐，可是她不想當天晚上就交換誓
言，因為這樣未免太倉促、太輕率，也太突兀了。

但是羅密歐還是急著要在當晚與她定情。茱麗葉說，
在他還沒提出要求前她就已經宣誓了──因為羅密歐早
已偷聽到她傾吐的情話了。不過茱麗葉還是決定要把那些

誓言收回，好重新享受許下盟誓的愉悅；因為她的感情就像海一樣無邊無際，她的愛意就像海一樣深不見底。

兩人正情話綿綿的時候，茱麗葉被她的奶媽給喚走了。天要亮了，跟她一道睡的奶媽覺得她得睡了。可是不一會兒茱麗葉又急忙跑回來對羅密歐說：如果他真心愛她、想要娶她，明天她立刻派人去見他並約定婚期，她要把自己的命運交給他、嫁給他、跟隨他到天涯海角。

他們商量著這件事的同時，奶媽不斷地喊著茱麗葉。她進去又出來，再進去，又出來，因為她捨不得羅密歐離去，就像一個小女孩捨不得放走她手裡的鳥兒一樣，她讓牠從手上跳出去，不久又用絲線把牠拉回來。羅密歐也捨不得離開她，因為在情人的耳裡，最甜蜜的樂音就是他們在深夜裡互相傾訴的甜言蜜語。可他們終須一別，於是各自祝福彼此能有一個安寧、香甜的夜晚後便離去。

他們分別的時候天已經亮了。羅密歐不願就此入眠，一心只想著他的情人和那幸福的會面。他沒有直接回家，而是繞路到附近的修道院找勞倫斯神父。這位善良的神父早已起床做禱告了，當他看到年輕的羅密歐一大清早出現，他猜想一定是愛情煩惱使他夜不能寐。羅密歐確實因為愛情整夜沒睡，可是神父猜錯他愛戀的對象了，他以為羅密歐是為了羅瑟琳才睡不著。當羅密歐告訴勞倫斯神父他愛上茱麗葉，並且請神父於婚禮當天替他們主持婚禮時，這位聖潔的神父抬起頭，舉起手，對於羅密歐的感情

忽然起了這麼大的變化感到驚訝,因為神父清楚羅密歐對羅瑟琳的愛,而且屢次埋怨羅瑟琳對他太冷漠。

於是神父說年輕人的愛只放在眼眸裡,卻不真正放在心裡。可是羅密歐卻說,神父不是經常責備他不該對不愛他的羅瑟琳那麼癡情嗎?如今,他愛茱麗葉,茱麗葉也愛著他。神父認同他部分的說詞,同時心想,也許可以藉由年輕的茱麗葉和羅密歐的婚姻,修補卡帕萊特和蒙特鳩兩家之間的嫌隙。這位善良的神父是這兩家人的朋友,時常替他們調解卻從未成功,因此沒有人比他更替這兩家人感到惋惜了。因此他一方面為了達到自己的目的,另一方面則是因為他喜歡年輕的羅密歐,所以對他的要求難以拒絕,於是答應替他們主持婚禮。

此時的羅密歐真是幸福極了,茱麗葉依約派人前去,透過那人,令她明白羅密歐的心意後,便盡速趕到勞倫斯神父修道院裡的密室,他們在那裡舉辦了一場神聖的婚禮。神父祈求上帝祝福他們的婚姻,並且藉著年輕的蒙特鳩和年輕的卡帕萊特的結合,埋去這兩家昔日的紛爭和長期的不合。

婚禮結束後,茱麗葉趕緊回家去,焦急地盼著天黑,因為羅密歐答應天一黑就會到他們定情的那個果園與她相會。這段時間真是太難熬了,就像節日前夕焦急的孩子,雖然做了新衣服,卻得等到第二天早上才能穿似的令人心急不已。

　　當天大約中午的時候，羅密歐的朋友班弗里和莫枯修在維洛那街上遇到卡帕萊特家的人。走在前頭的是脾氣暴躁的提拔特。在老卡帕萊特大人的宴會上想和羅密歐打架的，正是這個氣沖沖的提拔特。他一看到莫枯修，就粗魯地責備他不該跟蒙特鳩家的羅密歐來往。莫枯修也和提拔特一樣血氣方剛，性情暴躁，他尖刻地回覆這個指責。雖然班弗里竭力勸解，希望能平息他們的怒氣，兩個人卻還是吵起來了。

　　此時羅密歐正巧從那經過，於是凶悍的提拔特丟開莫枯修，找起羅密歐的麻煩，並且用「惡棍」這樣侮蔑的話罵羅密歐。羅密歐本想避免與提拔特起衝突，因為茱麗葉很愛他這位親戚。同時，這個年輕的蒙特鳩為人聰明溫和，從來沒有涉入家族間的爭吵，而且卡帕萊特現在是他愛妻的姓，這個姓與其說是會引起憤怒的口號，不如說是消解仇恨的靈符。所以他竭力和提拔特講理，和藹地稱他「好卡帕萊特」，雖然他是蒙特鳩家的一員，但唸著卡帕萊特這個姓氏時，讓他暗暗地有些愉悅。

　　可是提拔特恨蒙特鳩家所有人，好像他們都是地獄來的惡魔似，誰說什麼他都聽不下去，一下子就拔劍了。莫枯修不知道羅密歐想跟提拔特講和的原因，只把當前他這種容忍看作怕事、不體面的屈服，於是講了許多輕蔑的話來激怒提拔特，惹得兩人爭吵不休。最後提拔特和莫枯修交手了。羅密歐和班弗里竭力把這兩位格鬥者分開的時

候，莫枯修受到致命的一擊而倒下。莫枯修一死，羅密歐就再也忍不住了，他用提拔特罵他「惡棍」這輕蔑的話回罵提拔特。很快地他們也動手打了起來，直到提拔特死在羅密歐手中。

這是中午時分發生在維洛那市中心的可怕鬥爭。消息一傳出，馬上吸引大批群眾聚集此處，其中也少不了老卡帕萊特夫婦和老蒙特鳩夫婦。

過不久，親王也來了。親王與被提拔特殺死的莫枯修是親戚，而卡帕萊特和蒙特鳩兩家的爭吵時常擾亂他領地的安寧，於是便下令查辦違法之人並加以嚴懲。班弗里是親眼目睹這場爭執的人，親王叫他說說事情的來龍去脈。他在不連累羅密歐的情形下盡量描述了實情，還竭力替他的朋友求情。卡帕萊特夫人非常痛心提拔特遭人殺害，無論如何都要報復，要求親王嚴辦凶手，不要理會班弗里的話──說他既是羅密歐的朋友，又是蒙特鳩家的人，他的言論一定有所偏頗。因此她主張逮捕她的新女婿，雖然她還不知道他的新身份：茱麗葉的丈夫。

另一方面，蒙特鳩夫人肯求親王饒恕她的孩子，她振振有辭地爭辯說：儘管羅密歐殺了提拔特，但他不應該受罰，因為是提拔特先殺了莫枯修，是他自己犯法在先。親王並沒有被這兩個女人激動的發言所影響，他仔細調查了事實後，宣布他的判決：將羅密歐逐出維洛那。

對年輕的茱麗葉來說，這是個無比沉痛的消息。她才

剛做了幾個小時的新娘，如今親王的一道命令，等於是讓她永遠離了婚。這個消息傳到她耳裡時，最初她生羅密歐的氣，因為他殺了她親愛的堂哥，她以「俊秀的暴君」、「天使般的魔鬼」、「像烏鴉的鴿子」、「性情像豺狼的羔羊」、「花一樣的臉蛋裡藏著一顆蛇一般的心」矛盾地指謫羅密歐，她的心在愛恨之間掙扎著。可是最後愛情還是佔了上風，她先前為堂哥所流下的傷心淚，後來卻變成了快樂的淚水，因為提拔特本來會殺死她丈夫，如今羅密歐依舊安好。隨後她又悲從中來，因為羅密歐要被流放了。對她來說，羅密歐被放逐的消息比聽見提拔特的死訊還要糟糕數倍。

那場格鬥發生後，羅密歐就躲到勞倫斯神父的密室裡。他在那獲知親王的判決後，覺得放逐比死刑可怕多了。因為羅密歐認為只要出了維洛那，外頭就是個沒有茱麗葉的世界，看不見茱麗葉的話他也活不下去。有茱麗葉在的地方是天堂，除此之外全是充滿酷刑的煉獄。那位好神父本來想用哲理安慰他，可是這個瘋狂的青年什麼也聽不進去。他像瘋子一樣揪著自己的頭髮，整個人僵直地躺在地上，說他正在丈量自己墳墓的長度。

當羅密歐沮喪又憔悴失意之時，忽然他親愛的妻子派人送信來了，他的精神終於恢復了一些。神父趁機規勸他說，他剛才那樣軟弱得一點男子氣概也沒有。他已經把提拔特殺了，難道他還要殺死自己，也殺了跟他相依為命的

愛妻嗎？他說：「人若只是外表高貴，內在卻沒有堅定的勇氣，那只不過是個蠟人。」法律對他是寬容的，他原先死罪難逃，但親王只輕判他放逐；原本提拔特想殺死他，結果他殺死了提拔特；這本身就相當走運。而茱麗葉不僅好好地活著，還成為他親愛的妻子（萬萬也沒想到），在這一點上，他是無比幸福的。羅密歐聽到神父指出他受到上帝眷顧的種種事蹟後，他便不再像個乖張、不懂規矩的小姑娘了。神父要他當心，他說自暴自棄的人都沒有好下場。

等羅密歐稍微平靜了一些，神父勸他當天晚上先偷偷去跟茱麗葉告別，然後馬上就到曼多亞去，在那裡住下來，等神父找到合適的機會公布他和茱麗葉的婚事後，說不定這個喜訊能夠使兩家和解。神父相信到時一定可以懇求親王赦免他，因此，雖然現在必須忍痛分離，但之後他便可以歡天喜地回到維洛那了。羅密歐被神父賢明的勸告給說服，隨即向他告辭去看他的妻子，打算當天晚上同她共度一晚，天明前就獨自一人動身到曼多亞去。那位善良的神父答應羅密歐會時常為他捎信，讓他得以知曉家裡的情況好解相思之苦。

晚上，羅密歐就從茱麗葉對他傾吐愛意的那個果園，偷偷爬進她的閨房，跟他親愛的妻子共度一夜。那是個充滿愉悅與喜樂的一夜，可一想到兩人馬上就得分手，再回想起先前不幸的遭遇後，悲傷的情緒沖淡了他們那一夜的

歡樂和兩個人相處時的快活。不受歡迎的天明好像來得特別早。茱麗葉聽到雲雀晨起的歌聲,她還竭力說服自己那是夜晚歌唱的夜鶯呢。然而,那的確是雲雀的歌聲,而且那聲音聽起來很不和諧,非常不悅耳。同時,東方的曙光也清楚地指出,是時候讓這對情人分別了。羅密歐懷著一顆沉重的心跟他親愛的妻子分手,他答應到曼多亞後一定時時刻刻寫信給她。羅密歐從她閨房的窗戶爬下,並站在屋外抬頭看她,茱麗葉懷著滿是凶兆、悲愴的心情送走她的丈夫,在她看來,他彷彿已成墳墓裡的一具屍首。羅密歐對茱麗葉也有同樣的錯覺,不過他現在必須趕快離開,如果天亮後被人發現他仍待在維洛那城裡,就會被處以死刑。

然而,這一對命運多舛的戀人的悲劇才剛剛開始!羅密歐離開後沒幾天,老卡帕萊特大人就替茱麗葉決定了一門親事。他作夢也沒有料到女兒已結了婚,他替她挑的丈夫是巴里斯伯爵,是一位年輕英俊的高貴紳士,如果年輕的茱麗葉沒遇到羅密歐,他倒是個配得上她的情人。

茱麗葉一聽到父親在為她議婚,困惑苦惱極了。她央求說:她年紀還輕,不適宜結婚;又說最近提拔特的死讓她提不起精神來,沒法用笑臉去見未來的丈夫;而且卡帕萊特家喪事剛辦完就舉行婚筵,未免也太不成體統。她提出所有能想到的理由來反對這門親事,但沒有提出那個真正的理由:她已經結婚了。卡帕萊特大人完全不理睬她提

出的理由，他很堅決地吩咐她做好準備，因為下星期四她就得嫁給巴里斯。他既然給茱麗葉找到這樣一位年輕、有錢又高貴的丈夫，維洛那城裡眼光最高的女孩也會願意接受的一位人物，因此他把茱麗葉的拒絕當作她只是假作羞澀，他不能放任她如此阻撓自己的大好前途。

在這種走投無路的情形下，茱麗葉請教那位樂於幫助人的神父，遇到困境時，他總像她的顧問一樣。神父問她是否有足夠的決心採取一個迫不得已的辦法，她說她寧可讓人把她給活埋了，也不願在她親愛的丈夫還在世時就嫁給巴里斯。神父叫她先回去假裝很高興，並且遵照她父親的意願與巴里斯結婚。他交給她一小瓶藥，叫她第二天晚上，也就是婚禮的前夕，把它吞下去；之後的四十二小時裡，她看起來就會是僵冷、毫無生命跡象的屍體。這樣，第二天早晨新郎迎娶她的時候，就會認為她已經死了。然後，人們就會將她依照當地的習俗，臉也不蒙地放在柩車上運走，葬到家族的墓穴裡。如果她能克服人類膽怯的天性，同意這個可怕的考驗，那麼服藥的四十二小時以後她一定會醒過來（它的藥效就是如此），彷彿做了一場夢似的。在她醒過來之前，他先把這些安排告訴她丈夫，叫他夜裡趕來，把她帶到曼多亞去。對羅密歐的愛以及跟巴里斯結婚的恐懼，促使茱麗葉勇於嘗試這可怕的方法。她從神父手裡接過藥瓶，答應按照他的吩咐去做。

從修道院回來的路上，茱麗葉遇到年輕的巴里斯伯

爵，她裝成羞澀的樣子，答應嫁給他。對老卡帕萊特夫婦來說，這真是個天大的好消息。起初茱麗葉拒絕與伯爵結婚的時候，卡帕萊特大人對她很不諒解，現在她終於答應了，又開始對她百般寵愛。全家上下都為了即將舉行的婚禮奔忙著，卡帕萊特家豪擲千金籌備這場堪稱維洛那空前隆重的婚禮。

星期三晚上，茱麗葉立刻吞了那瓶藥。最初她仍有許多顧忌，她擔心神父害怕自己曾幫她和羅密歐證婚而遭受責難，給她吃的是毒藥，然而大家都知道他是個聖潔之人。她又害怕自己在羅密歐來之前清醒，而那個放滿卡帕萊特家屍骨的墳墓，還有滿身是

血、裹在屍衣裡正在腐爛的提拔特屍體會把她嚇壞。她又不禁想起以前聽過的一些鬼故事：鬼魂時常會到停放屍體的地方去。不過當她想起她對羅密歐的愛和對巴里斯的厭惡，便不顧一切把藥吞了下去，隨後就失去知覺。

年輕的巴里斯一大清早就來了，他想用音樂喚醒他的新娘子，然而房間裡呈現著可怕的景象，他看到的不是美麗動人的茱麗葉，而是茱麗葉的屍體。她的死對他是多麼大的打擊啊！卡帕萊特家陷入一片混亂，可憐的巴里斯非常悲痛，可惡的死神把他的新娘奪走了，甚至沒等他們完婚就拆散他們。老卡帕萊特夫婦的號哭更是悲痛，他們就只有這麼一個孩子，一個曾經帶給他們快樂和安慰的孩子。這兩位老人家眼看著自己的獨生女即將嫁給一位有前途、條件又好的女婿，從此地位非同小可，然而殘酷的死神卻奪走了她的生命。如今本來為喜事準備好的一切，現在得拿來改辦喪事了。婚宴變成了喪席，婚禮的頌詩變為沉痛的輓歌，輕快的樂器改成憂鬱的喪鐘；鮮花本來準備撒在新娘走過的路上，現在則拿來撒在她的屍體上。原本請來主持婚禮的神父，現在卻必須主持葬禮了。她的確被抬到教堂去，然而卻不是為了增添生者的快樂與希望，而是為了給亡者增添一個不幸之人。

勞倫斯神父已派人通知羅密歐葬禮是造假的，不必為此擔憂，他親愛的妻子只是暫時躺在墓穴裡，她希望羅密歐趕快來把她從那座陰森森的巨室裡解救出來。可是壞消

息總是傳得比好消息快，勞倫斯神父派去的人還沒到，羅密歐就在曼多亞聽到茱麗葉死去的消息了。在這之前，羅密歐本來分外地高興，因為他夢到自己死了（這真是個奇怪的夢，在夢裡死人還能想事情），他的妻子趕來看他，使勁地吻他，把生命吐進他的嘴裡，然後他又活過來了，而且成為國王。

　　就在這時候，他收到來自維洛那城的消息了，他期待會是一個應證他夢中預兆的好消息。可是他聽到的和他夢到的事情正好相反，原來死的是他的妻子茱麗葉，而且任憑他怎麼吻也吻不活了。於是他立刻備馬，決定當天晚上就去維洛那，到他妻子的墳墓裡看她。

　　人陷入絕境時，很容易產生壞念頭，他想起曼多亞有一個可憐的藥師，他最近還從他的藥房經過。那人像個乞丐，好像快餓死了，他那骯髒的架上擺著一些空盒子，使店裡顯得更加不堪，觸目所見皆證明了他的貧困。羅密歐當時看到這景象就說（也許他正擔憂多災多難的自己，最終也會落到這般絕望的下場）：「根據曼多亞的法律，賣毒藥的人要處死刑，但要是有誰需要毒藥，這個可憐蟲一定肯賣他。」現在他想起自己曾經說過的話。他找到那個藥師說明來意，他假裝猶豫了一會兒，等羅密歐把錢拿出來，現實的貧苦便使他再也無法抵抗了。他將藥賣給羅密歐，說要是吃了這藥，哪怕他有二十條命，也會就此與世長辭。

　　羅密歐帶著毒藥前往維洛那，到墓穴裡去看他親愛的妻子，他打算看了她最後一眼就服下毒藥，然後葬在她的旁邊。他半夜潛進維洛那，找到教堂的墓地，卡帕萊特家族的古墳就在正中間。他準備了火把、鏟子和鐵鉗，正準備打開墓門的時候，一個聲音打斷了他。

　　「卑鄙的蒙特鳩！」那個聲音叫住他，命令他立刻停止這種不法行為。說話的人正是年輕的巴里斯伯爵，想不到他也剛好在午夜的此時來到茱麗葉的墓上撒些鮮花，到這個本該成為他新娘的茱麗葉墳前哭泣。他不知道羅密歐和茱麗葉的關係，只知道他是蒙特鳩家的人（他的認知也沒錯），是卡帕萊特家的仇人，他猜想羅密歐在深更半夜跑來，一定是想汙辱屍體。因此，他發怒地制止他，並且說羅密歐是被維洛那判刑的罪犯，進了城就要被處以死刑，他要將他繩之以法。

　　羅密歐勸巴里斯走開，否則他的下場會和葬在那裡的提拔特一樣。他警告巴里斯不要惹火他，逼他再殺一個人，再犯一次罪。可是伯爵輕蔑地無視他的警告，把他當罪犯似的捉住他。羅密歐想掙脫，於是兩人打了起來，結果巴里斯倒下了。羅密歐藉著燈光看了看他殺死的是誰，發現是原先要迎娶茱麗葉的巴里斯（他從歸途上得知的），便一把拉起他的手，把巴里斯當成同病相憐的夥伴，說要把巴里斯葬在勝利的墳墓裡──他指的是茱麗葉的墳墓。

這時羅密歐打開了墓門，他的妻子茱麗葉就躺在那裡，她仍然是那樣動人，死神好像一點也無法改變她美麗的容貌和膚色，或者死神也愛上了她，所以這個削瘦、討厭的惡魔故意把她保存下來，在那裡守著她，因為她仍然是那樣美麗、有生氣，就像剛服用了麻醉藥睡著似的。她的身邊躺著裹了屍衣的提拔特，羅密歐向已成為屍體的提拔特道歉，並且因為茱麗葉的緣故，稱呼他一聲「堂哥」，並說他一定會替他殺了仇人（指羅密歐自己）。

羅密歐吻了他妻子的嘴唇，跟她永別。他從疲憊的身軀上卸除了沉重且不幸的負擔，一口氣把那藥師給他的毒藥吞了下去。羅密歐服的這帖藥是種致命的毒藥，跟茱麗葉服的那瓶假毒藥可不一樣，而她那瓶藥的藥效已經快退了，過不久她就會甦醒過來，抱怨羅密歐不守時，或者應該說他來得太早了。

茱麗葉甦醒的時刻即將來臨。神父聽說他派到曼多亞送信的人在路上耽擱了，一直沒有把信送到羅密歐手裡，所以他親自帶著燈籠和鏟子趕來，準備把被關在墓穴裡的茱麗葉救出來。當他趕到的時候，靈堂已經點上火把，附近還有刀劍和血跡，又看到羅密歐和巴里斯倒在地上，已經沒了氣息。

神父大驚失色。他還沒弄清楚這不幸是怎麼發生時，茱麗葉便醒了過來。她看到神父，才恍然想起自己身在何處，以及為何來到此處的緣故。她問起羅密歐，可是神父

聽到外頭有聲音，就要她趕緊離開這個死亡之地，因為種種天意使然，他們的計畫失敗了。神父聽到有人走來的聲音，便驚恐地逃離了。茱麗葉看到她忠實的情人手裡拿著杯子，猜出他已服毒自盡了。如果杯子裡還有剩餘的毒藥，她也會吞下去的。她親吻著他那殘留餘溫的嘴唇，想舔舐一些剩餘的毒藥。她聽到人聲逐漸逼近，於是拔出身上佩帶的匕首刺向自己，倒在她深愛的羅密歐身旁。

　　這時候，看守人來了。原來是巴里斯伯爵的一個侍從看見他的主人和羅密歐發生爭執，便四處找人求救，消息傳遍了維洛那城，市民在街道上胡亂喊叫，有人喊著：「巴里斯！」有人喊著：「羅密歐！」有人喊著：「茱麗葉！」，因為只聽到傳言，所以沒有人清楚事情的全貌。喧擾的人聲把蒙特鳩大人和卡帕萊特大人吵醒了，他們和親王一同前來查看究竟發生了什麼事。這時神父已被看守人捉到了，他渾身顫抖地從墓地走出來，嘆著氣，流著淚，神色異常。卡帕萊特家族的墓地前被人群擠得水洩不通，親王命令神父在眾人面前據實陳述這樁離奇悲慘的事件。

　　於是神父當著老蒙特鳩大人和老卡帕萊特大人的面，把他們兩家兒女這場不幸的戀愛照實說出來。他也說出是他促成他們的婚姻，希望藉由這個結合來消除兩家多年來的仇恨。他說死在那裡的羅密歐是茱麗葉的丈夫，而死在那裡的茱麗葉是羅密歐忠誠的妻子。可是他還未找到適當

的機會宣布他們的婚姻，就又有人向茱麗葉提親了。為了避免犯下重婚罪，茱麗葉聽從他的建議服下安眠藥，因此大家都認為她死了。同時他寫信給羅密歐，叫他回來，等藥效退了之後再把茱麗葉帶走。可是送信的人誤了事，羅密歐一直沒有收到信。接下來的事神父就無法說明了，他只知道當他親自跑來，打算把茱麗葉救出去時，巴里斯和羅密歐已然身亡。

剩下的情節就由那個看到巴里斯和羅密歐打鬥的侍從和隨著羅密歐到維洛那來的僕人補充。忠實的情人羅密歐把他寫給父親的信交給這個僕人，並囑咐僕人：如果他死了，就替他把信送到家裡。羅密歐的信證實了神父所說的話，他承認跟茱麗葉結了婚，要求父母寬恕他，也提到自己從那個可憐的藥師手裡買到毒藥，又說他到墳墓這就是為了尋死，好跟茱麗葉一同長眠。一切說詞都與現場狀況吻合，把神父可能參與這場凶殺的嫌疑都洗清了，證明他原是一番好意，不過他想的方法太不湊巧了，只能說人算不如天算。

親王轉身指責老蒙特鳩大人和老卡帕萊特大人彼此不該懷著這種野蠻又毫無理性的仇恨，他們已經觸怒了上天，上天藉著他們子女無法相守的戀愛來懲罰他們這種無理的冤仇。

這兩家終於同意把多年來的仇恨埋進子女的墳墓裡，不再互相仇視了。卡帕萊特大人要求蒙特鳩大人跟他握

手，並稱呼他「兄弟」，似乎承認兩家藉著羅密歐與茱麗葉的結婚成了親家，他要求蒙特鳩大人把手伸向他（表示和好），算是給他女兒的唯一安慰吧。可是蒙特鳩大人說他願意給得更多，他要為茱麗葉鑄一座純金雕像，只要維洛那存在的一天，任何一座塑像都不會比真實忠誠的茱麗葉雕像更輝煌精緻。卡帕萊特大人則表示他也要替羅密歐鑄一座雕像。

這兩位可憐的老人家啊！事情都到了無可挽救的地步，彼此還在爭相展現禮數。過去他們的憤怒和仇恨是那樣地深，只有歷經他們子女的離世（成了他們仇恨的可憐犧牲品），才消除了這兩個貴族之間根深蒂固的仇恨和忌妒。

II.

威尼斯商人

　　猶太人夏洛克住在威尼斯，他是個放高利貸的守財奴。他靠著放高利貸給基督徒商人，累積了鉅額財富。夏洛克為人刻薄，討債方式十分凶惡，所以善良的人都討厭他。威尼斯有一位名為安東尼歐的年輕商人特別討厭夏洛克，而夏洛克也同樣痛恨他，因為安東尼歐時常借錢給遭逢困難的人，而且從來不收利息。因此，這個貪婪的猶太人跟慷慨的商人安東尼歐結下了樑子。只要安東尼歐在市場（就是交易所）碰到夏洛克，他總是責備夏洛克不該放高利貸，對人不該那麼刻薄。而那位猶太人表面上裝作很有耐心地聽訓，心裡卻暗自打算報復他。

　　安東尼歐可說是世界上最善良的人了，家境又好，總是樂意幫助人。事實上，所有住在義大利的人，沒有一個比他更能發揚古羅馬的光榮了。大家都非常愛戴他，而與他最接近、最親密的朋友則是威尼斯的一個貴族巴薩尼奧。巴薩尼奧只繼承了少許遺產，再加上他大肆地揮霍（地位高而財產少的年輕人，都有這種習性），他那為數

不多的家當差不多都花光
了。每當巴薩尼奧一缺錢
用，安東尼歐就會接濟
他，看來他們兩人真是一
條心，合用一只荷包。

　　有一天，巴薩尼奧
來找安東尼歐，說他想
跟一位他十分鍾愛的富
家千金結婚，好恢復他
的家境。這位小姐的
父親最近去世了，一
大片莊園都由她一
個人繼承。她父親
在世的時候，巴薩
尼奧常常到她家去
拜訪，他感覺她有
時候會含情脈脈地

望著他，好像在等待他求婚。可是他沒有錢擺出相稱的排場，去跟繼承了這麼多莊園的小姐談戀愛。於是他懇求安東尼歐，再幫他一次：借給他三千塊金幣。

當時，安東尼歐手頭上已沒有多餘的錢可借給他的朋友了，可是不久他就會有批船隻滿載貨物而歸。他說他要去找那個放高利貸、有錢的夏洛克，用那些船隻作擔保，向他借錢。

安東尼歐和巴薩尼奧一道去見夏洛克。安東尼歐向這個猶太人請求借三千塊金幣，利息依他的要求計算，將來自己會以海上那批船隻滿載的貨物來償還。

夏洛克心想：「要是讓我抓到他的把柄，我一定要狠狠地一報往日之仇。他恨我們猶太民族，他借錢給人不收利息，還在商人間辱罵我，說我辛辛苦苦賺來的錢是高利貸。我要是饒過他，我們的民族就會被詛咒。」

安東尼歐見夏洛克沉默不語，而他急需用錢，便說：「夏洛克，你聽見了嗎？你到底要不要借我錢？」

這位猶太人回說：「安東尼歐先生，您在交易所時常罵我在放高利貸，我都只是聳聳肩膀不予置評，因為忍耐一向是我們民族的特色。您還說我是異教徒，一條能咬死人的狗，往我的猶太衣裳上吐口水，還用腳踢我，好像我是一條野狗。哦，現在您有求於我了，跑到這兒來對我說：『夏洛克，借錢給我！』一條狗會有錢嗎？一條野狗拿得出三千塊金幣借人嗎？我是不是應該卑躬屈膝地說：

好先生，您上星期三朝著我吐口
水，還有一次罵我是狗。為了報答
您這些好意，我會借錢給您。」
　　安東尼歐回說：「我還是有
可能會那樣叫你，再吐你口

水，並且繼續鄙視你。你也不用想成是借錢給一個朋友，就當作借給一個仇人，要是到時候我沒錢還，你大可拉下臉來按照條約懲罰我。」

夏洛克說，「哎呀，您火氣也太大了啊！我當然願意跟您交朋友，得到您的友誼。我會忘掉您對我的侮辱。您要借多少，我就借給您多少，不收利息。」

這個聽起來很慷慨的提議使安東尼歐大吃一驚。夏洛克依舊假仁假義地說，他這樣做全是為了得到安東尼歐的友誼，並且表示願意借給他三千塊金幣，不收任何利息，只要安東尼歐跟他到律師那裡去，鬧著玩地簽下一張借據：如果到期未還，夏洛克即可挑選安東尼歐身體的任一部位割下一磅肉。

「好吧，」安東尼歐說，「我願意簽這樣的借據，而且還會說猶太人的心腸真好。」

巴薩尼奧勸安東尼歐不要簽這樣的借約，可是安東尼歐堅持簽下，因為他確信還款期限之前他的船就會回來，船上貨物的價值可比借款還要多出許多倍呢！

夏洛克聽到他們的爭論，大聲地說：「亞伯拉罕老祖宗啊！這些基督徒的疑心病真重呀！他們自己待人刻薄，所以老是懷疑別人。請問你，巴薩尼奧，要是他期限到了付不出錢來，我向他逼討一磅肉的處罰，對我有什麼好處啊？從人身上割下來的一磅肉，價值還比不上一磅羊肉或牛肉呢！我是為了討好他才提出這麼友善的一個辦法來，

他要是接受，那就這麼辦，要是不呢，那就再會吧！」

　　儘管這個猶太人口口聲聲說他是出於好意，巴薩尼奧還是不願意他的朋友為了他去冒險。可是安東尼歐不聽巴薩尼奧的勸告，還是簽了借據，心裡想，其實這不過是（如那個猶太人所說的）鬧著玩罷了。

　　巴薩尼奧想娶的那位小姐將要繼承一大筆遺產，她住在一個叫貝爾蒙的地方，離威尼斯不遠，她的名字叫波西亞。不論人品或才智，她絕對都比得上我們在書上讀過的那個波西亞──就是伽圖的女兒，布魯斯特的妻子。

　　巴薩尼奧得到安東尼歐冒著生命危險借到的慷慨資助後，就帶著豪華的行囊，並與一位名叫葛來西安諾的先生一同前往貝爾蒙。

　　巴薩尼奧求婚很順利，波西亞很快就答應嫁給他了。

　　巴薩尼奧老實地告訴波西亞說，他沒有什麼財產，他可以誇耀的只有高貴的出身以及貴族的血統罷了。波西亞會愛上他本來就是因為他那高尚的氣質，況且她自己很有錢，不在乎丈夫有沒有財富。她以優雅謙遜的態度表示，她希望自己再美麗一千倍，再富裕一萬倍，這樣才配得上他。多才多藝的波西亞還十分謙虛地說，她是個沒受過多少教育、沒讀過許多書、沒有什麼經驗的女孩，雖然涉世未深但她還年輕，還有很多機會可以學習，她要把自己柔順的心靈託付給他，事事聽從他的指導、教誨。她說：「我自己和我所有的一切，現在都成為您的了，巴薩尼

奧。昨天我還擁有這棟豪宅，我是我自己的女王，這些僕人也都聽我指揮；現在，我的夫君，這棟豪宅、這些僕人和我自己，都已經是您的了。憑著這只戒指，我將這一切獻給您。」她送了巴薩尼奧一只戒指。

高貴富有的波西亞謙遜大方地接受巴薩尼奧這樣一個家產微薄的丈夫，使得他分外感激和驚嘆。對於如此敬重他的小姐，他不知道該怎樣表示他的快樂以及敬意，他笨口拙舌地說了一些愛慕和感謝的話。他接過戒指，發誓永遠戴著它不離手。

當波西亞落落大方地答應嫁給巴薩尼奧，成為他忠實順從的妻子時，葛來西安諾和波西亞的侍女尼麗莎也在場，各自伺候著他們的少爺和小姐。葛來西安諾向巴薩尼奧和那位慷慨的小姐道了喜，並希望能准許他與他們同時舉行婚禮。

「我打從心底贊成，葛來西安諾，」巴薩尼奧說，「只要你能找到對象的話。」

葛來西安諾接著說，他愛上了波西亞那位漂亮的侍女尼麗莎，而她已經答應，只要她的女主人嫁給巴薩尼奧，她就答應嫁給他。

波西亞問尼麗莎是否真有此事。

尼麗莎回說：「是真的，只要小姐您贊成的話。」波西亞欣然同意了。巴薩尼奧歡喜地說：「葛來西安諾，你們的結合，將為我們的婚禮增添光彩。」

這時候，一個信差送來的信，
讓這兩對情人的幸福蒙上了陰影，
他帶來了安東尼歐的親筆信，信
裡傳達了可怕的消息。巴薩尼奧
看著安東尼歐的來信，臉色
變得慘白，波西亞擔心那
封信帶來的是他好朋友的
死訊，便問是什麼消息
讓他這樣難過，他說：
「啊，親愛的波西亞，
這封信裡寫的是最悲
慘的消息。親愛的

夫人，我最初向妳表露愛意的時候，就坦白地告訴過妳，我的貴族血統是我僅有的財產，可是我當時就應該告訴妳，我不但什麼都沒有，而且還負債呢。」

然後，巴薩尼奧把一切都告訴了波西亞，說他怎樣向安東尼歐借錢，和安東尼歐怎樣從猶太人夏洛克那裡借錢；也說安東尼歐簽了張借據，上頭註明期限一到，如果付不出錢，就得用一磅肉來償還。隨後，巴薩尼奧唸起安東尼歐的信來，信裡說：

> 親愛的巴薩尼奧，我的船全都沉了，我必須履行跟猶太人簽的那張借據，到期前如果無法償還，必須遵照合約上的規定受罰。若割去一磅肉，我應當性命難保，因此我希望臨死前能見你一面。不過我會尊重你的意願，若是我們的友誼不足以令你前來，那麼，你也不要因為這封信而來見我。

「啊，我親愛的，」波西亞說，「把事情安排一下，立刻去吧。你可以帶著比這筆債款多二十倍的錢去償還，絕不能因為我們巴薩尼奧的過失，讓這位好心的朋友損傷一絲一毫。你既然是我付出這麼大的代價換得的人，我一定格外珍惜你。」

波西亞接著說，她要在巴薩尼奧動身之前跟他完婚，

這樣他才有權合法使用她的錢財。於是他們當天就結婚，葛來西安諾也娶了尼麗莎。婚禮一結束，巴薩尼奧和葛來西安諾就匆忙地動身趕往威尼斯。巴薩尼奧在監牢裡見到了安東尼歐。

債務已經過期了，狠毒的猶太人不肯收巴薩尼奧的錢，堅持要安東尼歐身上的一磅肉。威尼斯公爵早已敲定審判這件駭人案子的日子，巴薩尼奧滿心擔憂地等候著這個審判日的到來。

丈夫出發前，波西亞愉快地跟他談話，囑咐他回來的時候一定要把他的好朋友也帶來。可是她擔心安東尼歐會凶多吉少，因此她開始思量著自己能作些什麼，好幫助他親愛的巴薩尼奧救救朋友的性命。儘管波西亞為了尊重她的巴薩尼奧，曾經用一個賢慧妻子該有的婉約態度對他說，他比她明智，凡事都會聽從他的指示，可是眼看她所敬重的丈夫的朋友即將送命，她非得採取行動不可。她一點也不懷疑自己的本事，而且憑藉著她那準確完美的判斷力，她立即下定決心親自到威尼斯去替安東尼歐辯護。

波西亞有個親戚是律師，名叫裴拉里。她寫了一封信給這位先生，向他說明案情、徵求他的意見，並請他回信時附上一套律師穿的衣服。派去送信的人回來之後，帶來裴拉里的建言和波西亞所需要的一切裝備。

波西亞和她的侍女尼麗莎換上男人的衣裳，波西亞還披上律師的長袍，讓尼麗莎作為她的書記員一同前往。她

們馬上動身出發，就在開庭的那天趕到了威尼斯。正當威尼斯公爵和元老們即將開審時，波西亞走進元老院這個高等法院。她遞上那位有學問的律師裴拉里寫給公爵的一封信，說他本想親自來替安東尼歐辯護，可是因病不能出庭，所以他請求公爵允許讓這位學識淵博的年輕博士鮑爾薩澤（他這樣稱呼波西亞）代表他出庭辯護。公爵批准了這個請求，一邊看著這個陌生年輕人的相貌一邊覺得納悶。她披著律師的袍子，戴著很大的一頂假髮，偽裝得很好。

此刻，一場重要的審判開始了。波西亞環顧四周，看到那個毫無仁慈之心的猶太人，也看到了巴薩尼奧，而他卻沒認出喬裝的波西亞。巴薩尼奧正站在安東尼歐旁邊，替他的朋友提心吊膽，十分擔憂且難受。

溫柔的波西亞想到這份艱鉅難的任務有多麼重要，內心便湧出源源不絕的勇氣。她大膽地執行了她擔下的職責。她先對夏洛克說話，承認根據威尼斯的法律，他有權索取借據裡註明的那一磅肉，然後她真誠地說起仁慈是多麼高貴的品德，除了冷酷無情的夏洛克之外，任誰聽了都會心軟。她說：仁慈就像天空降落在旱地的甘露，仁慈是雙重的幸福，對別人仁慈的人會感到幸福，蒙受別人仁慈恩惠的人也會感到幸福。仁慈是上帝專屬的特質，對君王來說，它比王冠還要可貴。當我們執行世俗權威之際，在公道之外凡事優先考量仁慈的人，就越接近上帝。她要夏

洛克記住，既然我們都會向上帝禱告，懇求祂對我們仁慈，那麼祂也應當教會我們對別人仁慈。

夏洛克依然堅持索取借約上規定的那一磅肉。

「難道他拿不出錢還你嗎？」波西亞問。於是巴薩尼奧趁機表示不只那三千塊金幣，隨便他要多少倍的錢都可以。可是夏洛克拒絕這個建議，仍然堅持要安東尼歐身上的一磅肉。巴薩尼奧央求這位學問淵博的年輕律師想辦法變通一下法律條文，救一救安東尼歐的性命。可是波西亞嚴肅地說，法律一旦訂立，就絕對不能更動。

夏洛克聽到波西亞說法律無法更動後，便覺得她是支持自己的人，便說：「但尼爾再世來審判啦！啊，聰明的年輕律師，我是多麼地敬重你呀！你的學問比你的年紀要大多了！」

這時，波西亞要求夏洛克讓她看一看那張借據。看完之後，她說：「的確應該依借據上規定的來償還借款。根據借據，這位猶太人能夠合法地從安東尼歐心窩的地方割下一磅肉來。」然後她又對夏洛克說，「你還是發發慈悲，把錢收下來，讓我把這張借據撕掉吧！」

可是狠毒的夏洛克還是不肯寬恕安東尼歐，他說：「我以我的靈魂發誓，任憑誰說什麼都不能改變我的決心。」

波西亞接著說，「既然如此，安東尼歐，你就準備讓他的刀子扎進你的胸膛吧！」夏洛克興奮地磨著一把長

刀，準備割那一磅肉時，波西亞對安東尼歐說：「你還有話要說嗎？」

安東尼歐帶著鎮定豁然的神情回答，他無話可說，因為他早已準備就死了。然後他對巴薩尼奧說：「巴薩尼奧，把你的手伸給我，再會了！不要為我因你遭到這種不幸而感到難過。替我問候尊夫人，告訴她我有多麼愛你！」

巴薩尼奧的心裡痛苦萬分，他回說：「安東尼歐，我娶了一個妻子，她對我來說，就跟生命一樣寶貴，可是我的生命、我的妻子和這整個世界，在我眼裡還沒有你的生命珍貴啊！如果能挽回你的性命，我情願丟掉這一切，把所有的一切都給這個惡魔。」

善良的波西亞聽到她丈夫用這麼強烈的言詞來表示他對安東尼歐這個忠實朋友的友情，儘管有一點兒不高興，但她還是不禁說了一句：「要是尊夫人在這兒，聽到您這番話，她可不會感激您吧！」

隨後，一舉一動都喜歡模仿他主人的葛來西安諾心想，他也應該說幾句像巴薩尼奧那樣的話。此時，喬裝成律師書記員的尼麗莎正在波西亞身邊記錄著什麼，葛來西安諾便對她說：「我有一個妻子，我發誓我愛她；可是我希望她現在就在天堂裡，好請求上帝改變這可惡猶太人的殘忍性格。」

尼麗莎說，「幸好你是背著她這麼說，不然你們家可

一定會鬧得天翻地覆。」

夏洛克不耐煩地大聲嚷道：「我們這是在浪費時間呢，請快點宣判吧！」

這時法庭上的人們都知道這裡即將發生可怕的事了，每顆心都在為安東尼歐感到悲痛。

波西亞先問秤肉的磅秤準備好了沒有，然後對那個猶太人說：「夏洛克，你得請一位外科醫生在旁邊看顧著，免得他流血過多送了命。」

夏洛克的本意就是要安東尼歐流血過多而喪命，因此他說：「借據裡可沒有這一條約定。」

波西亞回說：「借據上沒有這一條規定又有什麼關係呢？做點善事總是好的啊。」

針對這些請求，夏洛克只答道：「借據裡根本就沒有這一條。不請又有什麼關係呢？」

波西亞說，「那麼，安東尼歐身上的那一磅肉是你的了。法律允許你這麼做，法庭也判給你了。你可以從他胸脯上割下這塊肉。法律允許你這麼做，法庭也判給了你。」

夏洛克又大聲嚷道：「明智又正直的法官！但尼爾他來審判了！」說罷他又磨起他那把長刀，急切地望著安東尼歐說：「來，準備好吧！」

「等一等，這位猶太人」波西亞說，「有件事要提醒你。借據上可沒有允諾給你一滴血。條文寫的是『一磅

肉』。在割這磅肉的時候，如果你讓這位基督徒流出一滴血來，你的田地和財產就都要依法律的規定充公，歸給威尼斯政府。」

既然夏洛克無法割掉一磅肉的同時，又不讓安東尼歐流一滴血（波西亞的見解十分睿智——借據上只寫了肉卻沒有寫血）——便成功救下安東尼歐。大家都十分欽佩這位年輕律師的聰明機智，元老院裡歡聲雷動。葛來西安諾引用夏洛克的話大聲嚷道：「啊，明智又正直的法官！猶太人，你看吧，但尼爾來審判了！」

夏洛克發現他的詭計無法得逞後，只好帶著懊悔的神情說，他願意接受錢了。巴薩尼奧因為安東尼歐出乎意外地獲救，非常高興地嚷著：「錢拿去吧！」

可是波西亞攔住他說：「別急，慢一點！這個猶太人不能拿錢，只能割肉。因此，夏洛克，準備好割那塊肉吧。可是你得當心別讓他流出血來，而且割得不能超過一磅，也不能比一磅少。要是割得比一磅多一點或者少一點，那就要依照威尼斯的法律判你死罪，並且沒收你全部的財產，歸給元老院。」

「給我錢，然後讓我走吧！」夏洛克說。

「我已經準備好了，」巴薩尼奧說，「錢在這裡。」

夏洛克剛要接過錢來，波西亞又把他攔住了，她說：「等一等，猶太人。事情還沒結束。根據威尼斯的法律，你設下圈套，意圖謀害一位市民的性命，所以你的財產已

經充公,歸給政府了。你的死活就看公爵怎麼決定了。因此,你就在此下跪請求他的饒恕吧。」

公爵對夏洛克說:「為了讓你看看我們基督徒的精神有什麼不一樣,你不用開口求饒,我也會饒你不死。可是你的財產一半要歸給安東尼歐,另外一半要歸給政府。」

此時,寬宏大量的安東尼歐說,要是夏洛克肯簽個字據,答應在他臨死的時候把財產留給他女兒和女婿,他願意放棄夏洛克應該給他的那份財產。原來安東尼歐知道這個猶太人有個獨生女,她最近不顧他的反對嫁給一個年輕的基督徒,這個人名叫羅倫佐,是安東尼歐的朋友。夏洛克為此震怒不已,他已經宣布取消他女兒的財產繼承權了。

猶太人答應這個條件。他想要報復的陰謀不僅失敗,還折損了大半的財產,於是他說:「請讓我回家去吧,我不太舒服。字據寫好送到我家去,我會簽字並答應把一半財產分給我的女兒。」

「那你回去吧,」公爵說,「可是你一定要簽那張字據。要是你願意懺悔,發誓為人不再如此殘酷,並變成一個基督徒,那麼政府可以赦免你,把那一半財產還給你。」

公爵把安東尼歐釋放,宣布審判結束。然後他大大誇獎這個年輕律師的才智,並邀他到家裡去吃飯。波西亞一心想趕在丈夫前頭回到貝爾蒙去,便回說:「您這番盛情

我心領了，可是我必須馬上趕回去。」公爵聽到律師沒有
時間留下來一道吃飯後，覺得很可惜。他轉過身，對安東
尼歐補了一句：「好好酬謝這位先生吧，在我看來，你有
一份不小的人情要還。」

　　公爵和元老們退庭後，巴薩尼奧對波西亞說：「最令
人尊敬的先生，多虧您的機智，我和我這位朋友安東尼歐
今天才得以逃過一場痛苦的刑罰，請您收下本來應該還給
猶太人的三千塊金幣吧。」

　　「送給您這點薄酬後，我們依然對您感激不盡，」安
東尼歐說，「我們永遠不會忘記您的大恩大德，若您需要
幫助，我們必定赴湯蹈火，在所不辭。」

　　波西亞說什麼也不肯收那筆錢，但是巴薩尼奧再三懇
求他接受報酬，於是她說：「那麼把你的手套送給我吧，
我要戴著它作紀念。」於是，巴薩尼奧就把手套脫下來，
她一眼就看到他手指上那枚她送給他的戒指。原來這位機
靈的夫人是想把那枚戒指弄到手，等下次見到巴薩尼奧時
可以捉弄他，因此她才向他要手套。看見那枚戒指後，她
便說：「既然你想對我表示謝意，那就把這戒指也送給我
吧。」

　　巴薩尼奧十分為難，因為律師要的正是他唯一不能割
捨的東西。他神色慌張地說，這枚戒指實在不便奉送，因
為這是他妻子送給他的，他已經發過誓，要終身戴著它。
可是他願意公開徵求，找來威尼斯最貴重的戒指送給他。

　　聽到這句話，波西亞故意裝作被冒犯的樣子並走出法庭，說道：「您這是在教我怎樣應付一個乞丐！」

　　「親愛的巴薩尼奧，」安東尼歐說，「戒指就送給他吧！看在我們的情誼和他大力幫忙我的份上，就得罪你夫人一回吧。」

　　巴薩尼奧對於自己的忘恩負義感到很慚愧，於是讓步了。他派葛來西安諾拿著戒指去追波西亞。結果，曾給過葛來西安諾一枚戒指的書記員尼麗莎，也照樣向他要戒指，葛來西安諾隨手就給了她（他不甘心讓主人的慷慨專美於前）。

　　兩位夫人一想到回家之後，她們可以如何責備丈夫把戒指當作禮物送給別的女人時，不禁大笑起來。

　　行善後的心情總是特別愉快。在回家的路上，波西亞就是這樣。在這種快樂的心情下，她看到什麼都覺得無比美好：月光從沒比這晚更加皓潔。當那輪討人喜歡的月亮隱沒到雲彩後頭時，從貝爾蒙的家裡透出的一道燈光，逗引她奔放的幻想。她對尼麗莎說：「我們看見的這道燈光是從我們家廳堂裡照射出來的。小小一支蠟燭，它的光輝竟然可以照得這麼遠！同樣地，在這個罪惡的世界上，做一件好事也能散發出很大的光輝。」聽到家裡傳來音樂聲，她說：「我覺得那樂聲比白天的更好聽。」

　　回到家後，波西亞和尼麗莎進了房間，各自換上原來的衣裝，等候丈夫的歸來。過了一會兒，她們的丈夫帶著

安東尼歐一道回來了。巴薩尼奧把他的摯友介紹給他的夫人波西亞，波西亞剛祝賀完安東尼歐脫險，並且表示歡迎時，就看到尼麗莎和她的丈夫在屋內的一個角落裡吵了起來。

「怎麼這麼快就拌起嘴來了呢？」波西亞說：「發生了什麼事呀？」

葛來西安諾回說：「夫人，就為了尼麗莎給我的那枚不值幾個錢的鍍金戒指；上面刻著詩句，就跟刀匠刻在刀子上的一樣：愛我，不要離開我。」

「你問詩句跟戒指的價值何在？你不懂嗎？」尼麗莎說，「我送給你的時候，你對我發誓直到死去的那一刻為止，都會永遠戴在手上。如今，你卻說你送給律師的書記員了？我就知道你一定是把它送給其他女人了。」

「我向妳發誓，」葛來西安諾回說，「我給了一個年輕人，一個男孩子，一個矮矮的男孩子，個子不比妳高。他是那位年輕律師的書記，多虧那位律師聰明的辯護，才救了安東尼歐的命。那孩子滔滔不絕地向我索取它做為酬勞，我無論如何也不能拒絕他啊。」

波西亞說：「葛來西安諾，這就是你的錯了，你不應該把你妻子送你的第一件禮物給了別人。我也送給我丈夫巴薩尼奧一枚戒指，我敢說，不管發生什麼事，他都不會摘下它。」

為了掩飾自己的過失，葛來西安諾說：「我的主人巴

薩尼奧也把他的戒指送給那位律師了，所以那個辛苦抄寫的孩子（律師的書記員）才會跟我要那枚戒指的。」

波西亞聽見這番話後故意表現得很生氣，責備巴薩尼奧不該把她的戒指送給別人。她說，她相信尼麗莎的話，戒指一定是給了某個女人。

巴薩尼奧惹惱他親愛的夫人，他自己心裡也不好受，因此他十分真誠地說：「我以我的人格擔保，戒指並不是給了什麼女人，而是給了一位法學博士。他不肯接受我送的三千塊金幣，一定要那枚戒指。我不答應，他就氣呼呼地走了。親愛的波西亞，妳說我該怎麼辦呢？我看起來就像個忘恩負義的人，我慚愧得只好叫人追上去，把戒指給了他。饒恕我吧，我的好夫人。要是妳在場的話，我想妳一定會求我把戒指送給那位可敬的博士。」

「啊，」安東尼歐說，「都是我害得你們兩對夫妻吵架。」

波西亞請安東尼歐不要自責，不論如何，他們都很歡迎他。安東尼歐說：「我曾經為了巴薩尼奧，拿自己的身軀向人抵押。要不是多虧了接受您丈夫戒指的那位先生，如今我早已小命不保。現在我敢再立一張借據，用我的靈魂擔保，您的丈夫絕不會再做出失信於您的事了。」

「那麼您就是他的保證人了，」波西亞說，「請您把這枚戒指給他，要他必須加以妥善保存這枚戒指。」

巴薩尼奧一看，發現這枚戒指跟他送掉的那枚一模一

樣，不禁大吃一驚。這時，波西亞告訴他說，她就是那個年輕的律師，尼麗莎就是她的書記員。巴薩尼奧這才終於知道，原來救安東尼歐性命的，正是他愛妻卓越的勇氣和智慧，他的心裡真是說不出地又驚又喜。

波西亞再一次向安東尼歐表達歡迎之情，並且把幾封偶然落到她手裡的信給了他，信裡說，安東尼歐那批原先以為全部損失的船隻，已經順利入港了。

於是，這位富商的悲慘故事，就在後來出乎意料的好運氣中漸漸被遺忘了。他們日後不僅可以悠閒地談笑那兩枚戒指的趣事，還可以調侃那兩位認不出自己妻子的丈夫。葛來西安諾高興地吟出了一段短詩：

只要活著，什麼都不怕，
就怕丟了尼麗莎的戒指。

III.

仲夏夜之夢

　　雅典城明文規定市民高興把女兒嫁給誰，女兒就得嫁，市民有權利強迫女兒出嫁，如果女兒不肯嫁給父親為她挑選的丈夫，父親可以依法請求處死女兒。但是做父親的總不希望自己女兒失去性命，因此就算女兒真的有不太聽話的時候，也很少訴諸這條法律，做父母的只是有時候用這條可怕的法律來嚇唬嚇唬她們罷了。

　　話說有一回，有位叫伊吉斯的老人竟然真的跑到底修斯（當時管轄雅典的公爵）面前控訴說，他要把女兒荷米亞許配給雅典貴族家庭出身的青年德米崔斯，可是女兒卻拒絕這門婚事，說她已經愛上一位叫賴桑德的雅典青年。於是伊吉斯請求底修斯主持公道，依照這條嚴厲的法律來處置他的女兒。

　　荷米亞辯解說，她之所以違背父親的意旨，是因為德米崔斯曾經追求過她的好朋友海倫娜，而且海倫娜也瘋狂地迷戀著德米崔斯。荷米亞違抗父親命令的理由雖然十分充分，但偏偏嚴苛的伊吉斯就是不為所動。

　　底修斯雖然是個偉大又仁慈的公爵，但他也無權改變國家的法律。他能做的只有給荷米亞四天的時間考慮，四天後，若是她仍不肯嫁給德米崔斯，就只好依法判處她死刑。

　　荷米亞從公爵那裡退庭後就去找她的情人賴桑德，告訴他自己的困境，說她若不肯放棄他而嫁給德米崔斯，就只剩下四天可活。

　　賴桑德聽到這個壞消息後感到痛苦萬分。他想起有個姑媽住在離雅典城不遠的地方，在那裡，雅典城就不能對荷米亞施行這條殘酷的法律了（出了雅典城這條法律就失效了），於是他提議荷米亞當天晚上就從她父親的房子裡逃出來，跟他一起到姑媽家，然後在那裡結婚。「我在城外幾哩遠的林子裡等妳，」賴桑德說，「就是那個令人心曠神怡的林子，我們經常在宜人的五月和海倫娜去那裡散步。」

　　荷米亞欣然接受這個建議。除了好友海倫娜，她沒有告訴任何人這個逃跑計畫，可是海倫娜（女孩們總是會為了愛情做出傻事）非常沒義氣地決定把這件事告訴德米崔斯。洩露朋友的秘密對她自己並沒有什麼好處，她只不過是想跟著她不忠誠的愛人到樹林裡去，因為她知道德米崔斯一定會到那裡追趕荷米亞。

　　賴桑德和荷米亞約定見面的林子，是那些被稱為精靈的小東西們最喜歡出沒的地方。仙王奧伯龍和仙后泰坦妮

亞會帶著所有小隨從，在這個林子裡舉行午夜歡宴。

就在這個時候，仙王和仙后鬧翻了。每逢月光皎潔的夜晚，他們在這令人心曠神怡的林子裡漫步時總是一碰面就吵架，吵得所有小精靈都嚇得爬進橡實殼裡躲了起來。

他們這次鬧翻，是因為泰坦妮亞不肯把偷偷換來的小男孩交給奧伯龍，小男孩的母親是泰坦妮亞的朋友，她死後仙后就從奶媽那裡把小男孩偷走，帶回林子裡來撫養。

這對情人相約在樹林裡的那個晚上，泰坦妮亞正帶著幾個侍女在散步，碰巧遇見了也有侍臣伴行的奧伯龍。

「真不巧，又在月光下碰見妳了，驕傲的泰坦妮亞！」仙王說。

仙后回答：「怎麼，善妒的奧伯龍，是你嗎？仙子們，我們趕快走吧，我可不想和他待在同一個地方。」

奧伯龍說，「等一等，妳這魯莽的仙子。我不是妳的丈夫嗎？為什麼泰坦妮亞妳總要和自己的丈夫奧伯龍作對呢？快讓妳偷來的小男孩做我的僮僕吧！」

「你死了這條心吧！」仙后回說，「就算你拿整個仙國來跟我交換，我也不會給你我的孩子。」說完她就氣沖沖地離開了。

「好吧，就依妳！」奧伯龍說，「我會在天亮之前，讓妳為侮辱我一事付出代價。」

於是，奧伯龍把他最寵信的幕僚帕克叫來。

帕克（有時被稱為「好傢伙羅賓」）是個機伶狡猾的

精靈，他常在附近的村子裡搗蛋尋開心。有時候他會跑去
製乳場把乳脂給刮走；有時候他會把自己輕巧的身體鑽進
攪乳器裡，當他在裡面跳著奇妙的舞蹈時，製乳酪的姑娘
無論費多大力氣也無法把乳汁攪成奶油，就算是村裡的壯
丁也做不成。如果帕克到釀酒器裡惡作劇，那麥酒也鐵定
遭殃。當幾個好鄰居聚在一起舒舒服服地喝幾杯酒時，帕
克就像一隻烤螃蟹，跳進酒杯裡，趁著老太婆要喝的當
兒，在她的唇間彈上跳下，潑得她乾癟的
下巴滿是麥酒。又當老太婆準備莊重地
坐下，講個悲慘的故事給街坊們聽聽
時，帕克就把她屁股下的三腳凳

給抽走，讓那可憐的老太婆摔個正著，使那些長舌婦們看了捧腹大笑，還發誓自己從來沒笑得這麼開心過。

「帕克，你過來！」奧伯龍對這個快樂的小流浪者說。「去替我採朵姑娘們叫做『三色堇』的花來，只要把這種紫色小花的汁液滴在熟睡之人的眼皮上，他就會愛上醒來之後第一眼看見的東西。我要趁著泰坦妮亞睡著的時候，把這種花汁滴到她的眼皮上，那她醒來之後就會對第一眼看見的東西一見鍾情，管那東西是獅子、熊、愛搗蛋的猴子，還是瞎攪和的猩猩。我還知道另一種魔法，可以用來解除她眼皮上的這種魔法，不過她得先把那男孩給我當僮僕。」

喜歡惡作劇的帕克對主人玩的這個把戲，感到十分有趣，於是連忙跑去尋找那紫色小花。在等帕克回來的空檔，奧伯龍看見德米崔斯和海倫娜走進林子，無意中聽到了德米崔斯責備海倫娜不該跟著他。他說了許多無情的話，而海倫娜卻語氣溫柔，勸他回想當初他如何愛她，並且向她表示過忠誠，如今他卻把她扔給野獸（如他自己所說的），海倫娜只好拼命地追著他跑。

仙王一向對忠貞的愛人特別有好感，他對海倫娜深表同情。賴桑德說過，他們以前常在這個令人心曠神怡的林子裡散步，也許在德米崔斯還愛著海倫娜的那段快樂日子裡，奧伯龍就曾經看過她。總之，帕克帶回紫色小花後，奧伯龍就對他的寵臣說：「這花你拿一點去，樹林裡有一

個可愛的雅典女孩,她愛上了一個傲慢的小伙子。你要是
看見那個小伙子在睡覺,就滴些花的汁液在他的眼皮上,
可是要等到那女孩在他附近的時候才滴,那麼他醒來之後
第一眼看見的就會是這位受他輕視的女孩。你只要看誰穿
著雅典衣服,就可以知道是哪個小伙子了。」

帕克答應會俐落地辦妥這件事,接著,奧伯龍趁著泰
坦妮亞不注意時潛入了她的臥房,這時她正準備就寢。她
的仙室是座花壇,長滿了野生百里香、野櫻草和芬芳的紫
羅蘭,架著野忍冬、麝香玫瑰和野薔薇攀成的篷頂。泰坦
妮亞每晚都會在這裡休息一會兒,把油亮的蛇皮拿來當被
子,蛇皮雖然很小一塊,但要裹起一個精靈已綽綽有餘。

奧伯龍看見泰坦妮亞正囑咐她的仙子們在她睡覺時該
做的工作。「你們當中,」仙后說,「一些人去殺死麝香
玫瑰花苞裡的蟲子,另一些人去跟蝙蝠打仗,把牠們的皮
翅膀拿回來給我的小精靈做外套,剩下的去監視每天晚上
都吵鬧鳴叫的貓頭鷹,不要讓牠靠近我。不過,現在首先
要做的是唱歌哄我睡覺。」於是,他們開始唱起這首歌
來:

> 雙舌的花蛇和扎手刺蝟,走遠吧;
> 蠑螈和蜥蜴,不要來搗蛋,
> 不要靠近我們的仙后。
> 夜鶯,用甜蜜的腔調,為我們唱一支催眠曲吧。

睡吧，睡吧，快睡吧！
睡吧，睡吧，快睡吧！
災害、魔法和符咒都走開，
不許靠近美麗的仙后，
催眠曲，晚安吧。

　　仙子們唱著這首可愛的催眠曲哄仙后進入夢鄉後，就去執行她吩咐的重要任務。這時奧伯龍悄悄走近泰坦妮亞，在她的眼皮上滴了些花液，然後說：

不管妳睜開眼睛看到什麼，
妳都會把他當作妳的情人。

　　我們再回來說說荷米亞吧。她為了逃避不嫁給德米崔斯而被判下的死罪，那天晚上從父親家裡逃了出來。她一走進樹林裡，就看見她親愛的賴桑德已經在那裡等著她，準備把她帶到姑媽家。可是他們還沒走完半個樹林，荷米亞就已經筋疲力竭了。賴桑德細心呵護著這位可愛的姑娘，而荷米亞則為了他，連自己的性命都不屑一顧。賴桑德勸荷米亞先在一片柔軟的草地上休息，等天亮再走，他自己則在離她不遠的地方躺下來，他們兩人很快便睡去。

　　就在這時，帕克發現了他們。他看到一個美少年在睡覺，又見他穿著雅典式衣裳，離他不遠處還睡著一個可愛的女孩，就斷定他們是奧伯龍要他找的那個雅典女孩和她

那個傲慢的情人。既然只有他們兩人在一起，帕克自然推想，那男的醒來第一眼看到的一定會是那個女孩。於是，帕克毫不猶豫就往他的眼皮上滴了一些紫色小花的汁液。

可是事情跟他想的完全不一樣。誰知海倫娜竟在此時出現，結果賴桑德睜開眼睛第一眼看到的不是荷米亞，而是海倫娜。說來真是不可思議，花液的魔力真強大，賴桑德對荷米亞的愛居然在一剎那全都消失了，他愛上了海倫娜。

要是賴桑德醒來時第一眼看見的是荷米亞，那麼即使帕克粗心弄錯也沒什麼關係，因為他本來就對那位忠貞的女孩十分癡情。可是精靈花液的魔力硬是讓可憐的賴桑德遺忘了真愛荷米亞，轉而追求另一個女孩，深更半夜卻把荷米亞獨自一人丟在樹林裡睡覺，這真是個不幸的意外。

因此，不幸的事就這樣發生了。正如前面所說的，德米崔斯粗魯地從海倫娜身邊跑開後，海倫娜竭力想追趕上他，可是她跑沒多久就跑不動了，因為在長程賽跑上，男人總是比女人強。過了一會兒，海倫娜就看不到德米崔斯了，她又沮喪又孤單地四處徘徊，後來就走到賴桑德睡覺的地方。

「啊！」她說，「躺在地上的不是賴桑德嗎？他是死了還是在睡覺呢？」她輕輕地碰了他一下說，「先生啊，如果你還活著的話，就醒醒吧！」

聽到這話，賴桑德睜開了眼睛（花液的魔力開始生

效），他立即狂熱地對她傾訴衷心，說她的美貌遠勝荷米亞，好比鴿子美過烏鴉一般，說他為了美麗的海倫娜情願赴湯蹈火，還說了許多類似的癡情話。海倫娜知道賴桑德是她的好朋友荷米亞的情人，也知道他已經跟她訂婚，所以聽到賴桑德對她說的話感到非常氣憤（這也怪不得她），以為賴桑德在愚弄她。

「啊！為什麼我生來就要被人嘲弄和輕視呢？德米崔斯從來不肯溫柔地看我一眼，也不肯對我說句甜蜜的話，難道這還不夠嗎，還不夠嗎？先生，你還要用這般嘲諷我的方式假意向我求愛。賴桑德，我還以為你是一個正人君子呢！」她氣沖沖地說完這些話後便跑開了，賴桑德緊跟在她後面，把他那還在睡夢中的荷米亞忘得一乾二淨。

荷米亞醒來後，發現只剩下自己一個人，既害怕又難過。她在樹林裡到處徘徊，不知道賴桑德出了什麼事，也不知道該上哪兒去找他。

與此同時，奧伯龍看見德米崔斯躺在樹下睡得正熟；德米崔斯沒找到荷米亞和他的情敵賴桑德，這場沒有結果的尋覓也讓他累得睡著了。奧伯龍問了帕克一些話，知道他滴錯人的眼皮了。現在找到了原本要找的那個人，於是奧伯龍用花液碰了一下德米崔斯熟睡的眼皮，德米崔斯旋即醒了過來，一眼就看見海倫娜。他就像賴桑德先前那樣，也對她傾吐愛意。就在這個時候，賴桑德出現了，後面跟著荷米亞（由於帕克不幸的過失，讓荷米亞現在追著

羅密歐與茱麗葉

情人跑）。於是，賴桑德和德米崔斯同時開口向海倫娜求愛，因為他們都被同一種強力的魔法所支配。

　　海倫娜大為吃驚，以為德米崔斯、賴桑德和昔日的好友荷米亞串通好來愚弄她。

　　荷米亞也和海倫娜一樣吃驚，賴桑德和德米崔斯本來都愛著她，為什麼現在卻都成了海倫娜的情人。荷米亞覺得這件事並不是玩笑。

　　這兩個女孩一向是最好的朋友，現在竟然開始怒言相向。

　　「殘忍的荷米亞啊！」海倫娜說，「是妳叫賴桑德用虛偽的甜言蜜語來惹我生氣，妳的另一個情人德米崔斯恨不得把我踩在腳下，而妳現在也要他稱我是女神、仙女、絕世美人、寶貝、天人？他恨我，若不是妳唆使他來嘲弄我，他是不會跟我說這種話的。殘忍的荷米亞，妳竟然和男人聯合起來欺負妳可憐的朋友。我們往日的同窗情誼妳全都忘了嗎？荷米亞啊，有多少次我們坐在同一張椅墊，唱著同一首歌，繡著同一種花朵。我們就像並蒂的櫻桃般一塊兒長大，永不分開呀！荷米亞，妳跟男人聯合起來嘲弄妳可憐的朋友，這豈不是太不顧情誼、也有失身分的事嗎？」

　　「妳這些話真是莫名其妙。」荷米亞說。「我並沒有嘲弄妳，我倒覺得是妳在嘲弄我！」

　　「唉，繼續吧！」海倫娜回說：「你們儘管繼續偽裝

下去吧,一副假惺惺的模樣,等我轉過身去就對我扮鬼臉;然後你們又擠眉弄眼,繃著臉把這個有趣的玩笑開下去。要是你們還有點憐憫之心,稍微有一點風度或禮貌,就不會這樣對我了。」

當海倫娜和荷米亞吵嘴的時候,德米崔斯和賴桑德轉身離開她們,為了爭奪海倫娜的愛而到樹林裡決鬥去了。

一發現男人不在,她們隨即分道揚鑣,再度疲倦地在樹林裡四下徘徊,尋找她們的情人。

仙王和小帕克偷聽了她們的對話。她們一離開,仙王就對帕克說:「帕克,你是不小心的,還是故意搞鬼?」

帕克回道:「您要相信我,精靈之王!是失誤啊。您不是告訴我說,從那個男人穿的雅典式衣裳就認得出他來嗎?不過,事情演變成這樣,我一點都不會過意不去,我倒覺得他們這樣吵吵鬧鬧很有趣。」

「你也聽見了,」奧伯龍說,「德米崔斯和賴桑德已經去找一個適合地方決鬥了。我命令你用濃霧把黑夜籠罩起來,把這些吵架的戀人引到黑暗裡,讓他們找不到彼此。你模仿他們的聲音,用難聽的話激他們,讓他們以為聽到的是情敵的聲音,引誘他們跟著你走,讓他們疲憊得再也走不動。等他們睡著了,你就把另一種花的汁液滴進賴桑德的眼睛裡,他醒來後就會忘記剛才對海倫娜產生的愛意,恢復從前對荷米亞的迷戀。這麼一來,這兩個美麗的女孩就都能快快樂樂地和她們所愛的男人在一起了,他

們都會以為剛剛發生的一切只是一場惱人的夢。快去吧，帕克，我要去看看我的泰坦妮亞找到什麼樣的情人了。」

此時泰坦妮亞還在睡覺，奧伯龍看見她旁邊有一個鄉巴佬，這個人在樹林裡迷路，而且也睡著了。「這傢伙，」他說，「讓他成為我泰坦妮亞的真愛吧！」說完就拿了一個驢子頭套在鄉巴佬的頭上，驢頭大小剛剛好，好像原本就長在他脖子上似的。雖然奧伯龍很小心地把驢頭套上去，不過還是把他吵醒了。他站起身來，完全沒有意識到奧伯龍在他身上搞鬼，就朝仙后睡覺的花壇（寢宮）走去。

「啊！我看見的是什麼天使呀！」泰坦尼亞睜開眼睛，那紫色小花的魔力開始起作用了。「你的智慧也和你的美貌一樣超凡嗎？」

「啊，太太。」愚蠢的鄉巴佬說，「要是我夠聰明，能夠走出這座樹林，那我就心滿意足了。」

「請不要離開這座樹林，」著迷的仙后說，「我是個不凡的精靈。我愛你。跟我一塊兒走吧，我會派仙子來伺候你的。」

於是，她喚來了四名仙子，他們的名字分別是：豌豆花、蜘蛛網、飛蛾和芥子。

「你們好好伺候這位可愛的先生，」仙后說，「他走路的時候你們就在他周圍飛舞，在他面前嬉戲，餵他吃葡萄和杏果，把蜜蜂的蜂蜜偷來給他。」她又對鄉巴佬說：

「過來，跟我坐在一塊兒。我俊俏的驢子，讓我摸摸你那毛茸茸的可愛臉蛋！我溫柔的寶貝，讓我吻吻你那漂亮的大耳朵！」

「豌豆花在哪裡？」驢頭鄉巴佬問。他不太理會仙后對他的追求，但是對擁有新侍從感到很得意。

「我在這兒，先生。」小豌豆花說。

「幫我搔搔頭。」鄉巴佬說，「蜘蛛網在哪兒？」

「我在這兒，先生。」蜘蛛網回答。

「蜘蛛網，」愚蠢的鄉巴佬說，「把薊樹上那隻紅色的小蜜蜂弄死，然後把蜜囊拿來給我。不要慌慌張張，要留心別把蜜囊打破了，要是你打翻了蜜囊，我可是會難過的。芥子在哪兒？」

「是的，先生。」芥子說，「您有何吩咐？」

　　「沒什麼。」鄉巴佬說，「芥子，你就和豌豆花一起替我搔搔癢吧。我該去理髮了，我覺得臉上的毛長得太長了。」

　　「親愛的，」仙后說，「你想吃點什麼？我有個喜愛冒險的仙子，他可以找到松鼠的儲糧，給你拿些新鮮的堅果來。」

　　「我倒是比較想吃一大把乾豌豆。」鄉巴佬說，他戴上驢頭之後，胃口也變得跟驢子一樣了。「但是拜託妳，不要叫妳那些人來吵我，我想睡了。」

　　「那就睡吧。」仙后說，「我會把你摟在我懷裡。啊，我多麼愛你！我多麼疼你呀！」

　　看到鄉巴佬睡在仙后的懷裡，仙王走到她面前，責備她不該把感情濫用在一頭驢子身上。

　　她沒法否認，因為鄉巴佬就睡在她懷裡，而且她還在他的驢頭上戴了花冠呢。

　　奧伯龍嘲笑她一番之後，又向她要那個偷換來的孩子。被丈夫撞見自己和新歡在一起，她覺得很羞愧，也就不敢再拒絕他的要求了。

　　就這樣，奧伯龍終於讓那個他要了好久的小男孩做他的僮僕。但是奧伯龍開始可憐起泰坦妮亞來，由於自己的惡作劇，才害她落入這般丟臉的處境。於是奧伯龍把另一種花的汁液滴在她的眼裡，仙后立刻恢復神志。她對自己剛才的意亂情迷很是驚訝，此時的她一見這畸形的怪物就

感到噁心。

奧伯龍把鄉巴佬頭上的驢頭拿下來，讓他頂著自己肩上那顆愚蠢的腦袋繼續睡覺。

現在，奧伯龍和泰坦妮亞言歸於好了，他把那兩對戀人的故事和他們半夜吵架的經過都告訴她，於是她跟他一起去看看這段奇遇的結果。

仙王和仙后找到那兩個男子和他們美麗的女孩，他們都睡在地上，彼此相距不遠。帕克為了補救先前的過錯，想盡辦法讓他們在不知不覺中被引到同一個地方，然後用仙王給他的解藥小心翼翼地解除賴桑德眼裡的魔咒。

荷米亞最先醒過來，看到迷失的賴桑德就睡在不遠的地方，她望著他，對他的怪異無常感到疑惑不已。此時，賴桑德也睜開眼睛，一看到他親愛的荷米亞，被施了魔咒的他立刻清醒過來，恢復了神志，也恢復了對荷米亞的愛。他們談起夜裡的奇遇，弄不清究竟這些事情是真的發生過，或者他們只是做了一場相同而怪異的夢。

此時，海倫娜和德米崔斯也都醒了，睡了一場大覺之後，海倫娜苦惱憤怒的情緒已經平靜下來，現在又聽到德米崔斯對她依然表示愛慕，她非常開心，尤其看出他說的是真心話之後，她心裡既驚奇又高興。

這兩位在樹林裡夜遊的美麗女孩已經不再是情敵了，她們重修舊好，彼此寬恕對方脫口而出的惡言，心平氣和地商量眼前的對策。不久，大家都同意，既然德米崔斯已

經不願再娶荷米亞，他就應該竭力去說服她父親撤銷那早已判下的殘酷死刑。為了幫助朋友，德米崔斯準備返回雅典。就在這時，他們驚訝地看到荷米亞的父親伊吉斯，他到樹林裡尋找他逃家的女兒。

伊吉斯知道德米崔斯已經不想娶他女兒後，也就不再反對她嫁給賴桑德了。他答應讓他們四天後舉行婚禮，也就是荷米亞原本要被處死的那一天。而海倫娜所愛的德米崔斯現在對她十分忠誠，她滿心歡喜地答應在同一天嫁給他。

由於奧伯龍的幫助，這兩對愛人的戀情都得到了圓滿的結果，仙王和仙后躲在一旁觀看這場和解，為此感到非常欣慰。於是，這些善良的精靈決定在仙國舉行歡宴，以慶祝即將到來的婚禮。

現在，要是這些精靈和他們戲耍的故事讓誰不高興，認為事情太荒謬、太難以置信，那麼就當自己是在做夢，當這些奇遇都是夢裡發生的故事就好。我希望沒有讀者會這麼不近人情，被這一場美妙的、無傷大雅的仲夏夜之夢所激怒。

IV.

李爾王

　　不列顛國王李爾有三個女兒：奧本尼公爵的妻子剛乃綺、康瓦爾公爵的妻子里根，還有未婚的考地利亞。法蘭西國王和勃艮第公爵這時候都在李爾的宮殿裡，他們兩人都是為了向考地利亞求婚而來。

　　老國王已經八十多歲了，他年事已高，政務繁忙，決定把國事交給年輕有為的人去治理，不再過問，這樣他就有時間準備後事，因為不久後他即將面對死亡。有了這樣的打算後，國王就把三個女兒都叫到跟前來，看看誰最敬愛他，這樣他才好依照她們愛他的程度將國土分配給她們。

　　大女兒剛乃綺說，她對父親的愛是無法用言語來表達的，她說她愛父親勝過愛她自己的眼睛，勝過愛她自己的生命和自由。其實，她只要老實地說幾句真心話就夠了，可正因為她並非出自真心，所以信口編了一套花言巧語。聽到女兒親口保證，國王信以為真，十分高興。於是，父愛油然而生，國王就把廣大國土的三分之一賜給了她和她

的丈夫。

　　國王接著把二女兒喚來，讓她表白一下自己的心思。里根跟姊姊一樣虛偽，說的一點也不比姊姊差。她說她姊姊的話還不足以表達她對父王的愛，因為沉浸在父王的父愛裡，世界上一切的歡樂都變得索然無味了。

　　看到孩子們都這樣愛他，李爾為自己感到慶幸。聽完里根動人的話，他也同樣把三分之一的國土賜給她和她的丈夫，跟他剛才賜給剛乃綺的一樣大。

　　然後李爾轉向他快樂的泉源：小女兒考地利亞。他問她有沒有什麼想說的話，心想她一定也會跟姊姊們一樣說出動人的話來討他歡心，也許她的話會比她們的還要動聽，因為他一向最寵愛她。可是考地利亞對於姊姊們的奉承感到非常厭惡，她知道姊姊們根本言不由衷，她們只是為了從年老的父王手裡騙取國土，這樣不必等到國王去世，她們和她們的丈夫就可以接管王國。因此，考地利亞只回說：她的愛恰如其分，她對父王的愛乃出於作女兒的本分。

　　聽到自己最寵愛的女兒說出這番不知感恩的話，國王大吃一驚，他要求考地利亞重新修正自己的話，以免自毀前程。

　　考地利亞告訴父親說，他身為父親，養育她、也深愛她；她也盡自己的孝心來報答他、服從他、愛他，且非常尊敬他。可是她無法像姊姊們那樣誇大其詞，或保證父親

是她世上唯一所愛的人。如果姊姊們如她們所說的，真的只愛父親一人，那怎麼又會有丈夫呢？如果有一天她結婚了，相信她的丈夫也想擁有她一半的愛和關懷，要她善盡做妻子的責任。如果她只愛父親一人，她就永遠不會像姊姊那樣嫁人了。

事實上，考地利亞才是真心如姊姊們所佯言地那樣深愛著年邁的父親。平常她會用為人女兒的態度，說些更親熱的話，更毫無保留地向父親表示敬愛。然而，看到姊姊們藉著虛偽的奉承而得到了豐厚的賞賜，她就保留了自己的態度，說出了不重聽的話——因為她認為她所能做的，就是默默地愛著父親，以表明她對父親的愛沒有沾染貪圖色彩，也不求任何回報。她的話雖然不動聽，卻比姊姊們說得真摯誠懇。

然而，老國王李爾卻認為考地利亞說出這番泛泛之詞的態度十分驕傲，因此非常生氣。國王年輕的時候脾氣就很暴躁，如今年紀大了，腦子更糊塗了，根本分辨不出誰是真誠還是奉承，誰的話是謊言還是實話。他一怒之下，就把原來預留給考地利亞的那三分之一國土收回來，平分給兩個姊姊和她們的丈夫奧本尼公爵和康瓦爾公爵。李爾把他們叫過來，在所有朝臣面前將王冠賜給他們，並且把所有權柄、稅收和國政一併交給他們管理。他釋出國王的一切政權，僅保留國王的頭銜和一百名騎士做為侍從，打算每個月輪流住在兩個女兒的王宮裡。

　　看到李爾行事如此衝動草率，如此荒唐地處置國土，
群臣無不震驚難過。然而，除了肯特伯爵，誰也不敢去冒
犯這位正在氣頭上的國王。肯特伯爵替考地利亞說了幾句
好話，暴跳如雷的李爾卻要他閉嘴，不然就要他的命，但
忠實善良的肯特並沒有因此退卻。他一向對李爾忠心耿
耿，敬他如君，愛他如父，從他如主；他從來不看重自己
的生命，他活著只為了擊退李爾的敵人，為了保衛李爾的
安全，他視死如歸。

　　如今，李爾的敵人就是李爾自己，這個忠實的臣僕本
著自己的原則，為了李爾好，毅然地反對他。他現在對李
爾無禮，那是因為李爾已經失去了理智。他一向是國王最
忠誠的諫臣，所以他請求國王接受他的諫言，同以往在做
許多重大決策時一樣，接納他的忠告。他勸國王三思，收
回他那草率的成命，並用他的性命擔保，李爾的小女兒對
他的孝心絕對不亞於她的姊姊們，她的回答之所以低調冷
漠，那是因為她真實，絲毫沒有虛情假意。在位者如果被
讒言所迷惑，正直的朝臣就顯得直言無諱，不管李爾怎麼
恫嚇，肯特都沒有退卻，因為他隨時都準備為國王犧牲自
己的性命，再大的威脅也封不住有責任感的人的嘴。

　　然而，善良的肯特伯爵直率的諫言只會更加激怒國
王。國王此時就像一個發瘋的病人，愛上了使自己致命的
疾病，準備殺掉自己的醫生。國王下令放逐這個忠僕，限
他五天內離開，如果他第六天仍在不列顛，就要將他處以

死刑。

　於是肯特向國王告辭，表示既然自己選擇這種直諫的方式，留在那裡也跟流放在外一樣。臨走前，他祝福正直慎言的考地利亞，並且希望她的兩個姊姊能將她們說的話付諸行動。他離去時又說，即使身在異鄉，他對國王依然忠誠。

　法蘭西國王和勃艮第公爵被召進宮，以聽取李爾對他小女兒所做的決定。考地利亞失去了父親的寵愛，分不到任何財產，國王想知道，他們是否還想娶她為妻？勃艮第公爵聽了之後便婉拒婚事，表示在這種狀況下他就不想娶她為妻了。至於法蘭西國王，他知道考地利亞失去父親的寵愛是因為她直言，不像她姊姊那樣善於諂媚，他牽起這位年輕姑娘的手，說她的美德勝過一份國王的嫁妝。他請考地利亞跟兩個姊姊告別，也告別待她刻薄的父親，跟他一起走，做他的皇后，也做法蘭西王國的皇后，他統治的王國要比她兩個姊姊們的更輝煌。最後，他用輕蔑的口吻稱勃艮第公爵為「如水的公爵」，因為他對這位年輕姑娘的愛就像流水般一轉眼便消逝了。

　考地利亞淌著淚水和姊姊們告別，同時囑咐她們要照她們所宣稱的那樣愛護父親。她的姊姊繃著臉不悅地說，她們會盡自己的本分，用不著她多嘴，還譏笑地說，她的丈夫已經把她視為命運賜給他的施捨了，她只管好好伺候她丈夫就行了。最後考地利亞帶著沉重的心情離去，她知

道姊姊們為人狡猾，她多麼希望把父親託付給比較可靠
的人，而不是離他而去。但眼下除了兩位姊姊，她父親
誰也不信任，因此考利亞只能懷著擔憂，與法蘭西國王
一同返回他的國家。

　　考地利亞一走，她的姊姊們就露出了邪惡的
真面目。依照約定，李爾頭一個月住在
大女兒剛乃綺那裡，可是不到一
個月，李爾就發現她的行為
和她的諾言大相逕庭。

這個卑鄙的女兒已經得到了她
父親賞賜給她的一切，但她還是
不知足，甚至還把父親頭上
戴的皇冠摘下來，連老人
家為了使自己還像個國
王而保留的排場都不能
忍受。她一看到父王和
他那一百名騎士就生氣；
每逢看到父王，她總是皺
著眉頭。而且，當老人家想
跟她說話時，她就假裝生病，
或找其他理由迴避他。很顯然地，她
已經把老人家當成是一個累贅，把他的侍從
當作是一種浪費。由於她對國王的怠慢，（恐怕）還有
她暗地裡的唆使，她的僕人也冷落他，不聽從他的命
令，甚至傲慢地佯裝沒聽到。李爾當然不可能沒有發現
女兒態度上的轉變，但是他盡量假裝沒看到，因為人們

總是不願承認痛苦的後果是自己的錯誤和頑固所導致。

　　一個人若是真誠忠實，就算待他刻薄，他也不會離開；一個人若是虛偽狡詐，就算對他再好，他也不會感激。這一點用在忠誠的肯特伯爵身上是最適合不過了。肯特被李爾流放，假使被發現他仍在不列顛，將會因此葬送性命。然而，只要還有機會對國王效命，他就甘願冒死留下。看啊！可憐的忠僕有時候被情勢所迫，不得不打扮成低賤的樣子來掩飾自己的身分，不過這並不卑賤可恥，因為他是為了恪盡職責。

　　這個伯爵放下尊嚴，喬裝成一名僕人，請求服侍國王。國王並不知道這個人就是肯特，應話的時候肯特故意答得很直爽，甚至有些粗魯，可是這卻使國王很高興（因為這跟那些油腔滑調的讒言大不相同，李爾看到女兒的口是心非後，讓他對那種花言巧語感到厭惡了）。於是，李爾答應讓肯特待在身旁服侍。肯特化名為凱爾斯，國王怎麼也沒料到，他就是自己曾經最鍾愛的臣子，位高權大的肯特伯爵。

　　凱爾斯很快就找到機會來表現他對國王的忠誠與敬愛：就在那一天，剛乃綺的管家對李爾十分侮慢，神情和言語都很無理，這無疑是他的主人私下教唆的。凱爾斯不能忍受他這樣公然侮辱國王，就故意用腳將他絆倒，把這個沒有禮貌的僕人扔進狗窩裡。凱爾斯如此護衛主人，讓李爾和他越來越親近。

李爾的朋友並不只有肯特一個人。依照習俗，國王和權貴身邊都有豢養「弄臣」（一般都這樣稱呼他們），在繁重的公務之後替他們解悶。在李爾還擁有宮殿時，他的宮廷裡也有這麼一個弄臣，他的地位低微，卻對李爾非常忠誠。在李爾放棄王位之後，這個卑微的弄臣仍然跟隨著他，時常以詼諧的話語來逗李爾開心。但是他偶爾也會忍不住揶揄國王，嘲笑他輕率地把一切都給了女兒。他作了首打油詩來描繪李爾的處境：

　　　　因驚喜而掉淚，
　　　他卻唱歌訴說悲傷；
　　　　堂堂一國之君，
　　　竟跟弄臣玩捉迷藏。

　　他多的是這種荒誕不經的詞曲，當著剛乃綺的面，這位逗趣正直的弄臣也照樣吐真言，他會用尖銳犀利的話諷刺她。譬如，他把國王比喻為籬雀，說牠把布穀鳥養大後，布穀鳥為了報答養育之恩，卻把籬雀的腦袋咬下來。又說，一隻笨驢也看得出來，現在是馬車拉著馬匹走（意思是，女兒本應該聽從父親的，現在卻欺凌父親）。他還說，李爾已經不再是李爾了，他只是李爾的影子。因為這些放肆的言詞，弄臣也受到一兩次小心挨鞭子的警告。

　　李爾開始感受到女兒對他的冷落和不敬，但是這個糊塗老人受到不肖女兒的惡劣待遇還不只這些。她現在清楚地對他說，如果他堅持要保留那一百名騎士，那他就不便繼續住在她的王宮裡。她說這些排場既沒意義又浪費錢，那些騎士只會在她的宮裡吵吵鬧鬧，吃吃喝喝。她要求把人數減少，只留下一些像他那樣上了歲數的人，這樣才跟他相稱。

　　李爾起初不敢相信自己的眼睛和耳朵，他不相信說出這樣刻薄話的竟然是自己的女兒。他不敢相信他給了她皇冠，她卻要裁掉他的侍從，不願讓他安享晚年。她堅持她那不孝的要求，李爾大發脾氣，罵她是「可惡的鳶」，說她都在瞎扯。的確，那一百名騎士都是品行優良的一時之選，他們謹守本分，並不像她說的那樣只會吃喝喧鬧。

　　李爾命人備妥馬匹，他要帶那一百名騎士到二女兒里根的住處。他嘴裡叨唸大女兒的忘恩負義，形容她是鐵石心腸的惡魔，還說一個孩子若是忘恩負義，比海裡的妖怪還可怕。他用可怕的字眼詛咒大女兒剛乃綺，詛咒她絕子絕孫，就算她有小孩，長大後也會用同樣鄙視侮辱的態度來回報她，讓她知道有個忘恩負義的孩子比被毒蛇咬到還要痛苦。

　　這時候，剛乃綺的丈夫奧本尼公爵擔心李爾會認為他也參與了這不義的行為，於是替自己辯解起來，但是李爾沒等他把話說完，就忿忿地叫人備妥馬鞍，帶著他的隨侍

動身到二女兒里根家去了。李爾心想,考地利亞的過錯（如果那算是過錯的話）比起她這個姊姊的行徑,是多麼微不足道啊!於是,他的倦眸不禁流下淚水。他覺得無比羞愧,自己是個大丈夫,竟然被剛乃綺這樣的禍害氣得流下淚來。

里根和她的丈夫把皇宮裝潢得富麗奢華。李爾先派遣僕人凱爾斯給二女兒帶封信,以便準備迎接他和他的衆隨侍們。不過,剛乃綺似乎搶先一步派人送信給里根,她在信中責備父親剛愎自用,脾氣乖張,還勸妹妹不要收留他隨身的一大群侍從。

剛乃綺的信差和凱爾斯同時抵達,兩個人碰了頭。那個信差原來就是凱爾斯的死對頭管家,凱爾斯曾為了他對李爾態度蠻橫而把他絆倒。凱爾斯很不喜歡這傢伙的神氣,而且懷疑他此行不懷好意,開口便斥罵他,要和他決鬥。那傢伙不肯決鬥,凱爾斯氣憤不已,狠狠地揍了他一頓,誰叫他製造禍端,送來這惡毒的信。里根和她的丈夫聽聞這件事,儘管凱爾斯是父王派來的信差,應該受到最高的禮遇,他們卻命人把凱爾斯銬上腳鐐。這樣,國王進入城堡時首先看到的,就是他這個受到屈辱的忠實僕人凱爾斯。

這只不過是國王即將受到的惡劣待遇中的開頭罷了,緊接著還有更過分的事呢。李爾表示要見他的女兒和女婿,僕人卻回說,他們趕了一整夜的路,累得無法迎接

他。最後，在李爾憤然地堅持之下，他們才出來接見他。可是，陪他們一道出來的，竟然是那個可恨的剛乃綺！她跑來跟妹妹說自己的事，並且慫恿妹妹反抗父王。

老人家看到這一幕時激動不已，尤其看到里根還牽著剛乃綺的手。他問剛乃綺，看看他這一大把灰白的鬍子，難道她一點都不覺得慚愧嗎？里根則勸他和剛乃綺回去，裁掉一半的侍從，要求剛乃綺原諒他，兩人和平共處，因為他年紀大了，缺乏明辨是非的能力，必須由見識較廣的人來管教他、帶領他。

要他屈膝下跪乞求自己的女兒供他衣食，李爾覺得這實在是太荒唐了。他拒絕這種違背人倫的依靠，表示永遠不會再回到剛乃綺那裡，他要和他那一百名騎士留在里根這裡。他說里根沒有忘記他把半個王國給了她，而且她的眼神溫和善良，不像剛乃綺那樣凶狠。李爾還說，要他裁掉一半的侍從，回到剛乃綺那裡，他寧可到法國，請求那個娶了他的小女兒卻不要嫁妝的國王給他一筆可憐的養老金。

李爾以為里根待他會比她姊姊好，可是他錯了。里根好像有意要贏過姊姊的忤逆行為，她說用五十名騎士來伺候父親太多了，二十五名就夠了。這時候，李爾的心幾乎要碎了。他轉過身來對剛乃綺說，自己願意和她回去，五十個還比二十五個多一倍，可見她對他的愛也比里根多一倍。可是剛乃綺卻又推諉說，為什麼需要二十五個這麼

多呢？連十個、五個也用不著，因為他大可使喚她或妹妹的僕人呀！

這兩個沒有良心的姊妹好像在比賽，看看誰對一向疼愛她們的老父親比較殘酷，她們一步步地奪走他的隨從，還有那些代表他曾經是個國王的尊嚴（對曾經統治過一個國家的他來說，根本毫無尊嚴可言）。並不是非得要有體面的侍從排場才算幸福，可是從國王淪落成為乞者，從統治幾百萬人到連一個侍從都沒有，的確是個很難堪的變化。然而，真正讓這個國王傷透心的，不是他沒有了隨從，而是他女兒的忘恩負義。李爾一方面受到這雙重的虐待，一方面又懊悔自己分配王國的昏庸，他的神志開始有些不正常了。雖然他說著連自己都不清楚的話，但仍發誓要報復這兩個不孝的妖婦，要她們遭受到慘絕人寰的報應。

正當李爾這樣信口恫嚇威脅時，天幕已黑，颳起了一陣暴風雨。他的女兒們仍然堅持不給他隨從，於是李爾叫人把馬拉過來，他寧可到外面被狂風暴雨吹打，也不願意跟這兩個無情無義的女兒待在同一個屋簷下。她們說，一個人如果剛愎自用而使自己受到傷害，那也是剛好而已。於是她們關上大門，任李爾在那樣的天候下離去。

風颳得很急，雷雨越下越大，老人家和大自然搏鬥著。然而，風雨的襲擊畢竟沒有女兒們的不義那樣叫人痛心。李爾走了好幾哩路，一路上幾乎連個灌木叢都沒有，

他就這樣在黑夜的荒原裡遊蕩，和狂風暴雨奮戰。他要風把陸地捲入海裡，或是大海揚起巨浪把大地淹沒，好讓所有像人類一樣忘恩負義的動物絕跡。現在，唯一陪伴老國王的只剩下那卑微的弄臣了，他依然跟著國王，竭力想用詼諧怪誕的話來消遣這不幸的遭遇。他說這樣糟糕的夜晚並不適合游泳，國王最好還是回去乞求女兒們的祝福！

IV.李爾王

只怪自己沒大腦，

嘿呀，又是風吹又是雨淋！

別怨天也別尤人，

任它風呀雨呀天天下不停。

　　他發誓，這樣的夜絕對是個讓一名女人不再傲慢的最佳時機。

　　李爾曾是堂堂的一國之君，如今卻只有一個弄臣孤零零地陪著他。這時候，忠實的僕人肯特伯爵找到國王，肯特一直喬裝成凱爾斯緊隨著他，但是國王始終沒有認出他來。肯特說：「國王，您在這裡啊？就算喜歡黑夜的動物也不會喜歡這樣的夜，可怕的暴風雨把野獸都嚇得躲回巢穴裡去了，人類也承受不了這樣的折磨和恐懼的呀！」

　　李爾反駁說，這樣的災難根本不算什麼，他懷抱的是更大的痛苦。內心平靜的時候，才有閒功夫讓肉體變得嬌貴，而他內心裡的風暴已經奪走了一切知覺，只能感覺到心跳。他談到女兒的忘恩負義，說那就像嘴巴把拿東西給它吃的手咬下來一樣，因為對兒女來說，父母就是他們的手、他們的食物和一切呀！

　　忠心的凱爾斯仍然一再請求國王不要待在屋外，最後終於說服他到荒原上的一間茅草屋裡去。弄臣先行入屋，不一會兒就慌慌張張地跑了出來，直嚷著說看見了鬼。仔

細一看，他所說的鬼只不過是個可憐的瘋乞丐，他躲進這沒人住的茅草屋裡來避雨。他說了些可怕的話，弄臣聽了很害怕。像這種可憐的瘋子，不是真的瘋了就是裝瘋，意圖迫使心腸軟的鄉下人給點施捨。他們給自己取名叫「可憐的湯姆」或「不幸的圖力古」，在鄉間四處遊蕩，嘴裡嘟囔著：「哪位賞點什麼東西給可憐的湯姆吧！」然後用針、釘子或迷迭香的樹枝把自己的手臂戳得流血。他們靠這種嚇人的舉動，一邊祈禱，一邊瘋言瘋語地詛咒，使那些無知的鄉下人見了感動或害怕，不得不給他們一點施捨。這個可憐的傢伙就是這種瘋子。他全身赤裸，只在腰上圍了一條毯子，國王看見他處境這樣淒慘，就斷定他也是把自己所有的財產都給了女兒，所以才會落得這步田地。除了有個不孝的女兒，李爾想不出還有什麼原因可以讓一個人如此悲慘。

聽到李爾說的這些瘋話，好心的凱爾斯看出他的精神狀態顯然不是很穩定，女兒的虐待真的把他氣瘋了。這時候，可敬的肯特伯爵又有了一個好機會，可以在關鍵時刻表現他的忠誠。天亮的時候，在一些仍然忠心耿耿的隨侍的協助下，肯特伯爵把國王送到多佛城堡去，因為伯爵的朋友和人脈大都在那裡。他自己則搭船前往法國，趕往考地利亞的宮廷，向她敘述她父親的悲慘境遇，並且鉅細靡遺地闡述她兩個姊姊慘無人道的行為。這個善良孝順的孩子聽了不禁流下淚來，她要求國王（她的丈夫）允許她搭

船到英格蘭，帶足人馬去討伐這兩個殘忍的姊姊和她們的丈夫，讓老父王復位。她的丈夫同意後，考地利亞隨即出發，帶著一支皇家軍隊在多佛登陸。

好心的肯特伯爵派人照顧發瘋的李爾，李爾卻趁機躲開那些人溜了出去。當他正在多佛附近的田野徘徊時，正好被考地利亞的隨侍發現。李爾當時的情況真是悽慘，他完全瘋了，一個人大聲唱著歌，頭上帶著用稻草、蕁麻和麥田裡撿來的野草編成的王冠。

考地利亞急著想見父親，可是大夫勸她暫時先不要見面，最好等李爾睡過覺、服過藥，精神穩定後再相見比較好。考地利亞承諾，要是這些精通醫術的大夫能讓老國王康復，她就把所有的金子和珠寶都送給他們。過不久，李爾便康復到可以和女兒見面的狀況了。

他們父女團聚的情景令人感動。可憐的老國王百感交集，再見到自己曾經深愛的孩子，他欣喜不已，可是想到當初他為了些小錯便在一怒之下遺棄她，而今她卻如此孝順，使他感到羞愧不已。李爾喜慚交雜，加上病痛的折磨，他半瘋半癲的頭腦忘了自己身在何處，搞不清楚吻著他、親切地和他說話的人是誰。他說，這位女子想來是他的女兒考地利亞，如果他弄錯了，也請大家不要見笑。接著李爾就跪了下來，乞求女兒原諒他。善良的考地利亞則一直跪在他身旁，祈求上帝保佑他。她對父親說，他不應當對她下跪，她只是盡她應盡的孝道，她是他的孩子，是

他如假包換的孩子考地利亞！她親吻他，想用她的吻來
撫平姊姊們對他的傷害。她還說，她們應該感到羞恥，
竟然把白髮蒼蒼的慈祥老父親趕到寒冷的屋外，即使是
敵人的狗咬了自己，在
那樣寒冷的夜晚，她
也會讓牠依偎在
火爐旁取暖，

更何況是疼愛自己的父親。

考地利亞告訴父親,她這次從法國回來是為了幫助他。李爾請她務必忘記過去的事並且原諒他,因為他老了,糊塗了,不知道自己在做什麼;她的確有理由不愛他,可是她的姊姊沒有理由不孝順他。考地利亞告訴他,她跟姊姊們一樣,沒有理由不愛他。

我們暫時把老國王託付給這個真心孝順、愛他的孩子去保護吧。老國王被他那兩個殘忍的女兒逼得精神錯亂,終於靠考地利亞和大夫的力量,用睡眠和醫藥把他治好了。現在我們再來說說那兩個狠毒的女兒。

這兩個忘恩負義的妖魔,對自己的父親都這樣無情無義了,又怎麼可能對自己的丈夫忠誠呢?過不了多久,她們連表面上假裝恩愛和履行妻子的義務都厭倦了,還公然表示她們愛上其他人。湊巧的是,她們兩人愛上的是同一個人,他就是已故的葛羅斯特伯爵的私生子愛德蒙。他用計謀奪取了原本屬於他兄長愛德嘉的爵位,靠卑鄙的手段當上了伯爵。這個惡劣的傢伙跟剛乃綺、里根這兩個人勾搭,正是一丘之貉。

里根的丈夫康瓦爾公爵恰巧在這時候死了,於是里根馬上宣布要跟葛羅斯特伯爵結婚。原來,這個卑鄙的伯爵不僅向里根示愛,同時也屢次向剛乃綺表白,這使得剛乃綺妒火中燒,竟想方設法將里根毒死。後來這件事被剛乃綺的丈夫奧本尼公爵知道了,又聽說她跟葛羅斯特伯爵有

曖昧關係,就把她打入牢裡。在失去所愛之人的折磨和憤恨之下,剛乃綺不久後便自盡了。天理公道就這樣應證在這兩個壞女兒的身上。

　　事情發生後一時譁然,大家都認為這兩人死有餘辜,正義得以伸張。然後他們又轉移焦點,驚愕地看到命運之神,竟也賜予善良的女兒考地利亞悲慘的未來。考地利亞的善行理應得到更多的善報,然而,殘酷的真理是:在這個世上,純潔善良的人並不一定會得到好報。剛乃綺和里根派的軍隊在邪惡的伯爵葛羅斯特統領之下獲勝了。這個卑鄙的伯爵不希望有人妨礙他篡奪王位,就把考地利亞害死在監獄裡。上天派考地利亞給世人示範盡孝的榜樣後,就把這個年輕善良的女孩召喚到祂身旁了。她死後不久,李爾也去世了。

　　從李爾受大女兒的虐待開始,到他最悲慘零落的這段期間,忠誠的肯特伯爵始終守護著他。李爾在世時,肯特曾企圖讓國王知道他一直化名成凱爾斯跟隨著他,可是李爾已經神智不清了,根本無法理解那是怎麼回事,搞不清楚肯特和凱爾斯怎麼可能是同一個人。肯特心想,事到如今也用不著去向他解釋了。李爾不久就撒手人寰,國王的這個忠僕,一方面因為自己上了年紀,一方面也為老主人悲傷,不久後也跟著走進墳墓裡。

　　上天最終還是懲罰了卑鄙的葛羅斯特伯爵,他謀反之事東窗事發,結果在合法伯爵繼承人的兄弟決鬥中被刺身

亡。至於剛乃綺的丈夫奧本尼公爵，他與考地利亞的死無
關，也沒有慫恿妻子去做違逆父親的事，於是，李爾死後
他就登基為不列顛的國王。他的事就用不著提了，因為本
則故事要講的是李爾和他三個女兒的事，如今他們都已離
世。

V.

無事生非

梅西那皇宮裡住著兩個姑娘，一個叫希柔，一個叫碧翠絲。希柔是梅西那總督里奧納多的女兒，碧翠絲是他的姪女。

碧翠絲個性活潑，希柔則較為拘謹，碧翠絲很喜歡說些俏皮話來逗堂妹開心。不管發生什麼事，無憂無慮的碧翠絲總能拿來消遣一番。

這兩個姑娘的故事是這樣開始的：幾個在軍隊裡官階頗高的年輕人來拜訪里奧納多，他們驍勇善戰，在一場剛結束的戰爭裡建功立業，在返家的路上正巧從梅西那經過。他們當中有阿拉貢親王唐佩卓、親王的佛羅倫斯貴族好友克勞迪歐，還有性格狂野卻機智的帕度亞貴族班奈狄克。

這些客人以前都來過梅西那，好客的總督待他們如故友舊識，把自己的女兒和姪女介紹給他們認識。

班奈狄克一進屋子，就跟里奧納多和親王熱絡地聊起話來。不喜歡被排除在談話之外的碧翠絲，打斷班奈狄克

的話說：「班奈狄克先生，我真好奇你怎麼還在講話，沒有人理你啊！」

雖然班奈狄克和碧翠絲講話一樣不經過大腦，但這種沒有禮貌的問候方式還是讓他很不高興。他覺得，一個出言不遜的姑娘想必不是很有教養。他想起上次到梅西那時，碧翠絲就常拿他開玩笑。

喜歡開別人玩笑的人，最不喜歡別人拿他們開玩笑了，班奈狄克和碧翠絲也是一樣。這兩個機靈嘴快的人以往只要一見面，就會彼此譏笑挖苦，唇槍舌戰一番，然後搞得不歡而散。因此，當班奈狄克話說到一半就被碧翠絲打斷，還說什麼沒有人在聽他說話，因此班奈狄克就假裝之前沒注意到她在場，說：「哎呀，我親愛的傲慢小姐，妳還活著啊？」

現在，他們倆人又展開舌戰，接著就是一場漫長又激烈的爭論。雖然碧翠絲認同班奈狄克在最近這場戰役中表現得相當英勇，她卻說她要把他在戰場上殺死的人一個個吃掉。她又注意到親王很喜歡聽班奈狄克說話，就稱他為「親王的弄臣」。這個嘲諷是碧翠絲有史以來最讓班奈狄克難堪的一句話。

為了諷刺他是個懦夫，她說她要把他殺死的人一個個吃光，這他倒不在乎，因為他知道自己是個勇敢的人。可是機智聰明的人最怕背上汙名，因為這種指責有時候會太接近事實，所以碧翠絲說他是「親王的弄臣」，班奈狄克

簡直恨透她了。

　　嫻靜的希柔在這些賓客面前默不作聲。克勞迪歐留意到她長得越來越漂亮了，他無法克制地注視著她那美麗的臉蛋和姣好的身材（她本來就是個叫人敬愛的年輕姑娘）。這時候，親王興致高昂地聽著班奈狄克和碧翠絲之間詼諧的談話，他小聲地對里奧納多說：「真是個開朗活潑的年輕姑娘，她倒可以成為班奈狄克的好妻子。」

　　聽到這個建議，里奧納多回說：「啊，殿下呀，殿下，他們若是結了婚，不出一個星期就會吵瘋的。」

　　儘管里奧納多認為他們並不相配，親王仍不放棄撮合這兩個機伶鬼的念頭。

　　親王和克勞迪歐從王宮回來的時候，親王發現，除了他認為該撮合的班奈狄克和碧翠絲之外，他們這一夥人當中還有另外一對也該撮合，因為克勞迪歐不斷提到希柔，這讓親王猜到他的心思，便問克勞迪歐：「你愛希柔嗎？」

　　對於這個問題，克勞迪歐回說：「啊，殿下，我上次去梅西那的時候，是以軍人的眼光來看待她，雖然心裡很喜歡她，可是沒有時間好談感情。如今，天下太平和樂，無需掛念戰事，我的腦子裡充斥著一縷縷纏綿的柔情，這種柔情告訴我年輕的希柔有多麼美，使我想起自己在出征以前，就已經愛上她了。」

　　聽到克勞迪歐表白他對希柔的感情，親王非常感動，

他立刻前去請求里奧納多同意讓克勞迪歐成為他的女婿。

里奧納多同意了這門親事，親王也沒費多大功夫就說服了溫柔的希柔接受克勞迪歐這位年輕有為之人的求婚。克勞迪歐是個天資聰穎、成就不凡的貴族，如今又有善良的親王幫忙撮合，他很快就說動了里奧納多盡早舉行他跟希柔的婚禮。

只需靜候幾日，克勞迪歐就可以跟他美麗的姑娘結婚了，可他仍不免抱怨等待的時日過於無趣。的確，大部分的年輕小伙子殷殷期盼著某件事完成時，總是會不耐煩。因此，親王為了轉移他的注意力，就提出一個有趣的點子：他想出一個妙計，讓班奈狄克和碧翠絲兩個人墜入愛河。

克勞迪歐很高興地參與了親王這個突發奇想的計畫，里奧納多也答應幫忙，連希柔也說她願意盡棉薄之力，幫助堂姊得到一段良緣。

親王想出的計策是：男士們設法讓班奈狄克相信碧翠絲迷戀他，而希柔則想辦法讓碧翠絲相信班奈狄克也愛上她。

親王、里奧納多和克勞迪歐率先行動。他們等待著時機，當班奈狄克靜靜地坐在涼亭裡看書的時候，親王和他的幫手就走到涼亭後面的樹叢裡。他們故意站在離班奈狄克很近的地方，近得讓他一定聽得到他們全部的談話。一陣閒聊之後，親王說：「里奧納多，那天你告訴我什麼

啊……你是說你的姪女碧翠絲愛上了班奈狄克先生嗎？我怎麼也想不到這位姑娘會對他那樣的男人動情啊。」

里奧納多回說，「是啊，殿下，我也沒想到。尤其想不到她竟對班奈迪克這麼多情，她表面上看起來相當厭惡他呀。」

為了證實這些話，克勞迪歐還在一旁說希柔告訴他碧翠絲迷戀班奈狄克，如果班奈迪克拒絕她，她一定會很傷心。但是，里奧納多和克勞迪歐似乎都認為班奈迪克是不可能愛上她的，因為他對漂亮的女孩一向很苛薄，尤其是碧翠絲。

親王聽了這些話，假裝同情碧翠絲，於是說：「要是可以將這件事情告訴班奈狄克就好了。」克勞迪歐接著說，「告訴他有什麼用呢？他會把它當作一椿笑話，那只會讓那可憐的姑娘更難堪罷了。」

親王又說：「他要真是這樣，就把他吊死算了，因為碧翠絲是個非常出色的姑娘，她做任何事都表現得很有智慧，除了愛上班奈狄克這件事例外。」然後，親王示意同伴繼續向前走，留班奈狄克在那兒仔細想想他偷聽到的話。

班奈狄克果真聽到了這場對話，聽到碧翠斯愛上他時，還自言自語地說：「有可能嗎？風會從角落裡吹來嗎？」

他們離開之後，他一個人這樣推論著：「這不像是在

騙人！他們的樣子看起來很認真，話又是從希柔那裡聽來的，而且他們好像很同情那個姑娘。愛上我？那我一定要好好回報她！我從來沒想過要結婚，當初我發誓要做一輩子的單身漢，那是因為我沒想到會有結婚的一天。他們說這個姑娘品性好，長得又漂亮，她的確是啊。還說除了愛上我這件事之外，她凡事都很精明。可是，愛上我也不代表她愚蠢啊。啊！碧翠絲來了！我對天發誓，她真是個美麗的姑娘！我敢肯定自己確實從她的臉上看出她對我有幾分的愛意。」

這時候碧翠絲走近他，以她慣有的尖酸語氣說：「他們硬是要我來叫你進去吃飯，這可違反了我自身的意願，我是很不情願的。」

班奈狄克從來沒想到自己會像現在這般客氣地同她說話，他說：「美麗的碧翠絲，謝謝妳，辛苦了。」碧翠絲又說了兩三句粗魯的話就離開了。班奈狄克認為，從她那些不客氣的話裡，他可以看出她隱藏的柔情，於是他大聲說：「我要是不憐惜她，我就是個壞蛋；我要是不愛她，我就是個猶太人。我要去弄一張她的肖像畫來。」

這位先生就這樣中了他們為他設下的圈套。現在輪到希柔來設計碧翠絲了。為了這件事，她派人喚來歐蘇拉和瑪格莉特這兩個侍女。她對瑪格莉特說：「好瑪格莉特，妳現在趕到客廳找我堂姊碧翠絲，她正在那裡跟親王和克勞狄歐談話，妳悄悄告訴她，說我和歐蘇拉正在果園裡散

步，我們聊的都是有關於她的事情。要她偷偷溜到那座舒適的涼亭裡去，那裡的金銀花被太陽曬得成熟了，卻像個忘恩負義的寵臣，反而不准太陽進來。」希柔讓瑪格莉特誘騙碧翠絲去的那座涼亭，就是班奈狄克剛才偷聽消息的那座舒適涼亭。

「我會讓她速速前去，我保證。」瑪格莉特說。

於是，希柔帶著歐蘇拉走進果園裡，對她說：「歐蘇拉，待會碧翠絲來的時候，我們就沿著這條小路來回走，我們談的必須都是班奈狄克的事。我一提到他的名字，妳就負責把他誇得好像他是全天下最好的男人。我會告訴妳班奈狄克是怎麼愛上碧翠絲的。我們現在就開始吧！妳看，碧翠絲像隻貼地的田鳧似的跑來聽我們說話了。」

她們兩人立即開始。希柔就像在回答歐蘇拉說的某個話題似的說：「不，真的，歐蘇拉，她太瞧不起人了，她就像岩石上的野鳥一樣忸怩作態。」

歐蘇拉道，「可是妳確定嗎？班奈狄克真的一心一意愛著碧翠絲嗎？」

希柔回說：「親王和我的未婚夫克勞狄歐都這麼說，他們要我一定得把這件事告訴她。可是我勸他們說，要是他們愛護班奈狄克，就永遠不要讓碧翠絲知道這件事。」

歐蘇拉回道，「沒錯，可別讓她知道班奈狄克愛她，免得碧翠絲去嘲弄他。」

希柔說：「唉，說實在的，我從沒見過這樣聰明、高

貴、年輕及英俊的男子，她卻把他說得一文不值。」

「沒錯，沒錯，如此吹毛求疵真是不可取。」歐蘇拉說。

「是啊，」希柔回說，「可是誰敢這麼跟她說呢？要是我去跟她說，她肯定會挖苦我的。」

歐蘇拉道，「喔，妳誤會妳堂姊了，她不會這麼沒眼光，拒絕像班奈狄克這樣一位難得的紳士。」

「他的名望很好，」希柔說，「老實說，除了我親愛的克勞狄歐之外，在義大利就屬他最優秀。」

這時候，希柔暗示她的侍女該換換話題了，於是歐蘇拉道：「小姐，您什麼時候結婚呢？」希柔說她明天就要跟克勞狄歐結婚，她還要求歐蘇拉跟她一塊兒去挑幾件新衣裳，她想跟她商量一下該穿什麼好。

碧翠絲一直屏氣凝神地偷聽著她們的談話。她們走了之後，她便喊說：「我的耳朵怎麼會這麼熱？難道這是真的嗎？輕蔑和嘲笑，永別了！再見吧，少女的驕傲！班奈狄克，愛下去吧！我不會辜負你的，用你柔情的雙手馴服我這野馬似的心吧。」

看到這一對老冤家變成親愛的新朋友，看到風趣幽默的親王施展的妙計使得這兩人互相愛上對方，看到兩人彼此中意後初次見面的情形，想必令人感到無比歡喜。

可是現在我們要談談希柔所遭遇的可悲命運了。第二天本來是希柔結婚的大喜之日，卻給她和她的好父親里奧

納多帶來傷痛。

親王有個同父異母的弟弟，他跟親王一起從戰場上來到梅西那。這個弟弟（他的名字叫唐‧約翰）是個既可悲又不安分的人，他專門喜歡設計陰謀陷害別人。

他恨他哥哥阿拉貢親王，恨克勞迪歐，因為克勞迪歐跟親王交情很好，他決定阻擾克勞迪歐跟希柔結婚，他要讓克勞迪歐和親王感到痛苦，因為他知道親王一心一意想成全這樁親事，對於這件事，他的熱心不亞於克勞迪歐本人。為了達到這個毒辣的目的，他雇了一個跟他自己一樣壞的人，名叫柏拉契奧，他唆使這個人破壞他們的好事，並允諾給他一大筆錢。

而這個柏拉契奧正在跟希柔的侍女瑪格麗特談戀愛。唐‧約翰知道了這件事，就慫恿他設法讓瑪格莉特答應，當天晚上等希柔睡了之後，在小姐臥室的窗戶邊跟他聊天，並且穿上希柔的衣裳，好欺騙克勞迪歐，使他相信那就是希柔。唐‧約翰設下這個毒計，想達到的正是這個目的。

唐‧約翰接著就到親王和克勞迪歐那兒去，告訴他們希柔是個不檢點的姑娘，說她深更半夜在臥室的窗台跟男人聊天。此時正是婚禮的前夕，他提議當天夜裡就帶他們去看看，讓他們親眼目睹希柔的不軌行徑。他們同意跟他一塊兒去，克勞迪歐還說：「要是今天晚上我看到什麼讓我不該跟她結婚的事，那麼明天我就要在結婚的教堂裡當

眾羞辱她。」親王也說：「我既然幫助你把她追到手，我也要跟你一起羞辱她。」

唐・約翰當天晚上把他們帶到希柔的臥室附近，他們看見柏拉契奧站在窗子底下，還看見瑪格莉特從希柔的窗口往外看，並且聽見她跟柏拉契奧聊天。瑪格麗特身上穿的那套衣裳，親王和克勞迪歐也曾看見希柔穿過，於是他們便相信那是希柔姑娘本人了。

當克勞迪歐發現（他以為發現了）這件事之後，怒氣沖天。他對希柔的滿腔愛意立刻變成仇恨，如他曾經所言，他決定隔日要在教堂裡揭發這件事。親王表示同意，他認為無論把什麼樣的責罰加在這個不守規矩的姑娘身上都不算苛刻，因為就在她準備跟高貴的克勞狄歐結婚的前一天晚上，她居然還在窗戶邊和另一個男人聊天。

第二天，眾人聚於此地慶祝這兩人的結合，克勞狄歐和希柔站在神父面前，正當神父開始唸頌誓詞時，克勞狄歐用最激動的言詞宣布了無辜希柔的罪狀。希柔聽到他說出這樣荒唐的話來，十分驚訝。她不解地說：「我的丈夫生病了嗎，他怎麼會說出這樣的話來？」

里奧納多非常震驚，他對親王說：「殿下，您怎麼不說話呢？」

「要我說什麼呢？」親王道，「我竭力促使我的好朋友跟一個不配為人妻的女人結合，我已經夠丟臉了。里奧納多，我以我的人格向你發誓，昨天晚上，我自己、我弟

弟和傷心的克勞迪歐，確實看到並且聽見她半夜在臥室的窗口跟一位男子聊天。」

班奈迪克聽到這些話十分震驚，他說：「這看起來不像在舉行一場婚禮啊！」

「的確，天啊！」傷心的希柔悲痛不已，接著這位不幸的姑娘便昏厥過去，看起來像是死了一樣。親王和克勞迪歐不管希柔是否甦醒，也毫不理會他們帶給里奧納多的痛苦，就逕自離開了教堂。憤怒使他們改變，變得如此鐵石心腸。

班奈狄克留下來幫忙碧翠絲讓希柔甦醒過來。他說：「希柔姑娘不會有事吧？」

「我想，她死了。」碧翠絲非常苦惱地回答，因為她很愛她的堂妹，她清楚知道她的堂妹品行端莊，一點也不相信剛才聽到的那些指控。

那可憐的老父親卻不是這樣想，他相信他孩子做了丟臉的事。當希柔像個死人一樣躺在他面前，他對著女兒唉聲歎氣，希望她再也不要睜開雙眼。那情景真是令人感到難受。

但老神父是個聰明人，他善於觀察人性。當這姑娘聽到別人對自己的指控時，他仔細地觀察她的神色，看到她臉上漲滿了羞辱的紅暈，又看到天神般的白色把羞紅的臉色趕走了，他在她的眼睛裡看到一種光火，他可以看出親王指責這個少女不貞的話毫無根據。於是，他對那個傷心

的父親說：「這位可愛的姑娘如果不是因誤會而冤枉地躺在這，那你就叫我傻子，別再相信我的學問、我的見識，也別再相信我的年歲、我的身分或是我的職務了。」

希柔從昏迷狀態甦醒後，神父對她說：「姑娘，他們指控妳跟哪個男人聊天呢？」

希柔回道：「那些指控我的人知道，但我並不知道啊。」然後她回過頭對里奧納多說：「啊，父親，您要是能夠證明我曾經在不適當的時候跟什麼人聊天，或是昨天晚上我跟什麼人說過一句話，那麼您就別認我這個女兒，您儘管恨我，把我折磨死吧。」

「親王和克勞狄歐，」神父說，「他們一定是誤會了什麼。」他建議里奧納多宣布希柔已經死了。他說，他們離開希柔的時候，她便進入昏死狀態，他們一定會相信的。他還勸他穿上喪服，為她立一座墓碑，凡是屬於葬禮的儀式皆一併辦理。

「為什麼要這樣呢？」里奧納多問：「這樣做有什麼用處呢？」

神父答道：「宣布她的死亡會把毀謗變成憐憫，這樣會有些好處的，可是我所盼望的好處不只這一點。克勞狄歐若是得知她是被他那些話逼死的，她生前可愛的模樣就一定會在他的腦海裡浮現。要是愛情曾經打動他的心，這時候他就會哀悼她，儘管他仍自以為揭發的是真相，他也會後悔不該那樣羞辱她。」

班奈迪克也說：「里奧納多，你就聽神父的話吧，雖然你知道我是多麼愛親王和克勞狄歐，但是我用我的人格擔保，絕不把這個秘密洩露給他們知道。」

經過這番勸說，里奧納多答應了。他悲痛道：「我已經傷心得一點主意也沒有了，你隨意用最細的一根線都能夠把我牽走。」於是，好心的神父就把里奧納多和希柔帶走，好好勸慰他們，只剩下碧翠絲和班奈狄克兩個人留下來。他們那幾位朋友布置的計策，原是為了讓這兩位能這樣聚在一起，並指望從那兩人身上大大地尋開心。如今，大家都垂頭喪氣，似乎再也沒心情開玩笑了。

班奈狄克先開口：「碧翠絲姑娘，妳一直在哭嗎？」

「是啊，而且我還會再哭一陣子呢。」碧翠絲說。

「這是當然的，」班奈狄克說，「我相信妳的好姊妹被冤枉了。」

「唉！」碧翠絲道，「要是誰替她伸冤，我一定好好酬謝他啊！」

班奈狄克說：「該怎麼解釋我們的友誼呢？這世界上我最愛的人就是妳了，我這麼說很奇怪嗎？」

「我也可以說，」碧翠絲道，「在這世界我最愛的人是你，這不是謊言，可是別相信我，不過我也沒有瞎說。我什麼也不承認，什麼也不否認。我只是替我堂妹感到相當難過。」

「以我的劍發誓，」班奈狄克說，「妳愛我，我也承

認我愛妳。來，儘管吩咐我為妳做事吧！」

「殺死克勞迪歐。」碧翠絲說。

「啊，那可不行。」班奈狄克說，因為他很愛他的朋友克勞迪歐，並且他相信克勞狄歐是被利用的。

「克勞迪歐信口毀謗、侮辱我的堂妹，破壞她的名譽，難道他不是個壞蛋嗎？」碧翠絲說，「啊，我要是個男人就好了！」

「聽我說，碧翠絲。」班奈狄克說。

可是他替克勞迪歐辯護的話，碧翠絲一句也不想聽，她逼著班奈狄克替她堂妹報仇。她說：「在窗戶邊跟一個男人聊天，說得真像回事！可愛的希柔，她被冤枉了，毀謗了，她這一輩子完了。但願我是個男人！或者有個朋友能夠為我當個男子漢！可是勇氣都已經融化成禮貌和客套話了。我既然不能如願變成男人，我只好作為女人家，傷心地死去。」

「等一等，善良的碧翠絲，」班奈狄克道，「我舉手向妳發誓，我愛妳。」

「要是你愛我，就別用手來發誓，拿它做點別的事吧。」碧翠絲說。

「憑心而論，妳認為克勞迪歐冤枉希柔了嗎？」班奈狄克問。

「是啊，」碧翠絲答道，「就像我知道我有思想，有一顆良心一樣地千真萬確。」

「那好，」班奈狄克說，「我答應妳去向他發起決鬥。讓我親一親妳的手再離開。我舉這隻手向妳發誓，我一定狠狠地給克勞迪歐吃點苦頭。請妳等我的消息，想著我的人。去吧！好好安慰妳的堂妹吧。」

正當碧翠絲慫恿班奈狄克，並用憤慨的話激發他的俠義之心，讓他為了希柔去向他親密的朋友克勞迪歐決鬥的時候，里奧納多也向親王和克勞迪歐挑戰，要他們用劍來平復他們帶給他女兒的傷害，說她已經傷心地死去了。

可是由於他們尊敬他的高齡，也同理他的悲傷，就說：「不，別跟我們吵架吧，老人家。」

這時候班奈狄克來了。班奈狄克也向克勞迪歐發起挑戰，要他用劍來償還對希柔造成的傷害。克勞迪歐和親王對彼此說：「這一定是碧翠絲唆使的。」儘管如此，要不是這時候公正的上天給無辜的希柔帶來了有力的證據，克勞迪歐一定會接受班奈狄克的挑戰。

親王和克勞迪歐還在談論班奈狄克的挑戰時，一個獄卒把變成犯人的柏拉契奧押到親王這兒來了。原來柏拉契奧跟他的同伴談起唐·約翰雇他去做壞事的時候，被人竊聽了。

柏拉契奧當著克勞迪歐的面，對親王招供一切原委。他說穿著小姐的衣裳在窗戶邊跟他聊天的是瑪格麗特，他們把她誤當成希柔本人了。這麼一來，克勞迪歐和親王自然不再懷疑希柔的清白。即使他們還有什麼猜疑的話，

唐·約翰一逃跑，他們的懷疑也就一掃而空了。唐·約翰曉得事跡敗露後，他哥哥一定會震怒，便連忙從梅西那逃走了。

克勞迪歐知道自己冤枉希柔，心裡非常悲痛，他還以為希柔一聽到他那些殘酷的話真的當場身亡了。他腦海裡浮現希柔的身影，如他當初愛上她時那樣美麗。親王問他，剛才聽到那些話時，他的心是不是像被鋼鐵刺穿靈魂一樣。他回應親王的問話，當他聽見柏拉契奧所說的事實，他覺得自己就像是吃了毒藥似的，苦不堪言。

於是，悔恨不已的克勞迪歐請求里奧納多老人家寬恕他帶給他孩子的傷害。並承諾：他如此輕信他人對自己未婚妻的不實指控，實屬過錯，因此，不論里奧納多怎樣懲罰他，他都願意接受，這樣才對得起他親愛的希柔。

里奧納多對他的懲罰是要他隔日早晨跟希柔的堂妹結婚。他說這個姑娘現在是他的繼承人了，她長得十分像希柔。克勞迪歐為了遵守他對里奧納多的莊重誓言，就答應跟這個不相識的女子結婚，即使她是位異國女子也無所謂。可是他心裡非常難過。那天晚上他在里奧納多給希柔立的墓碑前落淚，徹夜懺悔自己的過錯。

到了早晨，親王陪著克勞迪歐來到教堂。那位好心腸的神父、里奧納多和他的「姪女」都已經聚在那兒，準備再次舉行婚禮。里奧納多把許配給克勞迪歐的新娘子介紹給他。她戴著面紗，克勞迪歐看不清她的臉孔。

　　克勞迪歐對這位戴著面紗的姑娘說：「在這位神聖的神父面前，把妳的手交給我；要是妳願意跟我結婚，我就是妳的丈夫。」

　　「我活著的時候，曾做過你的妻子。」這位陌生女子對他如此說道。然後，她把面紗揭開，原來她不是什麼姪女（她是偽裝的），而是里奧納多的親生女兒希柔本人。

　　想當然爾，這對克勞迪歐來說，是再愉快不過的驚喜了（他本來以為她已經死了），他快樂得幾乎無法相信自己的眼睛。親王看到這一切，也同樣吃驚，他大聲說：「這不是希柔嗎，不是那個死了的希柔嗎？」

里奧納多答道：「殿下，若你們仍不斷詆毀她的話，她才是真的死了呢。」

神父答應他們，儀式結束之後，他會向他們解釋眼前的這個奇蹟。而在他正要為他們進行儀式時，班奈狄克打斷他，說自己同時也要跟碧翠絲結婚。

碧翠絲對這個婚姻稍微表示反對之意，於是班奈狄克就提起碧翠絲對他表示過的愛情（這是他從希柔那兒聽來的）質問她。在一番有趣的解釋之後，他們這才發現原來他們兩人都上了當，以為對方愛上自己（其實原先兩人間的情意根本就不存在）。一個哄人的玩笑竟使他們成為真正的情人，在這個趣味計策哄騙之下所發生的感情，現在已然十分熱烈了，一本正經的解釋也動搖不了他們之間的愛情了。班奈狄克既然提議跟她結婚，不管人們用什麼辦法反對，他也不管。他繼續快活地開著玩笑，他對碧翠絲發誓：他只是可憐她才娶她，因為聽聞她憔悴得快要死了。而碧翠絲則回嘴：她是經過許久的勸說才讓步，而且是為了救他一命，因為聽說他患了相思病，就快死了。

於是，這兩個伶牙俐齒的機伶鬼和解了，並且，等克勞迪歐和希柔完婚後，他們也隨之結為夫妻了。為了將故事好好收尾，還要說明一下：設計這個陰謀的唐‧約翰在逃跑的路上遭逮，押回梅西那來了。對這個可悲又不安分的人而言，自己的詭計沒能得逞，還得看著梅西那宮裡一片歡樂和盛宴的景況，對他而言就是最嚴厲的懲罰了吧。

VI.

哈姆雷特

　　丹麥國王哈姆雷特猝死後不到兩個月，皇后葛楚德就改嫁國王的弟弟克勞迪。全國上下皆為之驚愕不已，人們議論紛紛，交頭接耳地指責她的輕率與寡情。更令人不能苟同的是，不論外表或個性，克勞迪都無法與她已故的丈夫相提並論。克勞迪外貌可憎，性情狡詐惡劣，有人不禁懷疑，他是為了娶皇嫂而篡奪王位，暗中謀殺國王。

　　母親這個輕率的舉動，讓年輕的王子深受打擊。他敬愛死去的父親，幾乎把他當作偶像一樣崇拜。王子注重榮譽，為人正直，言語舉止都非常優雅高尚，他為母親可恥的行為感到十分難過。以至於年輕的王子一面哀悼父親的去世，一面又為母親不恥的婚姻感到痛心疾首，他整日籠罩在沉重的憂鬱裡，任憑傷痛咬噬他的靈魂，容貌變得憔悴不堪，平日對讀書的愛好也都消失了。過往總能讓他興致勃勃的活動和遊戲，再也吸引不了他。他覺得這個世界成了一座野草叢生的花園，百花枯萎，只剩下叢生的雜草，讓他十分厭倦。

　　並不是因此失去繼承王位的合法權力才令他心頭沉重，雖然對一個年輕高傲的王子來說，這的確是一個刺骨的傷痛和屈辱，但是真正讓他憤怒不已，並且再也開心不起來的，是母親竟然那麼快就遺忘他的父親。他是一個多麼好的父親啊！而且也是一位溫柔體貼的好丈夫。她對丈夫一向也是多情、柔順，兩人如膠似漆，好像她對他的愛是日益增加似的。如今，以年輕的哈姆雷特的角度來看，不到兩個月的時間母親就改嫁了，嫁的還是他的叔父，她愛夫的弟弟。他們的關係這麼親近，這椿婚姻本來就十分不恰當，而且有違法令。尤其母親這麼倉促就結婚，更是不登大雅之堂，而且還選了這麼不配作國王的人來當她的枕邊人，共享王權。

　　這件事比失去十個王國更叫這位可敬的年輕王子意志消沉，悲痛欲絕。

　　母親葛楚德和國王想盡辦法要讓他快樂起來，卻徒勞無功。他在皇宮裡仍然穿著深黑色的衣服，哀悼死去的父王，甚至在母親結婚那天，他也不願換件衣服祝賀他們。在那不名譽的一天（以他的角度來看），任何歡慶宴會他都拒絕參加。

　　最叫他苦惱的，是他父親死因成謎。克勞迪宣布國王是被毒蛇咬死的，可是年輕的哈姆雷特強烈懷疑克勞迪就是那條毒蛇。簡單來說，他認為克勞迪一定是為了篡奪王位而謀殺國王，現在坐在王位上的，正是螫死他父親的那

條毒蛇。

　　他的猜測究竟有幾分正確？他應該如何看待自己的母親？這樁謀殺案她涉入多少？她是否同意或知情？這些問題不斷困擾著他，使得他心神不寧。

　　小哈姆雷特聽到一個謠言，說一連兩三個晚上，守衛的哨兵都在宮殿前的高台上看見一個鬼魂，鬼魂的樣子跟他死去的父王一模一樣。

　　鬼魂出現的時候，總是穿著一身盔甲，和死去的國王所穿的一樣。凡是看到鬼魂的人（哈姆雷特的心腹何瑞修就是其中一個），談起鬼魂出現的時間和模樣都一致：鬼魂在鐘響十二下時出現，他的臉色慘白，悲傷多於憤怒；他的鬍子蒼白得可怕，在黑暗中看起來略帶些許銀色，和國王生前的樣子如出一轍；他們跟他說話，他都不回答，但是有一次他們看到他抬起頭，似乎有話要說，可是這時候公雞晨啼了，他也立刻從他們眼前消失不見。

　　年輕的王子聽到這件事後非常驚訝，他們的說法前後一致，讓他不得不相信。他判斷他們看到的一定是他父親的鬼魂，於是決定當晚跟士兵一道去守哨，也許有機會可以看到鬼魂。他心想，鬼魂不會無緣無故出現，他一定有話要說，儘管他一直沒開口，但是他會對自己說的。王子迫不及待地等待夜晚來臨。

　　天一黑，哈姆雷特就跟何瑞修和守衛馬賽勒斯登上鬼魂經常出沒的高台。那是個寒冷的夜晚，空氣異常陰濕刺

骨。哈姆雷特、何瑞修和一道守哨的人聊起了夜晚的寒冷，忽然，何瑞修打斷了談話，他說鬼魂出現了。

突然看到父親的鬼魂，哈姆雷特感到又驚奇又害怕。他呼喊天使和守護神來保佑他，因為他不知道這個鬼魂是好是壞，也不知道他的出現是吉是凶，不過，後來他的膽子漸漸大了起來。他的父親（他覺得那是他父親）面帶悲傷地望著他，似乎很想跟他說話。從各方面來看，鬼魂都跟他父親活著的時候一樣，於是他不禁叫出他的名字，他說道：「哈姆雷特，國王，父親！」並且懇求鬼魂告訴他為什麼不好好地睡在墳墓裡，要到人間來，出現在月光下？他請鬼魂告訴他們，要如何才能讓他的靈魂得到安息。於是，鬼魂招了招手要哈姆雷特跟他到僻靜的地方去，好單獨談話。

何瑞修和馬賽勒斯都勸王子不要去，他們擔心他也許是個惡鬼，故意把他引誘到附近的海邊，或是可怕的懸崖上，然後露出猙獰的面貌，把王子嚇瘋。可是他們這些勸告絲毫改變不了哈姆雷特的決心，他早已把生死置之度外，他並不怕死。至於他的靈魂，跟鬼魂同樣是永生不滅的，鬼魂又怎能加害於他呢？他覺得自己就如同獅子一樣強壯，儘管他們使勁拉住他，他還是掙脫了，任憑鬼魂帶他到任何地方。

等到他們獨處的時候，鬼魂打破沉寂，說他正是哈姆雷特父親的鬼魂，他是被人害死的，並且說出他如何被謀

殺。正如哈姆雷特早先懷疑的那樣，正是父王的親弟弟（哈姆雷特的叔叔）克勞迪阿斯下的毒手，他的目的就是為了霸佔皇后和王位。

那天下午，他一如往常地在花園裡睡覺，他那個起了歹心的弟弟，趁機偷偷溜到他身邊，把毒草汁倒進他的耳朵裡。那種毒汁是會要人命的，它會像水銀一樣快速地流進全身的血管裡，把血液燒乾，使全身肌膚都長起一層硬殼似的癩。就這樣，國王在入眠的時候，他的弟弟親手奪走他的王位、他的王后和他的生命。

鬼魂懇求哈姆雷特，要是他真確愛他的父親，就一定得為他報仇。鬼魂對著他的兒子哀嘆，想不到他母親如此不守貞節，居然背棄相愛多年的丈夫，嫁給謀殺他的凶手。可是鬼魂囑咐哈姆雷特，在對叔父進行報復的時候，千萬不要傷害他的母親，上天自會審判她，讓她自己受良心的譴責就行了。

哈姆雷特答應一切都照鬼魂吩咐的去做，然後，鬼魂就消失了。

等到剩下哈姆雷特一個人的時候，他下定決心要立刻把他記得的一切事情，把他從書本和閱歷中所學到的東西都忘得一乾二淨，讓腦子裡只記著鬼魂告訴他的話和吩咐他做的事。

哈姆雷特和鬼魂這段談話的細節，除了哈姆雷特的好朋友何瑞修之外，他沒有告訴任何人。他囑咐何瑞修和馬

賽勒斯，對於晚上所看到的一切，絕對要嚴加保密。

哈姆雷特的身體本就相當羸弱，鬼魂的出現以及所訴說的事實幾乎使他精神錯亂，他快發瘋了。哈姆雷特很擔心自己這樣下去會惹人注意，引起他叔叔的戒心。哈姆雷特為了防止叔叔懷疑自己要對付他，或是他根本早已知曉他父親猝死之因，於是他做了一個決定：他決定從那時候起開始裝瘋賣傻。他想，這樣一來他叔叔會鬆懈對他的防範，也就不至於猜忌他這個人了。再加上，偽裝成瘋癲的同時，他可以把自己內心真正的不安巧妙地隱藏起來。

從這時候起，哈姆雷特在服裝、言談舉止上，都裝成狂妄怪誕的模樣，完美地偽裝成一個瘋子，國王和皇后都被他成功蒙騙過去。他們不知道鬼魂出現的事，所以認為他發瘋不光是因為父親的死。他們認為他一定是為了愛情才精神失常，而且他們還以為他們知道他愛上的是誰。

在哈姆雷特還沒有變得沮喪憂鬱以前，他非常迷戀一個叫奧菲莉亞的美麗姑娘，她是御前大臣普洛尼斯的女兒。他曾經寫信給她，送她戒指，對她傾吐愛意，正大光明地向她求愛，而她也相信他的誓言和追求都是真心的。

可是近來他為許多事煩擾，因而對她變得相當冷淡。自他決定裝瘋開始，他便故作對她十分無情的樣子，甚至十分粗暴。不過這位善良的女孩並沒有責備他變心，她竭力說服自己，哈姆雷特之所以對她沒有像以前那樣好，並不是由於他冷酷無情，而是因為他的心生病了，並非有意

傷害她。她覺得他以前高貴的心靈和卓越的理智，就好比一串美妙的鈴鐺，能奏出悅耳動聽的樂章。可是現在，他的心靈和理智被深切的哀愁壓抑著、損害著，要是搖得不成調子或是搖得粗暴些，就只能發出一片刺耳不悅的聲響，使聽者痛苦。

哈姆雷特著手進行的事（報復殺死他父親的凶手）十分艱辛，跟求愛的輕快心情很不相稱，同時愛情在目前看來也是一種太閒散的感情，他不能容許自己有這種情感，可是有時候他仍不免兒女情長，思念他的奧菲莉亞。有一回，他覺得自己對那位溫柔的姑娘太殘酷了，就寫了一封狂熱激動的信給她。信裡措詞十分誇張，符合他裝瘋的神態，可是字裡行間也微微流露出些許柔情，讓這位可敬的姑娘不得不覺得哈姆雷特仍深愛著她。

他說她儘管懷疑星星其實是一團火，懷疑太陽並不會移動，懷疑真理是謊言，可是永遠不要懷疑他的愛，諸如此類的誇張言語。奧菲莉亞老實地把這封信拿給她父親看，老人家覺得有義務把這件事報告國王和王后，從那之後，國王和王后就認為愛情是致使哈姆雷特發瘋的真正原因。王后倒也很希望他是為了奧菲莉亞的美貌才瘋狂的，那樣，也許奧菲莉亞的美德能讓哈姆雷特幸運地復原，那對他們兩個人都有好處。

可是哈姆雷特的病比她所想得還嚴重，光憑這個辦法是無法治癒的。他腦子裡仍然盤踞著他父親的鬼魂，替父親報仇的那個神聖使命未完成前，他是不會感到安寧的。此仇一刻未報，每一刻都是罪過，對他而言如同違背父親的命令。

可是國王身邊隨時都有衛兵保護著，要想法子把他殺死並不是件容易的事。就算辦得到，哈姆雷特的母親總在國王身邊，使他無法下手，這個阻礙使他無法突圍。除此之外，篡奪王位的人正好是他母親的丈夫，這也使他感到有些痛心，動起手來更猶豫不決了。

哈姆雷特天性敦厚，要殺死一個人本來就是件可惡又可怕的事情。他自己長久下來的憂鬱和精神上的頹唐，促使他更加搖擺不定、躊躇不決，他一直沒能採取最後的行動。

而且，他對於自己所看到的鬼魂究竟真的是他父親，

還是個惡鬼，也不免有些遲疑。他聽說魔鬼想變成什麼就變成什麼，他也許是趁自己身體虛弱、意志消沉，打扮成他父親的樣子，驅使他去犯下殺人這樣可怕的事。於是，他決定不能單憑幻象或是幽靈的話行事，那也許是一時的錯覺，一定要找到更確切的證據。

正當他心裡這般猶豫不決的時候，宮裡來了一團戲班。哈姆雷特以前很喜歡看他們的表演，特別喜歡聽其中一個演員表演某段悲劇時的台詞，述說特洛伊的老國王普賴亞姆被殺和王后赫丘琶的悲痛。哈姆雷特對那些老朋友表示歡迎，然後想起過去他聽了那段台詞之後有多麼高興，就要求那個演員再表演一次。於是那個演員又很生動地表演了一遍，細說衰老的國王如何被人殘忍地謀害，全城和市民都被烈火燒毀，年老的王后難過得像發了瘋一樣，光著腳在宮裡狂奔。她原本戴著王冠的頭上包了一塊破布，本來披著王袍的腰上，只裹了一條慌忙中抓來的毯子。這場戲表演得十分生動，不但使觀眾集體落淚，認為他們看到的都是真實的情景，連演員講述台詞的時候都語帶哽咽，流下真正的眼淚。

這件事使哈姆雷特想到：只是一段虛構的台詞，就使得演員如此感動，為從來沒見過面的千百年前的古人赫丘琶流下眼淚，相較之下他自己是多麼麻木不仁，他有真正應該痛哭的理由和動機——一個真正的國王，一個親愛的父親被謀殺了——然而他竟然如此無動於衷，他的復仇心

沉寂了好久，幾乎快被他遺忘了！他想到演員的演出，想到維妙維肖的一齣好戲帶給觀眾的影響有多大。這時，他又記起曾聽說有些凶手在看到舞台上表演的謀殺後，受到感人的場面與相似情節的鼓舞。

於是他決定要這幾個演員在他叔叔面前，表演父親被謀殺的劇情，他要仔細觀察他叔叔的反應，從他的神色就可以判定他是不是凶手。他吩咐演員們遵照指示準備一齣戲，並邀請國王和王后前來觀賞。

這齣戲描寫的是維也納的一樁公爵謀殺案。公爵名叫貢查古，他的妻子叫巴蒂絲塔。劇情內容是公爵的近親琉西納貪圖他的財產，並在花園裡將他毒死，爾後沒多久這位凶手也擄獲貢查古妻子的芳心。

國王不知道這是布下的圈套，偕著王后以及整個宮廷的官員前來看戲。哈姆雷特坐得離他很近，好仔細觀察他的神色。這齣戲從貢查古和他的妻子兩人的談話開始。妻子一再表白她的愛，說假使貢查古在她之前死去，她也絕不會再嫁人，如果有一天她改嫁了，她就會受到詛咒。她還說，只有那些謀害親夫的壞女人才會改嫁。

哈姆雷特發現國王（他的叔父）聽到這段話時臉色就變了，這段台詞對國王和王后來說都像吃苦草一樣難受。琉西納按照劇情毒害了睡在花園裡的貢查古，這一幕跟國王在花園裡毒害他哥哥（已故的國王）的罪惡行為太過相似了，讓這個篡位之人受到了強烈的刺激，以致於再也無

法繼續坐著看戲。

　　國王突然喊人先點亮他寢室的火炬，佯裝（也許部份是真的）得了急病，要離開劇場。國王一走，戲也停了。哈姆雷特現在看到的，已經足夠使他斷定鬼魂所說的是事實，而不是他的幻覺。長久以來的疑惑、不安終於得到解答，哈姆雷特頓時感到十分高興。他對何瑞修發誓，鬼魂說的話毫無半點虛假，他確定父親是被他叔叔所謀害的。在他還沒決定好如何報仇之前，他的母親派人請他到她的內宮裡密談。

　　王后是奉國王的意旨要哈姆雷特去的，他要王后向哈姆雷特表示，他們對他剛才的舉動十分不滿。國王想知道他們談話的全部內容，也擔心皇后的報告會有所偏袒，可能會隱瞞一些重要的話，所以他吩咐御前大臣老普洛尼斯躲在王后內宮的帷幕後面偷聽他們的談話。這個計謀特別適合普洛尼斯的性格，他在充滿勾心鬥角、爾虞我詐的朝廷中混了大半輩子，他喜歡用不正當或是狡詐的手段來刺探內幕。

　　哈姆雷特來到他母親面前。她先是很婉轉地責備他的舉動魯莽，說他已經大大地冒犯了「他的父親」（她指的是國王，他的叔叔），因為他們結了婚，所以他要喚他「父親」。哈姆雷特非常生氣，聽到她把「父親」這樣一個親熱的、值得尊敬的稱呼用在一個卑鄙小人身上，而且那小人正是謀殺他生父的凶手，於是他用相當尖銳的口吻

答道：「母親，是您大大地冒犯了我的『父親』。」

王后說他的回答毫無意義。

哈姆雷特說：「用這句話回覆您的問題，則是再好不過了。」

王后斥責他是不是忘記自己在對誰說話了。

「唉！」哈姆雷特回道：「但願我能夠忘記呀！您是王后，您丈夫弟弟的妻子，又是我的母親。我但願您不是呀！」

「好吧，」王后說，「既然你對我如此無禮，我只好去找那些能言善道的人來了。」王后準備去找國王或普洛尼斯來跟哈姆雷特談話。

可是哈姆雷特不讓她走。現在他既然單獨跟她在一起了，他想試試，讓她了解她的所作所為相當不道德。他一把抓住他母親的手腕，緊緊挾著她，硬是叫她坐下。她被哈姆雷特急迫的神情嚇著了，擔心他會做出傷害她的事，於是她大喊了起來。同時，帷幕後頭也發出「救命呀！來救皇后呀！」的聲音。哈姆雷特聽到以後，以為是國王藏在那裡，就拔起劍，像是要戳一隻路過的老鼠一樣，朝那個發出聲音的地方插了過去。之後便再也沒了聲響，他斷定那個人已經死了。當他把屍體拖出來後，才知道原來刺死的不是國王，而是躲在帷幕後面當密探的御前大臣老普洛尼斯。

「天啊！」王后嚷著，「你幹了一件多麼魯莽殘忍的

事呀！」

「沒錯，母親，一件殘忍的事，」哈姆雷特答道，
「可是還比不上您幹的壞事呢。妳殺了一個國王，又嫁給
他的弟弟。」

哈姆雷特話說得過於露骨，以至於再也沒有回頭路
了。他當時就是想跟他母親攤牌，於是就那麼做了。雖然
做子女的應該盡量包容父母的過錯，然而父母如果犯下滔
天大罪，兒子還是可以嚴厲地斥責母親，只要出發點是為
了她好，為了讓她改邪歸正，而不光是為了斥責她。

此時，這位品德高尚的王子用感人的言詞指出皇后所
犯的惡行，說她不應該這麼輕易就忘掉他已故的父王，這
麼快就跟大家都認定的凶手結婚。她對她的前夫發過誓，
卻做出這樣的事來，讓人不再相信女人的誓言，懷疑那些
婦德不過是偽善而已，相守一生的誓約還比不上賭徒的一
句諾言，信仰也不過是開玩笑，一派空言罷了。他說她的
所為連上天都為她感到羞愧，連大地都厭棄她。

哈姆雷特拿出兩幅肖像畫給她看，一幅是已故的國
王，她第一任丈夫，另一幅是現在的國王，她第二任丈
夫。他要她仔細看看他們之間的差別。他的父親氣宇軒
昂，氣概非凡。他的鬈髮像太陽神阿波羅，前額像愛神邱
比特，眼睛像戰神馬斯，姿勢像剛降落在高聳入雲的山嶽
上的信使邁丘利。他說，這個人曾經是她的丈夫。然後他
又讓王后看看取代他父親的是怎樣一個人。他像是害蟲或

黴菌，因為他把他那健康強壯的哥哥給毀了。

由於哈姆雷特這番話，皇后看清了自己的靈魂，她感到十分慚愧，因為她終於認清自己的靈魂有多麼地骯髒醜陋。哈姆雷特問她怎麼能跟這個人一起生活，還成為他的妻子？他謀害了她的前夫，又像賊一樣用欺騙的手段奪取了王位——就在這時候，他父親的鬼魂出現了，樣子跟他生前一樣，也跟哈姆雷特日前看到的一樣。看到父親的鬼魂，哈姆雷特十分害怕，他問他來做什麼。鬼魂說，哈姆雷特似乎遺忘自己曾答應替他報仇雪恨的諾言，他是來提醒他的。鬼魂又要他去跟他母親談談，不然她會因為悲傷和恐懼而死去。

語畢，鬼魂就不見了。只有哈姆雷特一個人看得見鬼魂，不論他如何指出鬼魂站立的地方、形容他的樣貌，皇后還是誰都沒見著。她看見哈姆雷特對著空氣說話（這是她眼中所看到的景況），所以相當害怕，認為他已經發瘋了。

然而哈姆雷特要她不要替自己邪惡的靈魂找藉口，竟認為他父親的鬼魂能到人間來是因為他發瘋，而不是因為皇后自己的罪過。他請她摸一摸他的脈息跳動得多麼正常，一點也不像是瘋了。他流著淚，請求皇后對上天懺悔自己過去的罪過，以後不要再跟國王為伍，不要再對他盡妻子的本分。要是她能緬懷父親，以做母親的態度來對待他，他會以一個兒子的身分祈禱上天祝福她。她答應照他

的話去做後，他們的談話至此結束。

　　現在哈姆雷特可以好好來看看他一時魯莽殺死的人到底是誰。他走近一看，才知道被他所殺的是普洛尼斯，是他心愛的奧菲莉亞的父親，他趕緊把屍體拉開。這時，他的心神鎮定了一些，於是開始為自己所做的事落淚。

　　普洛尼斯的不幸給了國王將哈姆雷特驅逐出境的藉口。國王有感哈姆雷特對他來說是個威脅，滿心想把他處死，但人民相當愛戴哈姆雷特，他怕得罪人民；再加上他仍顧及王后的感受，儘管她有許多過錯，但她仍愛著她的兒子。因此，這個詭計多端的國王就以保護哈姆雷特的安全為由，派了兩個朝臣陪著他搭船到英國，避免他因殺死普洛尼斯而受到處分。當時英國是丹麥的屬邦，國王給英國皇室寫了封信，交給這兩個朝臣。他在信裡編造一些特殊理由，囑咐他們等哈姆雷特一在英國上岸，就立刻把他處死。

　　哈姆雷特心疑其中必定有詐，於是夜裡偷偷拿到那封信，巧妙地把自己的名字擦去，把要被處死的人名改成押送他的那兩個朝臣，然後又把信封起來，放回原處。

　　不久，他們的船受到海盜的襲擊，打了一場海戰。作戰的時候，哈姆雷特想展現自己的英勇，獨自拿著刀劍登上敵人的船，而他自己坐的那條船卻怯懦地逃走了。那兩個朝臣把他丟下，帶著信急急忙忙趕到英國去，但信的內容已被哈姆雷特竄改，於是他們自己遭到應有的報應。

　　海盜俘擄王子之後，對這個高貴的敵人十分客氣。既然曉得他們俘虜的是何人，就把哈姆雷特帶到離丹麥最近的一個港口，讓他上岸，他們希望王子可以在皇室裡幫一些忙，來回報他們這番好意。於是哈姆雷特就從那裡寫信給國王，告訴國王他因為一場奇妙的遭遇又回到祖國，並說他明天就要回宮見國王。回到家之後，迎接他的是令他感到十分衝擊的一幕──即是哈姆雷特曾經的愛人，年輕美麗的奧菲莉亞的葬禮。

　　自從奧菲莉亞可憐的父親死了之後，這個年輕姑娘就開始精神錯亂。普洛尼斯死得這般悽慘，而且竟然死在奧菲莉亞所愛之人的手裡，這件事傷透了這位溫柔姑娘的心，她的精神狀況迅速失常。她拿著花到處分給宮裡的婦女，說是要用在他父親的葬禮上。她唱著關於愛情和死亡的歌，有時候則唱著一些毫無意義的歌，好像所有的事情她全都忘得一乾二淨。

　　直到有一天，她趁沒人看見的時候來到一條小河邊，河邊斜長著一棵柳樹，樹影倒映在水面上。她用雛菊、蕁麻、野花和雜草編成一只花圈，然後爬到柳樹上，想把這個花圈掛在柳枝上，不料柳枝突然間折斷，這個美麗年輕的姑娘就連同她編的花圈和她採的花草一起掉進河裡去了。身上所穿的衣服讓她在水上漂浮了一陣子，她還唱了幾句古老的曲調，好像絲毫沒注意到自己所遭遇的災難，彷彿她本來就是水中的生物一樣。可是沒多久，她的衣服

被水浸濕，變得越來越沉重，於是她還沒唱完那首歌，就沉到汙泥裡慘死了。哈姆雷特到達的時候，她哥哥賴爾提斯正在為這個美麗的姑娘舉行葬禮，國王、皇后和所有的皇室成員也都在場。

哈姆雷特起初不曉得舉行的是什麼儀式，就只是站在一旁，不想去驚擾大家。他看到他們依照處女葬禮的規矩，在她墳上撒滿了花朵。花是由王后親自撒下的，她一邊撒一邊說：「鮮花應該撒在美人身上！可愛的姑娘，我本來希望用鮮花替妳妝點新娘床的，如今卻是撒在妳的墳頭上。妳本該是我兒子哈姆雷特的妻子。」

接著，哈姆雷特又聽到奧菲莉亞的哥哥說，希望她的墳裡長出紫羅蘭來，他看到賴爾提斯悲慟欲絕地跳進奧菲莉亞的墳墓裡去，並吩咐侍從們把土堆在他身上，讓他跟奧菲莉亞埋在一起。

哈姆雷特憶起自己對這位美麗姑娘的愛，他不能容忍一個做哥哥的如此悲哀，因為他認為他對奧菲莉亞的愛是她哥哥所不能及的！於是，哈姆雷特露面了，他也跳進奧菲莉亞的墳墓裡，跟他同樣瘋狂，甚至比他更失控。賴爾提斯認出他是哈姆雷特，他父親和妹妹都是因為這個人而死的，於是把他當作仇人，抓住他的脖子，最後還是侍從將他們拉開的。葬禮結束之後，哈姆雷特為自己剛才魯莽的行為道歉，讓人看了還以為他是要跟賴爾提斯打架，但其實他只是不能容忍有人對美麗的奧菲莉亞的死比他更

加傷心。很快地，這兩個高貴的青年就講和了。

可是國王（哈姆雷特那卑鄙的叔叔）利用賴爾提斯對他父親和妹妹的死所感到的悲憤，預謀殺害哈姆雷特。他慫恿賴爾提斯在言歸於好的掩飾下向哈姆雷特下戰帖，進行一場友誼的擊劍比賽。哈姆雷特接受這個挑戰，並且約好比賽的日子。

全皇室的人都前來觀賞這場比賽。在國王的指示下，賴爾提斯準備了一把毒劍。大家都知道哈姆雷特和賴爾提斯兩人皆精通劍術，所以大臣們都為這次比賽投下巨額的賭注。哈姆雷特挑了一把圓頭劍，他絲毫沒有懷疑賴爾提斯有什麼詭計，也沒有留意賴爾提斯的劍。賴爾提斯並沒有使用規定的圓頭劍或鈍劍，而是使用一把塗了毒藥的尖頭劍。

最初賴爾提斯並沒有認真和哈姆雷特比劍，因而讓他佔了些上風。於是國王故意誇張地讚賞哈姆雷特，為他的勝利乾杯，並且下了很大的賭注，打賭哈姆雷特鐵定獲勝。交手了幾個回合後，賴爾提斯攻擊得越來越猛烈，用毒劍刺向哈姆雷特，給了他致命的一擊。

哈姆雷特很氣憤，可是他還不清楚這場比賽背後的陰謀。正當他們打得激烈的時候，哈姆雷特用自己那把沒有毒的劍換成賴爾提斯那把毒劍，然後用賴爾提斯的劍回刺了他。就這樣，賴爾提斯罪有應得地落入自己的奸計。

就在這時候，皇后尖聲嚷著她被下毒了。原來國王給

哈姆雷特準備一碗水，打算等哈姆雷特擊劍運動後感到口渴的時候，好遞給他飲用。陰險的國王在水裡下了劇毒，如果賴爾提斯失敗的話，就可以用這個來把哈姆雷特毒死，結果這碗水卻被皇后無意中喝下。國王忘記事先告訴皇后水裡有毒，結果她喝下去之後馬上就死了，她用最後一口氣喊出自己遭人毒殺。

哈姆雷特懷疑事有蹊蹺，就命人把門關起來，他要查個水落石出。賴爾提斯告訴他不必查了，就是他下的毒手。他挨了哈姆雷特一劍，快要死了，於是招認他的奸計，並且說他自己是自作自受。他告訴哈姆雷特，劍頭塗了毒藥，哈姆雷特不消半個鐘頭便會死去，因為沒有解藥。他要求哈姆雷特饒恕他，臨死之前，他控訴這一切都是國王一手策劃的陰謀。

當哈姆雷特知道自己即將死亡，而劍上還殘有毒藥，他就猛地朝那個奸詐的叔叔撲過去，把劍頭刺進他的胸膛。這樣，他就完成了自己對死去父親的承諾，令那個卑鄙的殺人凶手得到應有的報應。

很快地，哈姆雷特覺得呼吸急促，眼看就要死去，他努力撐著身子轉了過來，用盡最後一口氣，要求親眼看到這場悲劇的好朋友何瑞修一定要活下去（當時何瑞修的樣子彷彿準備自盡般，想跟王子一起死），忠實地傳達這個故事給世人知道。作為一個清楚來龍去脈的人，何瑞修答應他，自己一定照他吩咐做。

VI.哈姆雷特

　　然後，哈姆雷特便安心地死去了。何瑞修和在場的人都流著淚，把這位親愛的王子的靈魂交給天使們去保護。因為哈姆雷特是一位仁慈寬厚的王子，他高貴的美德讓他深受人民的愛戴。他要是還活著，一定會是丹麥最令人尊敬、最稱職的國王。

I.

ROMEO AND JULIET

The two chief families in Verona were the rich Capulets and the Montagues. There had been an old quarrel between these families, which was grown to such a height, and so deadly was the enmity between them, that it extended to the remotest kindred, to the followers and retainers of both sides, insomuch that a servant of the house of Montague could not meet a servant of the house of Capulet, nor a Capulet encounter with a Montague by chance, but fierce words and sometimes bloodshed ensued; and frequent were the brawls from such accidental meetings, which disturbed the happy quiet of Verona's streets.

Old lord Capulet made a great supper, to which many fair ladies and many noble guests were invited. All the admired beauties of Verona were present, and all comers were made welcome if they were not of the house of Montague. At this feast of Capulets, Rosaline, beloved of Romeo, son to the old lord Montague, was present; and though it was dangerous for a Montague to be seen in this

assembly, yet Benvolio, a friend of Romeo, persuaded the young lord to go to this assembly in the disguise of a mask, that he might see his Rosaline, and seeing her, compare her with some choice beauties of Verona, who (he said) would make him think his swan a crow. Romeo had small faith in Benvolio's words; nevertheless, for the love of Rosaline, he was persuaded to go. For Romeo was a sincere and passionate lover, and one that lost his sleep for love, and fled society to be alone, thinking on Rosaline, who disdained him, and never requited his love, with the least show of courtesy or affection; and Benvolio wished to cure his friend of this love by showing him diversity of ladies and company. To this feast of Capulets then young Romeo with Benvolio and their friend Mercutio went masked. Old Capulet bid them welcome, and told them that ladies who had their toes unplagued with corns would dance with them. And the old man was light hearted and merry, and said that he had worn a mask when he was young, and could have told a whispering tale in a fair lady's ear. And they fell to dancing, and Romeo was suddenly struck with the exceeding beauty of a lady who danced there, who seemed to him to teach the torches to burn bright, and her beauty to show by night like a rich jewel worn by a blackamoor; beauty too rich for use, too dear for earth! like a snowy dove trooping with crows (he said), so richly did her beauty and perfections shine above the ladies her

companions. While he uttered these praises, he was overheard by Tybalt, a nephew of lord Capulet, who knew him by his voice to be Romeo. And this Tybalt, being of a fiery and passionate temper, could not endure that a Montague should come under cover of a mask, to fleer and scorn (as he said) at their solemnities. And he stormed and raged exceedingly, and would have struck young Romeo dead. But his uncle, the old lord Capulet, would not suffer him to do any injury at that time, both out of respect to his guests, and because Romeo had borne himself like a gentleman, and all tongues in Verona bragged of him to be a virtuous and well-governed youth. Tybalt, forced to be patient against his will, restrained himself, but swore that this vile Montague should at another time dearly pay for his intrusion.

The dancing being done, Romeo watched the place where the lady stood; and under favour of his masking habit, which might seem to excuse in part the liberty, he presumed in the gentlest manner to take her by the hand, calling it a shrine, which if he profaned by touching it, he was a blushing pilgrim, and would kiss it for atonement. 'Good pilgrim,' answered the lady, 'your devotion shows by far too mannerly and too courtly: saints have hands, which pilgrims may touch, but kiss not.' 'Have not saints lips, and pilgrims too?' said Romeo. 'Ay,' said the lady, 'lips which they must use in prayer.' 'O

then, my dear saint,' said Romeo, 'hear my prayer, and grant it, lest I despair.' In such like allusions and loving conceits they were engaged, when the lady was called away to her mother. And Romeo inquiring who her mother was, discovered that the lady whose peerless beauty he was so much struck with, was young Juliet, daughter and heir to the lord Capulet, the great enemy of the Montagues; and that he had unknowingly engaged his heart to his foe. This troubled him, but it could not dissuade him from loving. As little rest had Juliet, when she found that the gentleman that she had been talking with was Romeo and a Montague, for she had been suddenly smit with the same hasty and inconsiderate passion for Romeo, which he had conceived for her; and a prodigious birth of love it seemed to her, that she must love her enemy, and that her afflictions should settle there, where family considerations should induce her chiefly to hate.

It being midnight, Romeo with his companions departed; but they soon missed him, for, unable to stay away from the house where he had left his heart, he leaped the wall of an orchard which was at the back of Juliet's house. Here he had not been long, ruminating on his new love, when Juliet appeared above at a window, through which her exceeding beauty seemed to break like the light of the sun in the east; and the moon, which shone in the orchard with a faint light, appeared to Romeo as if sick and

pale with grief at the superior lustre of this new sun. And
she, leaning her cheek upon her hand, he passionately
wished himself a glove upon that hand, that he might
touch her cheek. She all this while thinking herself alone,
fetched a deep sigh, and exclaimed: 'Ah me!' Romeo,
enraptured to hear her speak, said softly, and unheard by
her: 'O speak again, bright angel, for such you appear,
being over my head, like a winged messenger from heaven
whom mortals fall back to gaze upon.' She, unconscious
of being overheard, and full of the new passion which that
night's adventure had given birth to, called upon her lover
by name (whom she supposed absent): 'O Romeo,
Romeo!' said she, 'wherefore art thou Romeo? Deny
thy father, and refuse thy name, for my sake; or if thou wilt
not, be but my sworn love, and I no longer will be a
Capulet.'

Romeo, having this encouragement, would fain have
spoken, but he was desirous of hearing more; and the lady
continued her passionate discourse with herself (as she
thought), still chiding Romeo for being Romeo and a
Montague, and wishing him some other name, or that he
would put away that hated name, and for that name which
was no part of himself, he should take all herself. At this
loving word Romeo could no longer refrain, but taking up
the dialogue as if her words had been addressed to him
personally, and not merely in fancy, he bade her call him

I. ROMEO AND JULIET

Love, or by whatever other name she pleased, for he was
no longer Romeo, if that name was displeasing to her.
Juliet, alarmed to hear a man's voice in the garden, did not
at first know who it was, that by favour of the night and
darkness had thus stumbled upon the discovery of her
secret; but when he spoke again, though her ears had not
yet drunk a hundred words of that tongue's uttering, yet so
nice is a lover's hearing, that she immediately knew him to
be young Romeo, and she expostulated with him on the
danger to which he had exposed himself by climbing the
orchard walls, for if any of her kinsmen should find him
there, it would be death to him, being a Montague.
'Alack,' said Romeo, 'there is more peril in your eye,
than in twenty of their swords. Do you but look kind upon
me, lady, and I am proof against their enmity. Better my life
should be ended by their hate, than that hated life should
be prolonged, to live without your love.' 'How came
you into this place,' said Juliet, 'and by whose
direction?' 'Love directed me,' answered Romeo: 'I
am no pilot, yet wert thou as far apart from me, as that vast
shore which is washed with the farthest sea, I should
venture for such merchandise.' A crimson blush came
over Juliet's face, yet unseen by Romeo by reason of the
night, when she reflected upon the discovery which she had
made, yet not meaning to make it, of her love to Romeo.
She would fain have recalled her words, but that was

impossible: fain would she have stood upon form, and have kept her lover at a distance, as the custom of discreet ladies is, to frown and be perverse, and give their suitors harsh denials at first; to stand off, and affect a coyness or indifference, where they most love, that their lovers may not think them too lightly or too easily won; for the difficulty of attainment increases the value of the object. But there was no room in her case for denials, or puttings off, or any of the customary arts of delay and protracted courtship. Romeo had heard from her own tongue, when she did not dream that he was near her, a confession of her love. So with an honest frankness, which the novelty of her situation excused, she confirmed the truth of what he had before heard, and addressing him by the name of fair Montague (love can sweeten a sour name), she begged him not to impute her easy yielding to levity or an unworthy mind, but that he must lay the fault of it (if it were a fault) upon the accident of the night which had so strangely discovered her thoughts. And she added, that though her behaviour to him might not be sufficiently prudent, measured by the custom of her sex, yet that she would prove more true than many whose prudence was dissembling, and their modesty artificial cunning.

Romeo was beginning to call the heavens to witness, that nothing was farther from his thoughts than to impute a shadow of dishonour to such an honoured lady, when she

stopped him, begging him not to swear; for although she joyed in him, yet she had no joy of that night's contract: it was too rash, too unadvised, too sudden. But he being urgent with her to exchange a vow of love with him that night, she said that she already had given him hers before he requested it; meaning, when he overheard her confession; but she would retract what she then bestowed, for the pleasure of giving it again, for her bounty was as infinite as the sea, and her love as deep. From this loving conference she was called away by her nurse, who slept with her, and thought it time for her to be in bed, for it was near to daybreak; but hastily returning, she said three or four words more to Romeo, the purport of which was, that if his love was indeed honourable, and his purpose marriage, she would send a messenger to him to-morrow, to appoint a time for their marriage, when she would lay all her fortunes at his feet, and follow him as her lord through the world. While they were settling this point, Juliet was repeatedly called for by her nurse, and went in and returned, and went and returned again, for she seemed as jealous of Romeo going from her, as a young girl of her bird, which she will let hop a little from her hand, and pluck it back with a silken thread; and Romeo was as loath to part as she; for the sweetest music to lovers is the sound of each other's tongues at night. But at last they parted, wishing mutually sweet sleep and rest for that night.

The day was breaking when they parted, and Romeo, who was too full of thoughts of his mistress and that blessed meeting to allow him to sleep, instead of going home, bent his course to a monastery hard by, to find friar Lawrence. The good friar was already up at his devotions, but seeing young Romeo abroad so early, he conjectured rightly that he had not been abed that night, but that some distemper of youthful affection had kept him waking. He was right in imputing the cause of Romeo's wakefulness to love, but he made a wrong guess at the object, for he thought that his love for Rosaline had kept him waking. But when Romeo revealed his new passion for Juliet, and requested the assistance of the friar to marry them that day, the holy man lifted up his eyes and hands in a sort of wonder at the sudden change in Romeo's affections, for he had been privy to all Romeo's love for Rosaline, and his many complaints of her disdain: and he said, that young men's love lay not truly in their hearts, but in their eyes. But Romeo replying, that he himself had often chidden him for doting on Rosaline, who could not love him again, whereas Juliet both loved and was beloved by him, the friar assented in some measure to his reasons; and thinking that a matrimonial alliance between young Juliet and Romeo might happily be the means of making up the long breach between the Capulets and the Montagues; which no one more lamented than this good friar, who was a friend to both the families and had often interposed his mediation to make up the quarrel without effect; partly moved by policy, and partly by his fondness for young Romeo, to whom he could deny nothing, the old man consented to join their hands in marriage.

Now was Romeo blessed indeed, and Juliet, who knew his intent from a messenger which she had despatched according to promise, did not fail to be early at the cell of friar Lawrence, where their hands were joined in holy marriage; the good friar praying the heavens to smile upon that act, and in the union of this young Montague and young Capulet to bury the old strife and long dissensions of their families.

The ceremony being over, Juliet hastened home, where she stayed impatient for the coming of night, at which time Romeo promised to come and meet her in the orchard, where they had met the night before; and the time between seemed as tedious to her, as the night before some great festival seems to an impatient child, that has got new finery which it may not put on till the morning.

That same day, about noon, Romeo's friends, Benvolio and Mercutio, walking through the streets of Verona, were met by a party of the Capulets with the impetuous Tybalt at their head. This was the same angry Tybalt who would have fought with Romeo at old lord Capulet's feast. He, seeing Mercutio, accused him bluntly of associating with

Romeo, a Montague. Mercutio, who had as much fire and youthful blood in him as Tybalt, replied to this accusation with some sharpness; and in spite of all Benvolio could say to moderate their wrath, a quarrel was beginning, when Romeo himself passing that way, the fierce Tybalt turned from Mercutio to Romeo, and gave him the disgraceful appellation of villain. Romeo wished to avoid a quarrel with Tybalt above all men, because he was the kinsman of Juliet, and much beloved by her; besides, this young Montague had never thoroughly entered into the family quarrel, being by nature wise and gentle, and the name of a Capulet, which was his dear lady's name, was now rather a charm to allay resentment, than a watchword to excite fury. So he tried to reason with Tybalt, whom he saluted mildly by the name of good Capulet, as if he, though a Montague, had some secret pleasure in uttering that name: but Tybalt, who hated all Montagues as he hated hell, would hear no reason, but drew his weapon; and Mercutio, who knew not of Romeo's secret motive for desiring peace with Tybalt, but looked upon his present forbearance as a sort of calm dishonourable submission, with many disdainful words provoked Tybalt to the prosecution of his first quarrel with him; and Tybalt and Mercutio fought, till Mercutio fell, receiving his death's wound while Romeo and Benvolio were vainly endeavouring to part the combatants. Mercutio being dead, Romeo kept his temper no longer, but returned

the scornful appellation of villain which Tybalt had given
him; and they fought till Tybalt was slain by Romeo. This
deadly broil falling out in the midst of Verona at noonday,
the news of it quickly brought a crowd of citizens to the
spot, and among them the old lords Capulet and Montague,
with their wives; and soon after arrived the prince himself,
who being related to Mercutio, whom Tybalt had slain, and
having had the peace of his government often disturbed by
these brawls of Montagues and Capulets, came determined
to put the law in strictest force against those who should be
found to be offenders. Benvolio, who had been eyewitness
to the fray, was commanded by the prince to relate the
origin of it, which he did, keeping as near the truth as he
could without injury to Romeo, softening and excusing the
part which his friends took in it. Lady Capulet, whose
extreme grief for the loss of her kinsman Tybalt made her
keep no bounds in her revenge, exhorted the prince to do
strict justice upon his murderer, and to pay no attention to
Benvolio's representation, who, being Romeo's friend and a
Montague, spoke partially. Thus she pleaded against her
new son-in-law, but she knew not yet that he was her son-
in-law and Juliet's husband. On the other hand was to be
seen Lady Montague pleading for her child's life, and
arguing with some justice that Romeo had done nothing
worthy of punishment in taking the life of Tybalt, which
was already forfeited to the law by his having slain

Mercutio. The prince, unmoved by the passionate exclamations of these women, on a careful examination of the facts, pronounced his sentence, and by that sentence Romeo was banished from Verona.

Heavy news to young Juliet, who had been but a few hours a bride, and now by this decree seemed everlastingly divorced! When the tidings reached her, she at first gave way to rage against Romeo, who had slain her dear cousin: she called him a beautiful tyrant, a fiend angelical, a ravenous dove, a lamb with a wolf's nature, a serpent-heart hid with a flowering face, and other like contradictory names, which denoted the struggles in her mind between her love and her resentment: but in the end love got the mastery, and the tears which she shed for grief that Romeo had slain her cousin, turned to drops of joy that her husband lived whom Tybalt would have slain. Then came fresh tears, and they were altogether of grief for Romeo's banishment. That word was more terrible to her than the death of many Tybalts.

Romeo, after the fray, had taken refuge in friar Lawrence's cell, where he was first made acquainted with the prince's sentence, which seemed to him far more terrible than death. To him it appeared there was no world out of Verona's walls, no living out of the sight of Juliet. Heaven was there where Juliet lived, and all beyond was purgatory, torture, hell. The good friar would have applied

the consolation of philosophy to his griefs: but this frantic young man would hear of none, but like a madman he tore his hair, and threw himself all along upon the ground, as he said, to take the measure of his grave. From this unseemly state he was roused by a message from his dear lady, which a little revived him; and then the friar took the advantage to expostulate with him on the unmanly weakness which he had shown. He had slain Tybalt, but would he also slay himself, slay his dear lady, who lived but in his life? The noble form of man, he said, was but a shape of wax, when it wanted the courage which should keep it firm. The law had been lenient to him, that instead of death, which he had incurred, had pronounced by the prince's mouth only banishment. He had slain Tybalt, but Tybalt would have slain him: there was a sort of happiness in that. Juliet was alive, and (beyond all hope) had become his dear wife; therein he was most happy. All these blessings, as the friar made them out to be, did Romeo put from him like a sullen misbehaved wench. And the friar bade him beware, for such as despaired, (he said) died miserable. Then when Romeo was a little calmed, he counselled him that he should go that night and secretly take his leave of Juliet, and thence proceed straightways to Mantua, at which place he should sojourn, till the friar found fit occasion to publish his marriage, which might be a joyful means of reconciling their families; and then he did not doubt but

the prince would be moved to pardon him, and he would return with twenty times more joy than he went forth with grief. Romeo was convinced by these wise counsels of the friar, and took his leave to go and seek his lady, proposing to stay with her that night, and by daybreak pursue his journey alone to Mantua; to which place the good friar promised to send him letters from time to time, acquainting him with the state of affairs at home.

That night Romeo passed with his dear wife, gaining secret admission to her chamber, from the orchard in which he had heard her confession of love the night before. That had been a night of unmixed joy and rapture; but the pleasures of this night, and the delight which these lovers took in each other's society, were sadly allayed with the prospect of parting, and the fatal adventures of the past day. The unwelcome daybreak seemed to come too soon, and when Juliet heard the morning song of the lark, she would have persuaded herself that it was the nightingale, which sings by night, but it was too truly the lark which sang, and a discordant and unpleasing note it seemed to her; and the streaks of day in the east too certainly pointed out that it was time for these lovers to part. Romeo took his leave of his dear wife with a heavy heart, promising to write to her from Mantua every hour in the day; and when he had descended from her chamber-window, as he stood below her on the ground, in that sad

foreboding state of mind in which she was, he appeared to her eyes as one dead in the bottom of a tomb. Romeo's mind misgave him in like manner: but now he was forced hastily to depart, for it was death for him to be found within the walls of Verona after daybreak.

This was but the beginning of the tragedy of this pair of star-crossed lovers. Romeo had not been gone many days, before the old lord Capulet proposed a match for Juliet. The husband he had chosen for her, not dreaming that she was married already, was count Paris, a gallant, young, and noble gentleman, no unworthy suitor to the young Juliet, if she had never seen Romeo.

The terrified Juliet was in a sad perplexity at her father's offer. She pleaded her youth unsuitable to marriage, the recent death of Tybalt, which had left her spirits too weak to meet a husband with any face of joy, and how indecorous it would show for the family of the Capulets to be celebrating a nuptial feast, when his funeral solemnities were hardly over: she pleaded every reason against the match, but the true one, namely, that she was married already. But lord Capulet was deaf to all her excuses, and in a peremptory manner ordered her to get ready, for by the following Thursday she should be married to Paris: and having found her a husband, rich, young, and noble, such as the proudest maid in Verona might joyfully accept, he could not bear that out of an affected coyness, as he

construed her denial, she should oppose obstacles to her own good fortune.

In this extremity Juliet applied to the friendly friar, always her counsellor in distress, and he asking her if she had resolution to undertake a desperate remedy, and she answering that she would go into the grave alive rather than marry Paris, her own dear husband living; he directed her to go home, and appear merry, and give her consent to marry Paris, according to her father's desire, and on the next night, which was the night before the marriage, to drink off the contents of a phial which he then gave her, the effect of which would be that for two-and-forty hours after drinking it she should appear cold and lifeless; and when the bridegroom came to fetch her in the morning, he would find her to appearance dead; that then she would be borne, as the manner in that country was, uncovered on a bier, to be buried in the family vault; that if she could put off womanish fear, and consent to this terrible trial, in forty-two hours after swallowing the liquid (such was its certain operation) she would be sure to awake, as from a dream; and before she should awake, he would let her husband know their drift, and he should come in the night, and bear her thence to Mantua. Love, and the dread of marrying Paris, gave young Juliet strength to undertake this horrible adventure; and she took the phial of the friar, promising to observe his directions.

Going from the monastery, she met the young count Paris, and modestly dissembling, promised to become his bride. This was joyful news to the lord Capulet and his wife. It seemed to put youth into the old man; and Juliet, who had displeased him exceedingly, by her refusal of the count, was his darling again, now she promised to be obedient. All things in the house were in a bustle against the approaching nuptials. No cost was spared to prepare such festival rejoicings as Verona had never before witnessed.

On the Wednesday night Juliet drank off the potion. She had many misgivings lest the friar, to avoid the blame which might be imputed to him for marrying her to Romeo, had given her poison; but then he was always known for a holy man: then lest she should awake before the time that Romeo was to come for her; whether the terror of the place, a vault of dead Capulets' bones, and where Tybalt, all bloody, lay festering in his shroud, would not be enough to drive her distracted: again she thought of all the stories she had heard of spirits haunting the places where their bodies were bestowed. But then her love for Romeo, and her aversion for Paris returned, and she desperately swallowed the draught and became insensible.

When young Paris came early in the morning with music to awaken his bride, instead of a living Juliet, her chamber presented the dreary spectacle of a lifeless corset

What death to his hopes! What confusion then reigned through the whole house! Poor Paris lamenting his bride, whom most detestable death had beguiled him of, had divorced from him even before their hands were joined. But still more piteous it was to hear the mournings of the old lord and lady Capulet, who having but this one, one poor loving child to rejoice and solace in, cruel death had snatched her from their sight, just as these careful parents were on the point of seeing her advanced (as they thought) by a promising and advantageous match. Now all things that were ordained for the festival were turned from their properties to do the office of a black funeral. The wedding cheer served for a sad burial feast, the bridal hymns were changed for sullen dirges, the sprightly instruments to melancholy bells, and the flowers that should have been strewed in the bride's path, now served but to strew her corset Now, instead of a priest to marry her, a priest was needed to bury her; and she was borne to church indeed, not to augment the cheerful hopes of the living, but to swell the dreary numbers of the dead.

Bad news, which always travels faster than good, now brought the dismal story of his Juliet's death to Romeo, at Mantua, before the messenger could arrive, who was sent from friar Lawrence to apprise him that these were mock funerals only, and but the shadow and representation of death, and that his dear lady lay in the tomb but for a short while, expecting when Romeo would come to release her from that dreary mansion. Just before, Romeo had been unusually joyful and light-hearted. He had dreamed in the night that he was dead (a strange dream, that gave a dead man leave to think), and that his lady came and found him dead, and breathed such life with kisses in his lips, that he revived, and was an emperor! And now that a messenger came from Verona, he thought surely it was to confirm some good news which his dreams had presaged. But when the contrary to this flattering vision appeared, and that it was his lady who was dead in truth, whom he could not

revive by any kisses, he ordered horses to be got ready, for he determined that night to visit Verona, and to see his lady in her tomb. And as mischief is swift to enter into the thoughts of desperate men, he called to mind a poor apothecary, whose shop in Mantua he had lately passed, and from the beggarly appearance of the man, who seemed famished, and the wretched show in his show of empty boxes ranged on dirty shelves, and other tokens of extreme wretchedness, he had said at the time (perhaps having some misgivings that his own disastrous life might haply meet with a conclusion so desperate), 'If a man were to need poison, which by the law of Mantua it is death to sell, here lives a poor wretch who would sell it him.' These words of his now came into his mind, and he sought out the apothecary, who after some pretended scruples, Romeo offering him gold, which his poverty could not resist, sold him a poison, which, if he swallowed, he told him, if he had the strength of twenty men, would quickly despatch him.

With this poison he set out for Verona, to have a sight of his dear lady in her tomb, meaning, when he had satisfied his sight, to swallow the poison, and be buried by her side. He reached Verona at midnight, and found the churchyard, in the midst of which was situated the ancient tomb of the Capulets. He had provided a light, and a spade, and wrenching iron, and was proceeding to break open the

monument, when he was interrupted by a voice, which by the name of vile Montague, bade him desist from his unlawful business. It was the young count Paris, who had come to the tomb of Juliet at that unseasonable time of night, to strew flowers and to weep over the grave of her that should have been his bride. He knew not what an interest Romeo had in the dead, but knowing him to be a Montague, and (as he supposed) a sworn foe to all the Capulets, he judged that he was come by night to do some villainous shame to the dead bodies; therefore in an angry tone he bade him desist; and as a criminal, condemned by the laws of Verona to die if he were found within the walls of the city, he would have apprehended him. Romeo urged Paris to leave him, and warned him by the fate of Tybalt, who lay buried there, not to provoke his anger, or draw down another sin upon his head, by forcing him to kill him. But the count in scorn refused his warning, and laid hands on him as a felon, which Romeo resisting, they fought, and Paris fell. When Romeo, by the help of a light, came to see who it was that he had slain, that it was Paris, who (he learned in his way from Mantua) should have married Juliet, he took the dead youth by the hand, as one whom misfortune had made a companion, and said that he would bury him in a triumphal grave, meaning in Juliet's grave, which he now opened: and there lay his lady, as one whom death had no power upon to change a feature or

complexion, in her matchless beauty; or as if Death were amorous, and the lean abhorred monster kept her there for his delight; for she lay yet fresh and blooming, as she had fallen to sleep when she swallowed that benumbing potion; and near her lay Tybalt in his bloody shroud, whom Romeo seeing, begged pardon of his lifeless corse, and for Juliet's sake called him cousin, and said that he was about to do him a favour by putting his enemy to death. Here Romeo took his last leave of his lady's lips, kissing them; and here he shook the burden of his cross stars from his weary body, swallowing that poison which the apothecary had sold him, whose operation was fatal and real, not like that dissembling potion which Juliet had swallowed, the effect of which was now nearly expiring, and she about to awake to complain that Romeo had not kept his time, or that he had come too soon.

For now the hour was arrived at which the friar had promised that she should awake; and he, having learned that his letters which he had sent to Mantua, by some unlucky detention of the messenger, had never reached Romeo, came himself, provided with the pickaxe and lantern, to deliver the lady from her confinement; but he was surprised to find a light already burning in the Capulets' monument, and to see swords and blood near it, and Romeo and Paris lying breathless by the monument.

Before he could entertain a conjecture, to imagine how

these fatal accidents had fallen out, Juliet awoke out of her trance, and seeing the friar near her, she remembered the place where she was, and the occasion of her being there, and asked for Romeo, but the friar, hearing a noise, bade her come out of that place of death, and of unnatural sleep, for a greater power than they could contradict had thwarted their intents; and being frightened by the noise of people coming, he fled: but when Juliet saw the cup closed in her true love's hand, she guessed that poison had been the cause of his end, and she would have swallowed the dregs if any had been left, and she kissed his still warm lips to try if any poison yet did hang upon them, then hearing a nearer noise of people coming, she quickly unsheathed a dagger which she wore, and stabbing herself, died by her true Romeo's side.

The watch by this time had come up to the place. A page belonging to count Paris, who had witnessed the fight between his master and Romeo, had given the alarm, which had spread among the citizens, who went up and down the streets of Verona confusedly exclaiming, A Paris! a Romeo! a Juliet! as the rumour had imperfectly reached them, till the uproar brought lord Montague and lord Capulet out of their beds, with the prince, to inquire into the causes of the disturbance. The friar had been apprehended by some of the watch, coming from the churchyard, trembling, sighing, and weeping, in a suspicious manner. A great multitude

being assembled at the Capulets' monument, the friar was demanded by the prince to deliver what he knew of these strange and disastrous accidents.

And there, in the presence of the old lords Montague and Capulet, he faithfully related the story of their children's fatal love, the part he took in promoting their marriage, in the hope in that union to end the long quarrels between their families: how Romeo, there dead, was husband to Juliet; and Juliet, there dead, was Romeo's faithful wife; how before he could find a fit opportunity to divulge their marriage, another match was projected for Juliet, who, to avoid the crime of a second marriage, swallowed the sleeping draught (as he advised), and all thought her dead; how meantime he wrote to Romeo, to come and take her thence when the force of the potion should cease, and by what unfortunate miscarriage of the messenger the letters never reached Romeo: further than this the friar could not follow the story, nor knew more than that coming himself, to deliver Juliet from that place of death, he found the count Paris and Romeo slain. The remainder of the transactions was supplied by the narration of the page who had seen Paris and Romeo fight, and by the servant who came with Romeo from Verona, to whom this faithful lover had given letters to be delivered to his father in the event of his death, which made good the friar's words, confessing his marriage with Juliet, imploring

the forgiveness of his parents, acknowledging the buying of the poison of the poor apothecary, and his intent in coming to the monument, to die, and lie with Juliet. All these circumstances agreed together to clear the friar from any hand he could be supposed to have in these complicated slaughters, further than as the unintended consequences of his own well meant, yet too artificial and subtle contrivances.

And the prince, turning to these old lords, Montague and Capulet, rebuked them for their brutal and irrational enmities, and showed them what a scourge Heaven had laid upon such offences, that it had found means even through the love of their children to punish their unnatural hate. And these old rivals, no longer enemies, agreed to bury their long strife in their children's graves; and lord Capulet requested lord Montague to give him his hand, calling him by the name of brother, as if in acknowledgment of the union of their families, by the marriage of the young Capulet and Montague; and saying that lord Montague's hand (in token of reconcilement) was all he demanded for his daughter's jointure: but lord Montague said he would give him more, for he would raise her a statue of pure gold, that while Verona kept its name, no figure should be so esteemed for its richness and workmanship as that of the true and faithful Juliet. And lord Capulet in return said that he would raise another statue to Romeo. So did these poor

old lords, when it was too late, strive to outgo each other in mutual courtesies: while so deadly had been their rage and enmity in past times, that nothing but the fearful overthrow of their children (poor sacrifices to their quarrels and dissensions) could remove the rooted hates and jealousies of the noble families.

II.

THE MERCHANT OF VENICE

Shylock, the Jew, lived at Venice: he was an usurer, who had amassed an immense fortune by lending money at great interest to Christian merchants. Shylock, being a hard-hearted man, exacted the payment of the money he lent with such severity that he was much disliked by all good men, and particularly by Antonio, a young merchant of Venice; and Shylock as much hated Antonio, because he used to lend money to people in distress, and would never take any interest for the money he lent; therefore there was great enmity between this covetous Jew and the generous merchant Antonio. Whenever Antonio met Shylock on the Rialto (or Exchange), he used to reproach him with his usuries and hard dealings, which the Jew would bear with seeming patience, while he secretly meditated revenge.

Antonio was the kindest man that lived, the best conditioned, and had the most unwearied spirit in doing courtesies; indeed, he was one in whom the ancient Roman honour more appeared than in any that drew breath in Italy. He was greatly beloved by all his fellow-citizens; but the friend who was nearest and dearest to his heart was Bassanio, a noble Venetian, who, having but a small patrimony, had nearly exhausted his little fortune by living in too expensive a manner for his slender means, as young men of high rank with small fortunes are too apt to do. Whenever Bassanio wanted money, Antonio assisted him; and it seemed as if they had but one heart and one purse between them.

One day Bassanio came to Antonio, and told him that he wished to repair his fortune by a wealthy marriage with a lady whom he dearly loved, whose father, that was lately dead, had left her sole heiress to a large estate; and that in her father's lifetime he used to visit at her house, when he thought he had observed this lady had sometimes from her eyes sent speechless messages, that seemed to say he would be no unwelcome suitor; but not having money to furnish himself with an appearance befitting the lover of so rich an heiress, he besought Antonio to add to the many favours he had shown him, by lending him three thousand ducats.

Antonio had no money by him at that time to lend his friend; but expecting soon to have some ships come home laden with merchandise, he said he would go to Shylock, the rich money-lender, and borrow the money upon the credit of those ships.

Antonio and Bassanio went
together to Shylock, and Antonio
asked the Jew to lend him three
thousand ducats upon any
interest he should require,
to be paid out of the

merchandise contained in his ships at sea. On this, Shylock thought within himself: 'If I can once catch him on the hip, I will feed fat the ancient grudge I bear him; he hates our Jewish nation; he lends out money gratis, and among merchants he rails at me and my well-earned bargains, which he calls interest. Cursed be my tribe if I forgive him!' Antonio finding he was musing within himself and did not answer, and being impatient for the money, said: 'Shylock, do you hear? will you lend the money?' To this question the Jew replied: 'Signior Antonio, on the Rialto many a time and often you have railed at me about my monies and my usuries, and I have borne it with a patient shrug, for sufferance is the badge of all our tribe; and then you have called me unbeliever, cut-throat dog, and spit upon my Jewish garments, and spurned at me with your foot, as if I was a cur. Well then, it now appears you need my help; and you come to me, and say, Shylock, lend me monies. Has a dog money? Is it possible a cur should lend three thousand ducats? Shall I bend low and say, Fair sir, you spit upon me on Wednesday last, another time you called me dog, and for these courtesies I am to lend you monies.' Antonio replied: 'I am as like to call you so again, to spit on you again, and spurn you too. If you will lend me this money, lend it not to me as to a friend, but rather lend it to me as to an enemy, that, if I break, you may with better face exact the penalty.' 'Why, look

you,' said Shylock, 'how you storm! I would be friends with you, and have your love. I will forget the shames you have put upon me. I will supply your wants, and take no interest for my money.' This seemingly kind offer greatly surprised Antonio; and then Shylock, still pretending kindness, and that all he did was to gain Antonio's love, again said he would lend him the three thousand ducats, and take no interest for his money; only Antonio should go with him to a lawyer, and there sign in merry sport a bond, that if he did not repay the money by a certain day, he would forfeit a pound of flesh, to be cut off from any part of his body that Shylock pleased.

'Content,' said Antonio: 'I will sign to this bond, and say there is much kindness in the Jew.'

Bassanio said Antonio should not sign to such a bond for him; but still Antonio insisted that he would sign it, for that before the day of payment came, his ships would return laden with many times the value of the money.

Shylock, hearing this debate, exclaimed: 'O, father Abraham, what suspicious people these Christians are! Their own hard dealings teach them to suspect the thoughts of others. I pray you tell me this, Bassanio: if he should break this day, what should I gain by the exaction of the forfeiture? A pound of man's flesh, taken from a man, is not so estimable, nor profitable neither, as the flesh of mutton or beef. I say, to buy his favour I offer this friendship: if he will take it, so; if not, adieu.'

At last, against the advice of Bassanio, who, notwithstanding all the Jew had said of his kind intentions, did not like his friend should run the hazard of this shocking penalty for his sake, Antonio signed the bond, thinking it really was (as the Jew said) merely in sport.

The rich heiress that Bassanio wished to marry lived near Venice, at a place called Belmont: her name was Portia, and in the graces of her person and her mind she was nothing inferior to that Portia, of whom we read, who was Cato's daughter, and the wife of Brutus.

Bassanio being so kindly supplied with money by his friend Antonio, at the hazard of his life, set out for Belmont with a splendid train, and attended by a gentleman of the name of Gratiano.

Bassanio proving successful in his suit, Portia in a short time consented to accept of him for a husband.

Bassanio confessed to Portia that he had no fortune, and that his high birth and noble ancestry was all that he could boast of; she, who loved him for his worthy qualities, and had riches enough not to regard wealth in a husband, answered with a graceful modesty, that she would wish herself a thousand times more fair, and ten thousand times more rich, to be more worthy of him; and then the accomplished Portia prettily dispraised herself, and said she was an unlessoned girl, unschooled, unpractised, yet not so

old but that she could learn, and that she would commit her gentle spirit to be directed and governed by him in all things; and she said: 'Myself and what is mine, to you and yours is now converted. But yesterday, Bassanio, I was the lady of this fair mansion, queen of myself, and mistress over these servants; and now this house, these servants, and myself, are yours, my lord; I give them with this ring'; presenting a ring to Bassanio.

Bassanio was so overpowered with gratitude and wonder at the gracious manner in which the rich and noble Portia accepted of a man of his humble fortunes, that he could not express his joy and reverence to the dear lady who so honoured him, by anything but broken words of love and thankfulness; and taking the ring, he vowed never to part with it.

Gratiano and Nerissa, Portia's waiting-maid, were in attendance upon their lord and lady, when Portia so gracefully promised to become the obedient wife of Bassanio; and Gratiano, wishing Bassanio and the generous lady joy, desired permission to be married at the same time.

'With all my heart, Gratiano,' said Bassanio, 'if you can get a wife.'

Gratiano then said that he loved the lady Portia's fair waiting gentlewoman Nerissa, and that she had promised to be his wife, if her lady married Bassanio. Portia asked Nerissa if this was true. Nerissa replied: 'Madam, it is so, if you approve of it.' Portia willingly consenting, Bassanio pleasantly said: 'Then our wedding-feast shall be much honoured by your marriage, Gratiano.'

The happiness of these lovers was sadly crossed at this moment by the entrance of a messenger, who brought a letter from Antonio containing fearful tidings. When Bassanio read Antonio's letter, Portia feared it was to tell him of the death of some dear friend, he looked so pale; and inquiring what was the news which had so distressed him, he said: **'O sweet Portia, here are a few of the unpleasantest words that ever blotted paper; gentle lady, when I first imparted my love to you, I freely told you all the wealth I had ran in my veins; but I should have told you that I had less than nothing, being in debt.'** Bassanio then told Portia what has been here related, of his borrowing the money of Antonio, and of Antonio's procuring it of Shylock the Jew, and of the bond by which Antonio had engaged to forfeit a pound of flesh, if it was not repaid by a certain day: and then Bassanio read Antonio's letter: the words of which were: 'Sweet Bassanio, my ships are all lost, my bond to the Jew is forfeited, and since in paying it is impossible I should live, I could wish to see you at my death; notwithstanding use your pleasure; if your love for me do not persuade you to come, let not my letter.' 'O, my dear love,' said Portia, 'despatch all business, and begone; you shall have gold to

pay the money twenty times over, before this kind friend shall lose a hair by my Bassanio's fault; and as you are so dearly bought, I will dearly love you.' Portia then said she would be married to Bassanio before he set out, to give him a legal right to her money; and that same day they were married, and Gratiano was also married to Nerissa; and Bassanio and Gratiano, the instant they were married, set out in great haste for Venice, where Bassanio found Antonio in prison.

The day of payment being past, the cruel Jew would not accept of the money which Bassanio offered him, but insisted upon having a pound of Antonio's flesh. A day was appointed to try this shocking cause before the duke of Venice, and Bassanio awaited in dreadful suspense the event of the trial.

When Portia parted with her husband, she spoke cheeringly to him, and bade him bring his dear friend along with him when he returned; yet she feared it would go hard with Antonio, and when she was left alone, she began to think and consider within herself, if she could by any means be instrumental in saving the life of her dear Bassanio's friend; and notwithstanding when she wished to honour her Bassanio, she had said to him with such a meek and wifelike grace, that she would submit in all things to be governed by his superior wisdom, yet being now called forth into action by the peril of her honoured husband's friend, she did nothing doubt her own powers, and by the sole guidance of her own true and perfect judgment, at once resolved to go herself to Venice, and speak in Antonio's defence.

Portia had a relation who was a counsellor in the law; to this gentleman, whose name was Bellario, she wrote, and stating the case to him, desired his opinion, and that with his advice he would also send her the dress worn by a counsellor. When the messenger returned, he brought letters from Bellario of advice how to proceed, and also everything necessary for her equipment.

Portia dressed herself and her maid Nerissa in men's apparel, and putting on the robes of a counsellor, she took Nerissa along with her as her clerk; and setting out immediately, they arrived at Venice on the very day of the trial. The cause was just going to be heard before the duke and senators of Venice in the senate-house, when Portia entered this high court of justice, and presented a letter from Bellario, in which that learned counsellor wrote to the duke, saying, he would have come himself to plead for Antonio, but that he was prevented by sickness, and he requested that the learned young doctor Balthasar (so he called Portia) might be permitted to plead in his stead. This the duke granted, much wondering at the youthful appearance of the stranger, who was prettily disguised by her counsellor's robes and her large wig.

And now began this important trial. Portia looked around her, and she knew the merciless Jew; and she saw Bassanio, but he knew her not in her disguise. He was standing beside Antonio, in an agony of distress and fear for his friend.

The importance of the arduous task Portia had engaged in gave this tender lady courage, and she boldly proceeded in the duty she had undertaken to perform: and first of all she addressed herself to Shylock; and allowing that he had a right by the Venetian law to have the forfeit expressed in the bond, she spoke so sweetly of the noble quality of merry, as would have softened any heart but the unfeeling Shylock's; saying, that it dropped as the gentle rain from heaven upon the place beneath; and how mercy was a double blessing, it blessed him that gave, and him that received it, and how it became monarchs better than their crowns, being an attribute of God Himself; and that earthly power came nearest to God's, in proportion as mercy tempered justice; and she bid Shylock remember that as we all pray for mercy, that same prayer should teach us to show mercy. Shylock only answered her by desiring to have the penalty forfeited in the bond. 'Is he not able to pay the money?' asked Portia. Bassanio then offered the Jew the payment of the three thousand ducats as many times over as he should desire; which Shylock refusing, and still insisting upon having a pound of Antonio's flesh,

Bassanio begged the learned young counsellor would
endeavour to wrest the law a little, to save Antonio's life.
But Portia gravely answered, that laws once established
must never be altered. Shylock hearing Portia say that the
law might not be altered, it seemed to him that she was
pleading in his favour, and he said: 'A Daniel is come to
judgment! O wise young judge, how I do honour you! How
much elder are you than your looks!'

Portia now desired Shylock to let her look at the bond;
and when she had read it, she said: 'This bond is
forfeited, and by this the Jew may lawfully claim a pound
of flesh, to be by him cut off nearest Antonio's heart.'
Then she said to Shylock: 'Be merciful: take the money,
and bid me tear the bond.' But no mercy would the cruel
Shylock show; and he said: 'By my soul I swear, there is
no power in the tongue of men to alter me.' 'Why then,
Antonio,' said Portia, 'you must prepare your bosom
for the knife' : and while Shylock was sharpening a long
knife with great eagerness to cut off the pound of flesh,
Portia said to Antonio: 'Have you anything to say?'
Antonio with a calm resignation replied, that he had but
little to say, for that he had prepared his mind for death.
Then he said to Bassanio: 'Give me your hand, Bassanio!
Fare you well! Grieve not that I am fallen into this
misfortune for you. Commend me to your honourable wife,
and tell her how I have loved you!' Bassanio in the

deepest affliction replied: 'Antonio, I am married to a wife, who is as dear to me as life itself; but life itself, my wife, and all the world, are not esteemed with me above your life; I would lose all, I would sacrifice all to this devil here, to deliver you.'

Portia hearing this, though the kind-hearted lady was not at all offended with her husband for expressing the love he owed to so true a friend as Antonio in these strong terms, yet could not help answering: 'Your wife would give you little thanks, if she were present, to hear you make this offer.' And then Gratiano, who loved to copy what his lord did, thought he must make a speech like Bassanio's, and he said, in Nerissa's hearing, who was writing in her clerk's dress by the side of Portia: 'I have a wife, whom I protest I love; I wish she were in heaven, if she could but entreat some power there to change the cruel temper of this currish Jew.' 'It is well you wish this behind her back, else you would have but an unquiet house,' said Nerissa.

Shylock now cried out impatiently: 'We trifle time; I pray pronounce the sentence.' And now all was awful expectation in the court, and every heart was full of grief for Antonio.

Portia asked if the scales were ready to weigh the flesh; and she said to the Jew: 'Shylock, you must have some surgeon by, lest he bleed to death.' Shylock, whose whole

intent was that Antonio should bleed to death, said: 'It is not so named in the bond.' Portia replied: 'It is not so named in the bond, but what of that? It were good you did so much for charity.' To this all the answer Shylock would make was: 'I cannot find it; it is not in the bond.'

'Then,' said Portia, 'a pound of Antonio's flesh is shine. The law allows it, and the court awards it. And you may cut this flesh from off his breast. The law allows it and the court awards it.' Again Shylock exclaimed: 'O wise and upright judge! A Daniel is come to judgment!' And then he sharpened his long knife again, and looking eagerly on Antonio, he said: 'Come, prepare!'

'Tarry a little, Jew,' said Portia; 'there is something else. This bond here gives you no drop of blood; the words expressly are 'a pound of flesh.' If in the cutting off the pound of flesh you shed one drop of Christian blood, your lands and goods are by the law to be confiscated to the state of Venice.' Now as it was utterly impossible for Shylock to cut off the pound of flesh without shedding some of Antonio's blood, this wise discovery of Portia's, that it was flesh and not blood that was named in the bond, saved the life of Antonio; and all admiring the wonderful sagacity of the young counsellor, who had so happily thought of this expedient, plaudits resounded from every part of the senate-house; and Gratiano exclaimed, in the words which Shylock had used:

'O wise and upright judge! mark, Jew, a Daniel is come to judgment!'

Shylock, finding himself defeated in his cruel intent, said with a disappointed look, that he would take the money; and Bassanio, rejoiced beyond measure at Antonio's unexpected deliverance, cried out: 'Here is the money!' But Portia stopped him, saying: 'Softly; there is no haste; the Jew shall have nothing but the penalty: therefore prepare, Shylock, to cut off the flesh; but mind you shed no blood: nor do not cut off more nor less than just a pound; be it more or less by one poor scruple, nay if the scale turn but by the weight of a single hair, you are condemned by the laws of Venice to die, and all your wealth is forfeited to the senate.' 'Give me my money, and let me go,' said Shylock. 'I have it ready,' said Bassanio: 'here it is.'

Shylock was going to take the money, when Portia again stopped him, saying: 'Tarry, Jew; I have yet another hold upon you. By the laws of Venice, your wealth is forfeited to the state, for having conspired against the life of one of its citizens, and your life lies at the mercy of the duke; therefore, down on your knees, and ask him to pardon you.'

The duke then said to Shylock: 'That you may see the difference of our Christian spirit, I pardon you your life before you ask it; half your wealth belongs to Antonio, the

other half comes to the state.'

The generous Antonio then said that he would give up his share of Shylock's wealth, if Shylock would sign a deed to make it over at his death to his daughter and her husband; for Antonio knew that the Jew had an only daughter who had lately married against his consent to a young Christian, named Lorenzo, a friend of Antonio's, which had so offended Shylock, that he had disinherited her.

The Jew agreed to this: and being thus disappointed in his revenge, and despoiled of his riches, he said: 'I am ill. Let me go home; send the deed after me, and I will sign over half my riches to my daughter.' 'Get thee gone, then,' said the Duke, 'and sign it; and if you repent your cruelty and turn Christian, the state will forgive you the fine of the other half of your riches.'

The duke now released Antonio, and dismissed the court. He then highly praised the wisdom and ingenuity of the young counsellor, and invited him home to dinner. Portia, who meant to return to Belmont before her husband, replied: 'I humbly thank your grace, but I must away directly.' The duke said he was sorry he had not leisure to stay and dine with him; and turning to Antonio, he added: 'Reward this gentleman; for in my mind you are much indebted to him.'

The duke and his senators left the court; and then

Bassanio said to Portia: 'Most worthy gentleman, I and my friend Antonio have by your wisdom been this day acquitted of grievous penalties, and I beg you will accept of the three thousand ducats due unto the Jew.' 'And we shall stand indebted to you over and above,' said Antonio, 'in love and service evermore.'

Portia could not be prevailed upon to accept the money; but upon Bassanio still pressing her to accept of some reward, she said: 'Give me your gloves; I will wear them for your sake' ; and then Bassanio taking off his gloves, she espied the ring which she had given him upon his finger: now it was the ring the wily lady wanted to get from him to make a merry jest when she saw her Bassanio again, that made her ask him for his gloves; and she said, when she saw the ring, 'and for your love I will take this ring from you.' Bassanio was sadly distressed that the counsellor should ask him for the only thing he could not part with, and he replied in great confusion, that he could not give him that ring, because it was his wife's gift, and he had vowed never to part with it; but that he would give him the most valuable ring in Venice, and find it out by proclamation. On this Portia affected to be affronted, and left the court, saying: 'You teach me, sir, how a beggar should be answered.'

'Dear Bassanio,' said Antonio, 'let him have the ring; let my love and the great service he has done for me

be valued against your wife's displeasure,' Bassanio,
ashamed to appear so ungrateful, yielded, and sent
Gratiano after Portia with the ring; and then the clerk
Nerissa, who had also given Gratiano a ring, she begged his
ring, and Gratiano (not choosing to be outdone in
generosity by his lord) gave it to her. And there was
laughing among these ladies to think, when they got home,
how they would tax their husbands with giving away their
rings, and swear that they had given them as a present to
some woman.

Portia, when she returned, was in that happy temper
of mind which never fails to attend the consciousness of
having performed a good action; her cheerful spirits
enjoyed everything she saw: the moon never seemed to
shine so bright before; and when that pleasant moon was
hid behind a cloud, then a light which she saw from her
house at Belmont as well pleased her charmed fancy, and
she said to Nerissa: 'That light we see is burning in my
hall; how far that little candle throws its beams, so shines a
good deed in a naughty world' ; and hearing the sound of
music from her house, she said: 'Methinks that music
sounds much sweeter than by day.'

And now Portia and Nerissa entered the house, and
dressing themselves in their own apparel, they awaited the
arrival of their husbands, who soon followed them with
Antonio; and Bassanio presenting his dear friend to the

lady Portia, the congratulations and welcomings of that lady were hardly over, when they perceived Nerissa and her husband quarrelling in a corner of the room. 'A quarrel already?' said Portia. 'What is the matter?' Gratiano replied: 'Lady, it is about a paltry gilt ring that Nerissa gave me, with words upon it like the poetry on a cutler's knife; Love me, and leave me not.'

'What does the poetry or the value of the ring signify?' said Nerissa. 'You swore to me when I gave it to you, that you would keep it till the hour of death; and now you say you gave it to the lawyer's clerk. I know you gave it to a woman.' 'By this hand,' replied Gratiano, 'I gave it to a youth, a kind of boy, a little scrubbed boy, no higher than yourself; he was clerk to the young counsellor that by his wise pleading saved Antonio's life: this prating boy begged it for a fee, and I could not for my life deny him.' Portia said: 'You were to blame, Gratiano, to part with your wife's first gift. I gave my lord Bassanio a ring, and I am sure he would not part with it for all the world.' Gratiano, in excuse for his fault, now said: 'My lord Bassanio gave his ring away to the counsellor, and then the boy, his clerk, that took some pains in writing, he begged my ring.'

Portia, hearing this, seemed very angry, and reproached Bassanio for giving away her ring; and she said, Nerissa had taught her what to believe, and that she knew some woman

had the ring. Bassanio was very unhappy to have so offended his dear lady, and he said with great earnestness: 'No, by my honour, no woman had it, but a civil doctor, who refused three thousand ducats of me, and begged the ring, which when I denied him, he went displeased away. What could I do, sweet Portia? I was so beset with shame for my seeming ingratitude, that I was forced to send the ring after him. Pardon me, good lady; had you been there, I think you would have begged the ring of me to give the worthy doctor.'

'Ah!' said Antonio, 'I am the unhappy cause of these quarrels.'

Portia bid Antonio not to grieve at that, for that he was welcome notwithstanding; and then Antonio said: 'I once did lend my body for Bassanio's sake; and but for him to whom your husband gave the ring, I should have now been dead. I dare be bound again, my soul upon the forfeit, your lord will never more break his faith with you.'

'Then you shall be his surety,' said Portia; 'give him this ring, and bid him keep it better than the other.'

When Bassanio looked at this ring, he was strangely surprised to find it was the same he gave away; and then Portia told him how she was the young counsellor, and Nerissa was her clerk; and Bassanio found, to his unspeakable wonder and delight, that it was by the noble courage and wisdom of his wife that Antonio's life was saved.

And Portia again welcomed Antonio, and gave him letters which by some chance had fallen into her hands, which contained an account of Antonio's ships, that were supposed lost, being safely arrived in the harbour. So these tragical beginnings of this rich merchant's story were all forgotten in the unexpected good fortune which ensued; and there was leisure to laugh at the comical adventure of the rings, and the husbands that did not know their own wives Gratiano merrily swearing, in a sort of rhyming speech, that

... while he lived, he'd fear no other thing
So sore, as keeping safe Nerissa's ring.

Ⅲ.

A MIDSUMMER NIGHT'S DREAM

There was a law in the city of Athens which gave to its citizens the power of compelling their daughters to marry whomsoever they pleased; for upon a daughter's refusing to marry the man her father had chosen to be her husband, the father was empowered by this law to cause her to be put to death; but as fathers do not often desire the death of their own daughters, even though they do happen to prove a little refractory, this law was seldom or never put in execution, though perhaps the young ladies of that city were not unfrequently threatened by their parents with the terrors of it.

There was one instance, however, of an old man, whose name was Egeus, who actually did come before Theseus (at that time the reigning duke of Athens), to complain that his daughter Hermia, whom he had commanded to marry Demetrius, a young man of a noble Athenian family, refused to obey him, because she loved another young Athenian, named Lysander. Egeus demanded justice of Theseus, and desired that this cruel law might be put in force against his daughter.

Hermia pleaded in excuse for her disobedience, that Demetrius had formerly professed love for her dear friend Helena, and that Helena loved Demetrius to distraction; but this honourable reason, which Hermia gave for not obeying her father's command, moved not the stern Egeus.

Theseus, though a great and merciful prince, had no power to alter the laws of his country; therefore he could only give Hermia four days to consider of it: and at the end of that time, if she still refused to marry Demetrius, she was to be put to death.

When Hermia was dismissed from the presence of the duke, she went to her lover Lysander, and told him the peril she was in, and that she must either give him up and marry Demetrius, or lose her life in four days.

Lysander was in great affliction at hearing these evil tidings; but recollecting that he had an aunt who lived at some distance from Athens, and that at the place where she lived the cruel law could not be put in force against Hermia (this law not extending beyond the boundaries of the city), he proposed to Hermia that she should steal out of her father's house that night, and go with him to his aunt's house, where he would marry her. 'I will meet you,' said Lysander, 'in the wood a few miles without the city; in

that delightful wood where we have so often walked with Helena in the pleasant month of May.'

To this proposal Hermia joyfully agreed; and she told no one of her intended flight but her friend Helena. Helena (as maidens will do foolish things for love) very ungenerously resolved to go and tell this to Demetrius, though she could hope no benefit from betraying her friend's secret, but the poor pleasure of following her faithless lover to the wood; for she well knew that Demetrius would go thither in pursuit of Hermia.

The wood in which Lysander and Hermia proposed to meet was the favourite haunt of those little beings known by the name of Fairies.

Oberon the king, and Titania the queen of the fairies, with all their tiny train of followers, in this wood held their midnight revels.

Between this little king and queen of sprites there happened, at this time, a sad disagreement; they never met by moonlight in the shady walks of this pleasant wood, but they were quarrelling, till all their fairy elves would creep into acorn-cups and hide themselves for fear.

The cause of this unhappy disagreement was Titania's refusing to give Oberon a little changeling boy, whose mother had been Titania's friend; and upon her death the fairy queen stole the child from its nurse, and brought him up in the woods.

The night on which the lovers were to meet in this wood, as Titania was walking with some of her maids of honour, she met Oberon attended by his train of fairy courtiers.

'I' ll met by moonlight, proud Titania,' said the fairy king. The queen replied: 'What, jealous Oberon, is it you? Fairies, skip hence; I have foresworn his company.'

'Tarry, rash fairy,' said Oberon; 'am not I thy lord? Why does Titania cross her Oberon? Give me your little changeling boy to be my page.'

Set your heart at rest,' answered the queen; 'your whole fairy kingdom buys not the boy of me.' She then left her lord in great anger. 'Well, go your way,' said Oberon 'before the morning dawns I will torment you for this injury.'

Oberon then sent for Puck, his chief favourite and privy counsellor.

Puck (or as he was sometimes called, Robin Goodfellow) was a shrewd and knavish sprite, that used to play comical pranks in the neighbouring villages; sometimes getting into the dairies and skimming the milk, sometimes plunging his light and airy form into the butter-churn, and while he was dancing his fantastic shape in the churn, in vain the dairymaid would labour to change her cream into butter: nor had the village swains any better success; whenever Puck chose to play his freaks in the brewing

copper, the ale was sure to be spoiled. When a few good
neighbours were met to drink some comfortable ale
together, Puck would jump into the bowl of ale in the
likeness of a roasted crab, and when some old goody was
going to drink he would bob against her lips, and spill the
ale over her withered chin; and presently after, when the
same old dame was gravely seating herself to tell her
neighbours a sad and melancholy story, Puck would slip her
three-legged stool from under her, and
down toppled the poor old woman,
and then the old gossips would
hold their sides and laugh at

her, and swear they never wasted a merrier hour.

'Come hither, Puck,' said Oberon to this little merry wanderer of the night; 'fetch me the flower which maids call Lore in Idleness; the juice of that little purple flower laid on the eyelids of those who sleep, will make them, when they awake, dote on the first thing they see. Some of the juice of that flower I will drop on the eyelids of my Titania when she is asleep; and the first thing she looks upon when she opens her eyes she will fall in love with, even though it be a lion or a bear, a meddling monkey, or a busy ape; and before I will take this charm from off her sight, which I can do with another charm I know of, I will make her give me that boy to be my page.'

Puck, who loved mischief to his heart, was highly diverted with this intended frolic of his master, and ran to seek the flower; and while Oberon was waiting the return of Puck, he observed Demetrius and Helena enter the wood: he overheard Demetrius reproaching Helena for following him, and after many unkind words on his part, and gentle expostulations from Helena, reminding him of his former love and professions of true faith to her, he left her (as he said) to the mercy of the wild beasts, and she ran after him as swiftly as she could.

The fairy king, who was always friendly to true lovers, felt great compassion for Helena; and perhaps, as Lysander said they used to walk by moonlight in this pleasant wood,

Oberon might have seen Helena in those happy times when she was beloved by Demetrius. However that might be, when Puck returned with the little purple flower, Oberon said to his favourite: 'Take a part of this flower; there has been a sweet Athenian lady here, who is in love with a disdainful youth; if you find him sleeping, drop some of the love-juice in his eyes, but contrive to do it when she is near him, that the first thing he sees when he awakes may be this despised lady. You will know the man by the Athenian garments which he wears.' Puck promised to manage this matter very dexterously: and then Oberon went, unperceived by Titania, to her bower, where she was preparing to go to rest. Her fairy bower was a bank, where grew wild thyme, cowslips, and sweet violets, under a canopy of wood-bine, musk-roses, and eglantine. There Titania always slept some part of the night; her coverlet the enamelled skin of a snake, which, though a small mantle, was wide enough to wrap a fairy in.

He found Titania giving orders to her fairies, how they were to employ themselves while she slept. 'Some of you,' said her majesty, 'must kill cankers in the musk-rose buds, and some wage war with the bats for their leathern wings, to make my small elves coats; and some of you keep watch that the clamorous owl, that nightly hoots, come not near me: but first sing me to sleep.' Then they began to sing this song:

'You spotted snakes with double tongue,
Thorny hedgehogs, be not seen
Newts and blind-worms do no wrong
Come not near our Fairy Queen.
Philomel, with melody
Sing in our sweet lullaby
Lulla, lulla, lullaby; lulla, lulla, lullaby;
Never harm, nor spell, nor charm,
Come our lovely lady nigh;
So good night with lullaby.'

When the fairies had sung their queen asleep with this pretty lullaby, they left her to perform the important services she had enjoined them. Oberon then softly drew near his Titania, and dropped some of the love-juice on her eyelids, saying:

'What thou seest when thou wake
Do it for thy true-love take.'

But to return to Hermia, who made her escape out of her father's house that night, to avoid the death she was doomed to for refusing to marry Demetrius. When she

entered the wood, she found her dear Lysander waiting for her, to conduct her to his aunt's house; but before they had passed half through the wood, Hermia was so much fatigued, that Lysander, who was very careful of this dear lady, who had proved her affection for him even by hazarding her life for his sake, persuaded her to rest till morning on a bank of soft moss, and lying down himself on the ground at some little distance, they soon fell fast asleep. Here they were found by Puck, who, seeing a handsome young man asleep, and perceiving that his clothes were made in the Athenian fashion, and that a pretty lady was sleeping near him, concluded that this must be the Athenian maid and her disdainful lover whom Oberon had sent him to seek; and he naturally enough conjectured that, as they were alone together, she must be the first thing he would see when he awoke; so, without more ado, he proceeded to pour some of the juice of the little purple flower into his eyes. But it so fell out, that Helena came that way, and, instead of Hermia, was the first object Lysander beheld when he opened his eyes; and strange to relate, so powerful was the love-charm, all his love for Hermia vanished away, and Lysander fell in love with Helena.

Had he first seen Hermia when he awoke, the blunder Puck committed would have been of no consequence, for he could not love that faithful lady too well; but for poor

Lysander to be forced by a fairy love-charm to forget his own true Hermia, and to run after another lady, and leave Hermia asleep quite alone in a wood at midnight, was a sad chance indeed.

Thus this misfortune happened. Helena, as has been before related, endeavoured to keep pace with Demetrius when he ran away so rudely from her; but she could not continue this unequal race long, men being always better runners in a long race than ladies. Helena soon lost sight of Demetrius; and as she was wandering about, dejected and forlorn, she arrived at the place where Lysander was sleeping. 'Ah!' said she, 'this is Lysander lying on the ground: is he dead or asleep?' Then, gently touching him, she said: 'Good sir, if you are alive, awake.' Upon this Lysander opened his eyes, and (the love-charm beginning to work) immediately addressed her in terms of extravagant love and admiration; telling her she as much excelled Hermia in beauty as a dove does a raven, and that he would run through fire for her sweet sake; and many more such lover-like speeches. Helena, knowing Lysander was her friend Hermia's lover, and that he was solemnly engaged to marry her, was in the utmost rage when she heard herself addressed in this manner; for she thought (as well she might) that Lysander was making a jest of her. 'Oh!' said she, 'why was I born to be mocked and scorned by every one? Is it not enough, is it not enough, young man,

that I can never get a sweet look or a kind word from Demetrius; but you, sir, must pretend in this disdainful manner to court me? I thought, Lysander, you were a lord of more true gentleness.' Saying these words in great anger, she ran away; and Lysander followed her, quite forgetful of his own Hermia, who was still asleep.

When Hermia awoke, she was in a sad fright at finding herself alone. She wandered about the wood, not knowing what was become of Lysander, or which way to go to seek for him. In the meantime Demetrius, not being able to find Hermia and his rival Lysander, and fatigued with his fruitless search, was observed by Oberon fast asleep. Oberon had learnt by some questions he had asked of Puck, that he had applied the love-charm to the wrong person's eyes; and now having found the person first intended, he touched the eyelids of the sleeping Demetrius with the love-juice, and he instantly awoke; and the first thing he saw being Helena, he, as Lysander had done before, began to address love-speeches to her; and just at that moment Lysander, followed by Hermia (for through Puck's unlucky mistake it was now become Hermia's turn to run after her lover) made his appearance; and then Lysander and Demetrius, both speaking together, made love to Helena, they being each one under the influence of the same potent charm.

The astonished Helena thought that Demetrius,

Lysander, and her once dear friend Hermia, were all in a plot together to make a jest of her.

Hermia was as much surprised as Helena; she knew not why Lysander and Demetrius, who both before loved her, were now become the lovers of Helena; and to Hermia the matter seemed to be no jest.

The ladies, who before had always been the dearest of friends, now fell to high words together.

'Unkind Hermia,' said Helena, 'it is you have set Lysander on to vex me with mock praises; and your other lover Demetrius, who used almost to spurn me with his foot, have you not bid him call me Goddess, Nymph, rare, precious, and celestial? He would not speak thus to me, whom he hates, if you did not set him on to make a jest of me. Unkind Hermia, to join with men in scorning your poor friend. Have you forgot our school-day friendship? How often, Hermia, have we two, sitting on one cushion, both singing one song, with our needles working the same flower, both on the same sampler wrought; growing up together in fashion of a double cherry, scarcely seeming parted! Hermia, it is not friendly in you, it is not maidenly to join with men in scorning your poor friend.'

I am amazed at your passionate words,' said Hermia: I scorn you not; it seems you scorn me.' 'Ay, do,' returned Hermia, 'persevere, counterfeit serious looks, and make mouths at me when I turn my back; then wink at each other, and hold the sweet jest up. If you had any pity, grace, or manners, you would not use me thus.'

While Helena and Hermia were speaking these angry words to each other, Demetrius and Lysander left them, to fight together in the wood for the love of Helena.

When they found the gentlemen had left them, they departed, and once more wandered weary in the wood in search of their lovers.

As soon as they were gone, the fairy king, who with little Puck had been listening to their quarrels, said to him: 'This is your negligence, Puck; or did you do this wilfully?' 'Believe me, king of shadows,' answered Puck, 'it was a mistake; did not you tell me I should know the man by his Athenian garments? However, I am not sorry this has happened, for I think their jangling makes excellent sport.' 'You heard,' said Oberon, 'that Demetrius and Lysander are gone to seek a convenient place to fight in. I command you to overhang the night with a thick fog, and lead these quarrelsome lovers so astray in the dark, that they shall not be able to kind each other. Counterfeit each of their voices to the other, and with bitter taunts provoke them to follow you, while they think it is their rival's tongue they hear. See you do this, till they are so weary they can go no farther; and when you find they are asleep, drop the juice of this other flower into Lysander's eyes, and when he awakes he will forget his new

love for Helena, and return to his old passion for Hermia; and then the two fair ladies may each one be happy with the man she loves, and they will think all that has passed a vexatious dream. About this quickly, Puck, and I will go and see what sweet love my Titania has found.'

Titania was still sleeping, and Oberon seeing a clown near her, who had lost his way in the wood, and was likewise asleep: 'This fellow,' said he, 'shall be my Titania's true love'; and clapping an ass's head over the clown's, it seemed to fit him as well as if it had grown upon his own shoulders. Though Oberon fixed the ass's head on very gently, it awakened him, and rising up, unconscious of what Oberon had done to him, he went towards the bower where the fairy queen slept.

'Ah! what angel is that I see?' said Titania, opening her eyes, and the juice of the little purple flower beginning to take effect: 'are you as wise as you are beautiful?'

'Why, mistress,' said the foolish clown, 'if I have wit enough to find the way out of this wood, I have enough to serve my turn.'

'Out of the wood do not desire to go,' said the enamoured queen. 'I am a spirit of no common rate. I love you. Go with me, and I will give you fairies to attend upon you.'

She then called four of her fairies: their names were, Pease-blossom, Cobweb, Moth, and Mustard-seed.

'Attend,' said the queen, 'upon this sweet gentleman; hop in his walks, and gambol in his sight; feed him with grapes and apricots, and steal for him the honey-bags from the bees. Come, sit with me,' said she to the clown, 'and let me play with your amiable hairy cheeks, my beautiful ass! and kiss your fair large ears, my gentle joy!'

'Where is Pease-blossom?' said the ass-headed clown, not much regarding the fairy queen's courtship, but very proud of his new attendants.

'Here, sir,' said little Pease-blossom.

'Scratch my head,' said the clown. 'Where is Cobweb?'

'Here, sir,' said Cobweb.

'Good Mr. Cobweb,' said the foolish clown, 'kill me the red humble bee on the top of that thistle yonder; and, good Mr. Cobweb, bring me the honey-bag. Do not fret yourself too much in the action, Mr. Cobweb, and take care the honey-bag break not; I should be sorry to have you overflown with a honey-bag. Where is Mustard-seed?'

'Here, sir,' said Mustard-seed: 'what is your will?'

'Nothing,' said the clown, 'good Mr. Mustard-seed, but to help Mr. Pease-blossom to scratch; I must go to a barber's, Mr. Mustard-seed, for methinks I am marvellous hairy about the face.'

'My sweet love,' said the queen, 'what will you have to eat? I have a venturous fairy shall seek the squirrel's hoard, and fetch you some new nuts.'

'I had rather have a handful of dried pease,' said the clown, who with his ass's head had got an ass's appetite. 'But, I pray, let none of your people disturb me, for I have a mind to sleep.'

'Sleep, then,' said the queen, 'and I will wind you in my arms. O how I love you! how I dote upon you!'

When the fairy king saw the clown sleeping in the arms of his queen, he advanced within her sight, and reproached her with having lavished her favours upon an ass.

This she could not deny, as the clown was then sleeping within her arms, with his ass's head crowned by her with flowers.

When Oberon had teased her for some time, he again demanded the changeling boy; which she, ashamed of being discovered by her lord with her new favourite, did not dare to refuse him.

Oberon, having thus obtained the little boy he had so long wished for to be his page, took pity on the disgraceful situation into which, by his merry contrivance, he had brought his Titania and threw some of the juice of the other flower into her eyes; and the fairy queen immediately recovered her senses, and wondered at her late dotage, saying how she now loathed the sight of the strange monster.

Oberon likewise took the ass's head from off the clown, and left him to finish his nap with his own fool's head upon his shoulders.

Oberon and his Titania being now perfectly reconciled, he related to her the history of the lovers, and their midnight quarrels; and she agreed to go with him and see the end of their adventures.

The fairy king and queen found the lovers and their fair ladies, at no great distance from each other, sleeping on a grass-plot; for Puck, to make amends for his former mistake, had contrived with the utmost diligence to bring them all to the same spot, unknown to each other: and he had carefully removed the charm from off the eyes of Lysander with the antidote the fairy king gave to him.

Hermia first awoke, and finding her lost Lysander asleep so near her, was looking at him and wondering at his strange inconstancy. Lysander presently opening his eyes, and seeing his dear Hermia, recovered his reason which the fairy charm had before clouded, and with his reason, his love for Hermia; and they began to talk over the adventures of the night, doubting if these things had really happened, or if they had both been dreaming the same bewildering dream.

Helena and Demetrius were by this time awake; and a

sweet sleep having quieted Helena's disturbed and angry spirits, she listened with delight to the professions of love which Demetrius still made to her, and which, to her surprise as well as pleasure, she began to perceive were sincere.

These fair night-wandering ladies, now no longer rivals, became once more true friends; all the unkind words which had passed were forgiven, and they calmly consulted together what was best to be done in their present situation. It was soon agreed that, as Demetrius had given up his pretensions to Hermia, he should endeavour to prevail upon her father to revoke the cruel sentence of death which had been passed against her. Demetrius was preparing to return to Athens for this friendly purpose, when they were surprised with the sight of Egeus, Hermia's father, who came to the wood in pursuit of his runaway daughter.

When Egeus understood that Demetrius would not now marry his daughter, he no longer opposed her marriage with Lysander, but gave his consent that they should be wedded on the fourth day from that time, being the same day on which Hermia had been condemned to lose her life; and on that same day Helena joyfully agreed to marry her beloved and now faithful Demetrius.

The fairy king and queen, who were invisible spectators of this reconciliation, and now saw the happy ending of the lovers' history, brought about through the good offices of Oberon, received so much pleasure, that these kind spirits resolved to celebrate the approaching nuptials with sports and revels throughout their fairy kingdom.

And now, if any are offended with this story of fairies and their pranks, as judging it incredible and strange, they have only to think that they have been asleep and dreaming, and that all these adventures were visions which they saw in their sleep: and I hope none of my readers will be so unreasonable as to be offended with a pretty harmless Midsummer Night's Dream.

IV.

KING LEAR

Lear, king of Britain, had three daughters; Goneril, wife to the duke of Albany; Regan, wife to the duke of Cornwall; and Cordelia, a young maid, for whose love the king of France and duke of Burgundy were joint suitors, and were at this time making stay for that purpose in the court of Lear.

The old king, worn out with age and the fatigues of government, he being more than fourscore years old, determined to take no further part in state affairs, but to leave the management to younger strengths, that he might have time to prepare for death, which must at no long period ensue. With this intent he called his three daughters to him, to know from their own lips which of them loved him best, that he might part his kingdom among them in such proportions as their affection for him should seem to deserve.

Goneril, the eldest, declared that she loved her father more than words could give out, that he was dearer to her than the light of her own eyes, dearer than life and liberty, with a deal of such professing stuff, which is easy to counterfeit where there is no real love, only a few fine words delivered with confidence being wanted in that case. The king, delighted to hear from her own mouth this assurance of her love, and thinking truly that her heart went with it, in a fit of fatherly fondness bestowed upon her and her husband one-third of his ample kingdom.

Then calling to him his second daughter, he demanded what she had to say. Regan, who was made of the same hollow metal as her sister, was not a whit behind in her profession, but rather declared that what her sister had spoken came short of the love which she professed to bear for his highness; insomuch that she found all other joys dead, in comparison with the pleasure which she took in the love of her dear king and father.

Lear blessed himself in having such loving children, as he thought; and could do no less, after the handsome assurances which Regan had made, than bestow a third of his kingdom upon her and her husband, equal in size to that which he had already given away to Goneril.

Then turning to his youngest daughter Cordelia, whom he called his joy, he asked what she had to say, thinking no doubt that she would glad his ears with the same loving speeches which her sisters had uttered, or rather that her expressions would be so much stronger than theirs, as she had always been his darling, and favoured by him above

either of them. But Cordelia, disgusted with the flattery of her sisters, whose hearts she knew were far from their lips, and seeing that all their coaxing speeches were only intended to wheedle the old king out of his dominions, that they and their husbands might reign in his lifetime, made no other reply but this, that she loved his majesty according to her duty, neither more nor less.

The king, shocked with this appearance of ingratitude in his favourite child, desired her to consider her words, and to mend her speech, lest it should mar her fortunes.

Cordelia then told her father, that he was her father, that he had given her breeding, and loved her; that she returned those duties back as was most fit, and did obey him, love him, and most honour him. But that she could not frame her mouth to such large speeches as her sisters had done, or promise to love nothing else in the world. Why had her sisters husbands, if (as they said) they had no love for anything but their father? If she should ever wed, she was sure the lord to whom she gave her hand would want half her love, half of her care and duty; she should never marry like her sisters, to love her father all.

Cordelia, who in earnest loved her old father even almost as extravagantly as her sisters pretended to do, would have plainly told him so at any other time, in more daughter-like and loving terms, and without these qualifications, which did indeed sound a little ungracious;

but after the crafty flattering speeches of her sisters, which she had seen drawn such extravagant rewards, she thought the handsomest thing she could do was to love and be silent. This put her affection out of suspicion of mercenary ends, and showed that she loved, but not for gain; and that her professions, the less ostentatious they were, had so much the more of truth and sincerity than her sisters' .

This plainness of speech, which Lear called pride, so enraged the old monarch who in his best of times always showed much of spleen and rashness, and in whom the dotage incident to old age had so clouded over his reason, that he could not discern truth from flattery, nor a gay painted speech from words that came from the heart--that in a fury of resentment he retracted the third part of his kingdom, which yet remained, and which he had reserved for Cordelia, and gave it away from her, sharing it equally between her two sisters and their husbands, the dukes of Albany and Cornwall; whom he now called to him, and in presence of all his courtiers bestowing a coronet between them, invested them jointly with all the power, revenue, and execution of government, only retaining to himself the name of king; all the rest of royalty he resigned; with this reservation, that himself, with a hundred knights for his attendants, was to be maintained by monthly course in each of his daughters' palaces in turn.

So preposterous a disposal of his kingdom, so little

guided by reason, and so much by passion, filled all his courtiers with astonishment and sorrow; but none of them had the courage to interpose between this incensed king and his wrath, except the earl of Kent, who was beginning to speak a good word for Cordelia, when the passionate Lear on pain of death commanded him to desist; but the good Kent was not so to be repelled. He had been ever loyal to Lear, whom he had honoured as a king, loved as a father, followed as a master; and he had never esteemed his life further than as a pawn to wage against his royal master's enemies, nor feared to lose it when Lear's safety was the motive; nor now that Lear was most his own enemy, did this faithful servant of the king forget his old principles, but manfully opposed Lear, to do Lear good; and was unmannerly only because Lear was mad. He had been a most faithful counsellor in times past to the king, and he besought him now, that he would see with his eyes (as he had done in many weighty matters), and go by his advice still; and in his best consideration recall this hideous rashness: for he would answer with his life, his judgment that Lear's youngest daughter did not love him least, nor were those empty-hearted whose low sound gave no token of hollowness. When power bowed to flattery, honour was bound to plainness. For Lear's threats, what could he do to him, whose life was already at his service? That should not hinder duty from speaking.

The honest freedom of this good earl of Kent only
stirred up the king's wrath the more, and like a frantic
patient who kills his physician, and loves his mortal disease,
he banished this true servant, and allotted him but five days
to make his preparations for departure; but if on the sixth
his hated person was found within the realm of Britain,
that moment was to be his death. And Kent bade farewell
to the king, and said, that since he chose to show himself
in such fashion, it was but banishment to stay there; and
before he went, he recommended Cordelia to the
protection of the gods, the maid who had so rightly
thought, and so discreetly spoken; and only wished that her
sisters' large speeches might be answered with deeds of
love; and then he went, as he said, to shape his old course
to a new country.

The king of France and duke of Burgundy were now
called in to hear the determination of Lear about his
youngest daughter, and to know whether they would persist
in their courtship to Cordelia, now that she was under her
father's displeasure, and had no fortune but her own
person to recommend her: and the duke of Burgundy
declined the match, and would not take her to wife upon
such conditions; but the king of France, understanding
what the nature of the fault had been which had lost her
the love of her father, that it was only a tardiness of
speech, and the not being able to frame her tongue to

flattery like her sisters, took this young maid by the hand, and saying that her virtues were a dowry above a kingdom, bade Cordelia to take farewell of her sisters and of her father, though he had been unkind, and she should go with him, and be queen of him and of fair France, and reign over fairer possessions than her sisters: and he called the duke of Burgundy in contempt a waterish duke, because his love for this young maid had in a moment run all away like water.

Then Cordelia with weeping eyes took leave of her sisters, and besought them to love their father well, and make good their professions: and they sullenly told her not to prescribe to them, for they knew their duty; but to strive to content her husband, who had taken her (as they tauntingly expressed it) as Fortune's alms. And Cordelia with a heavy heart departed, for she knew the cunning of her sisters, and she wished her father in better hands than she was about to leave him in.

Cordelia was no sooner gone, than the devilish dispositions of her sisters began to show themselves in their true colours. Even before the expiration of the first month, which Lear was to spend by agreement with his eldest daughter Goneril, the old king began to find out the difference between promises and performances. This wretch having got from her father all that he had to bestow, even to the giving away of the crown from off his head,

began to grudge even those small remnants of royalty
which the old man had reserved to himself, to please his
fancy with the idea of being still a king. She could not bear
to see him and his hundred knights. Every time she met
her father, she put on a frowning countenance; and when
the old man wanted to speak with her, she
would feign sickness, or anything to get
rid of the sight of him; for it was
plain that she esteemed his
old age a useless burden,

and his attendants an unnecessary expense: not only she herself slackened in her expressions of duty to the king, but by her example, and (it is to be feared) not without her private instructions, her very servants affected to treat him with neglect, and would either refuse to obey his orders, or still more contemptuously pretend not to hear them. Lear could not but perceive this alteration in the behaviour of his daughter, but he shut his eyes against it as long as he could, as people commonly are unwilling to believe the unpleasant consequences which their own mistakes and obstinacy have brought upon them.

True love and fidelity are no more to be estranged by ill, than falsehood and hollow-heartedness can be conciliated by good, usage. This eminently appears in the instance of the good earl of Kent, who, though banished by Lear, and his life made forfeit if he were found in Britain, chose to stay and abide all consequences, as long as there was a chance of his being useful to the king his master. See to what mean shifts and disguises poor loyalty is forced to submit sometimes; yet it counts nothing base or unworthy, so as it can but do service where it owes an obligation! In the disguise of a serving man, all his greatness and pomp laid aside, this good earl proffered his services to the king, who, not knowing him to be Kent in that disguise, but pleased with a certain plainness, or rather bluntness in his answers, which the earl put on (so different from that smooth oily flattery which he had so much reason to be sick of, having found the effects not answerable in his daughter), a bargain was quickly struck, and Lear took Kent into his service by the name of Caius, as he called himself, never suspecting him to be his once great favourite, the high and mighty earl of Kent.

This Caius quickly found means to show his fidelity and love to his royal master: for Goneril's steward that same day behaving in a disrespectful manner to Lear, and giving him saucy looks and language, as no doubt he was secretly encouraged to do by his mistress, Caius, not enduring to hear so open an affront put upon his majesty, made no more ado but presently tripped up his heels, and laid the unmannerly slave in the kennel; for which friendly service Lear became more and more attached to him.

Nor was Kent the only friend Lear had. In his degree, and as far as so insignificant a personage could show his love, the poor fool, or jester, that had been of his palace while Lear had a palace, as it was the custom of kings and great personages at that time to keep a fool (as he was called) to make them sport after serious business: this poor fool clung to Lear after he had given away his crown, and by his witty sayings would keep up his good humour, though he could not refrain sometimes from jeering at his master for his imprudence in uncrowning himself, and giving all away to his daughters; at which time, as he

rhymingly expressed it, these daughters

For sudden joy did weep
And he for sorrow sung,
That such a king should play bo-peep
And go the fools among.

And in such wild sayings, and scraps of songs, of which he had plenty, this pleasant honest fool poured out his heart even in the presence of Goneril herself, in many a bitter taunt and jest which cut to the quick: such as comparing the king to the hedge-sparrow, who feeds the young of the cuckoo till they grow old enough, and then has its head bit off for its pains; and saying, that an ass may know when the cart draws the horse (meaning that Lear's daughters, that ought to go behind, now ranked before their father); and that Lear was no longer Lear, but the shadow of Lear: for which free speeches he was once or twice threatened to be whipped.

The coolness and falling off of respect which Lear had begun to perceive, were not all which this foolish fond father was to suffer from his unworthy daughter: she now plainly told him that his staying in her palace was inconvenient so long as he insisted upon keeping up an establishment of a hundred knights; that this establishment

was useless and expensive, and only served to kill her court
with riot and feasting; and she prayed him that he would
lessen their number, and keep none but old men about him,
such as himself, and fitting his age.

Lear at first could not believe his eyes or ears, nor that
it was his daughter who spoke so unkindly. He could not
believe that she who had received a crown from him could
seek to cut off his train, and grudge him the respect due to
his old age. But she persisting in her undutiful demand, the
old man's rage was so excited, that he called her a detested
kite, and said that she spoke an untruth; and so indeed she
did, for the hundred knights were all men of choice
behaviour and sobriety of manners, skilled in all particulars
of duty, and not given to rioting or feasting, as she said.
And he bid his horses to be prepared, for he would go to
his other daughter, Regan, he and his hundred knights; and
he spoke of ingratitude, and said it was a marble-hearted
devil, and showed more hideous in a child than the sea-
monster. And he cursed his eldest daughter Goneril so as
was terrible to hear; praying that she might never have a
child, or if she had, that it might live to return that scorn
and contempt upon her which she had shown to him that
she might feel how sharper than a serpent's tooth it was to
have a thankless child. And Goneril's husband, the duke of
Albany, beginning to excuse himself for any share which
Lear might suppose he had in the unkindness, Lear would

not hear him out, but in a rage ordered his horses to be saddled, and set out with his followers for the abode of Regan, his other daughter. And Lear thought to himself how small the fault of Cordelia (if it was a fault) now appeared, in comparison with her sister's, and he wept; and then he was ashamed that such a creature as Goneril should have so much power over his manhood as to make him weep.

Regan and her husband were keeping their court in great pomp and state at their palace; and Lear despatched his servant Caius with letters to his daughter, that she might be prepared for his reception, while he and his train followed after. But it seems that Goneril had been beforehand with him, sending letters also to Regan, accusing her father of waywardness and ill humours, and advising her not to receive so great a train as he was bringing with him. This messenger arrived at the same time with Caius, and Caius and he met: and who should it be but Caius's old enemy the steward, whom he had formerly tripped up by the heels for his saucy behaviour to Lear. Caius not liking the fellow's look, and suspecting what he came for, began to revile him, and challenged him to fight, which the fellow refusing, Caius, in a fit of honest passion, beat him soundly, as such a mischief-maker and carrier of wicked messages deserved; which coming to the ears of Regan and her husband, they ordered Caius to be put in the stocks, though he was a messenger from the king her father, and in that character demanded the highest respect: so that the first thing the king saw when he entered the castle, was his faithful servant Caius sitting in that disgraceful situation.

This was but a bad omen of the reception which he was to expect; but a worse followed, when, upon inquiry for his daughter and her husband, he was told they were weary with travelling all night, and could not see him; and when lastly, upon his insisting in a positive and angry manner to see them, they came to greet him, whom should he see in their company but the hated Goneril, who had come to tell her own story, and set her sister against the king her father!

This sight much moved the old man, and still more to see Regan take her by the hand; and he asked Goneril if she was not ashamed to look upon his old white beard. And Regan advised him to go home again with Goneril, and live with her peaceably, dismissing half of his attendants, and to ask her forgiveness; for he was old and wanted discretion, and must be ruled and led by persons that had more discretion than himself. And Lear showed how preposterous that would sound, if he were to go down on his knees, and beg of his own daughter for food and raiment, and he argued against such an unnatural dependence, declaring his resolution never to return with

her, but to stay where he was with Regan, he and his hundred knights; for he said that she had not forgot the half of the kingdom which he had endowed her with, and that her eyes were not fierce like Goneril's, but mild and kind. And he said that rather than return to Goneril, with half his train cut off, he would go over to France, and beg a wretched pension of the king there, who had married his youngest daughter without a portion.

But he was mistaken in expecting kinder treatment of Regan than he had experienced from her sister Goneril. As if willing to outdo her sister in unequal behaviour, she declared that she thought fifty knights too many to wait upon him: that five-and-twenty were enough. Then Lear, nigh heart-broken, turned to Goneril and said that he would go back with her, for her fifty doubled five-and-twenty, and so her love was twice as much as Regan's. But Goneril excused herself, and said, what need of so many as five-and-twenty? or even ten? or five? when he might be waited upon by her servants, or her sister's servants? So these two wicked daughters, as if they strove to exceed each other in cruelty to their old father, who had been so good to them, by little and little would have abated him of all his train, all respect (little enough for him that once commanded a kingdom), which was left him to show that he had once been a king! Not that a splendid train is essential to happiness, but from a king to a beggar is a hard

change, from commanding millions to be without one
attendant; and it was the ingratitude in his daughters'
denying it, more than what he would suffer by the want of
it, which pierced this poor king to the heart; insomuch, that
with this double ill-usage, a vexation for having so foolishly
given away a kingdom, his wits began to be unsettled, and
while he said e knew not what, he vowed revenge against
those unnatural hags, and to make examples of them that
should be a terror to the earth!

While he was thus idly threatening what his weak arm
could never execute, night came on, and a loud storm of
thunder and lightning with rain; and his daughters still
persisting in their resolution not to admit his followers, he
called for his horses, and chose rather to encounter the
utmost fury of the storm abroad, than stay under the same
roof with these ungrateful daughters: and they, saying that
the injuries which wilful men procure to themselves are
their just punishment, suffered him to go in that condition
and shut their doors upon him.

The wind were high, and the rain and storm increased,
when the old man sallied forth to combat with the
elements, less sharp than his daughters' unkindness. For
many miles about there was scarce a bush; and there upon
a heath, exposed to the fury of the storm in a dark night,
did king Lear wander out, and defy the winds and the
thunder; and he bid the winds to blow the earth into the

sea, or swell the waves of the sea till they drowned the earth, that no token might remain of any such ungrateful animal as man. The old king was now left with no other companion than the poor fool, who still abided with him, with his merry conceits striving to outjest misfortune, saying it was but a naughty night to swim in, and truly the king had better go in and ask his daughter's blessing:

But he that has a little tiny wit
With heigh ho, the wind and the rain!
Must make content with his fortunes fit
Though the rain it raineth every day:

And swearing it was a brave night to cool a lady's pride.

Thus poorly accompanied, this once great monarch was found by his ever-faithful servant the good earl of Kent, now transformed to Caius, who ever followed close at his side, though the king did not know him to be the earl; and he said: 'Alas! sir, are you here? creatures that love night, love not such nights as these. This dreadful storm has driven the beasts to their hiding places. Man's nature cannot endure the affliction or the fear.' And Lear rebuked him and said, these lesser evils were not felt, where a greater malady was taxed. When the mind is at ease, the body has leisure to be delicate, but the temper in his mind did take all feeling else from his senses, but of that which beat at his heart. And he spoke of filial ingratitude, and said it was all one as if the mouth should tear the hand for lifting food to it; for parents were hands and food and everything to children.

But the good Caius still persisting in his entreaties that the king would not stay out in the open air, at last persuaded him to enter a little wretched hovel which stood upon the heath, where the fool first entering, suddenly ran back terrified, saying that he had seen a spirit. But upon examination this spirit proved to be nothing more than a poor Bedlam beggar, who had crept into this deserted hovel for shelter, and with his talk about devils frighted the fool, one of those poor lunatics who are either mad, or feign to be so, the better to extort charity from the compassionate country people, who go about the country, calling themselves poor Tom and poor Turlygood, saying: 'Who gives anything to poor Tom?' sticking pins and nails and sprigs of rosemary into their arms to make them bleed; and with such horrible actions, partly by prayers, and partly with lunatic curses, they move or terrify the ignorant countryfolks into giving them alms. This poor fellow was such a one; and the king seeing him in so wretched a plight, with nothing but a blanket about his loins to cover his nakedness, could not be persuaded but that the fellow was

some father who had given all away to his daughters, and brought himself to that pass: for nothing he thought could bring a man to such wretchedness but the having unkind daughters.

And from this and many such wild speeches which he uttered, the good Caius plainly perceived that he was not in his perfect mind, but that his daughters' ill usage had really made him go mad. And now the loyalty of this worthy earl of Kent showed itself in more essential services than he had hitherto found opportunity to perform. For with the assistance of some of the king's attendants who remained loyal, he had the person of his royal master removed at daybreak to the castle of Dover, where his own friends and influence, as earl of Kent, chiefly lay; and himself embarking for France, hastened to the court of Cordelia, and did there in such moving terms represent the pitiful condition of her royal father, and set out in such lively colours the inhumanity of her sisters, that this good and loving child with many tears besought the king her husband that he would give her leave to embark for England, with a sufficient power to subdue these cruel daughters and their husbands, and restore the old king her father to his throne; which being granted, she set forth, and with a royal army landed at Dover.

Lear having by some chance escaped from the guardians which the good earl of Kent had put over him to ' take care of him in his lunacy, was found by some of Cordelia's train, wandering about the fields near Dover, in a pitiable condition, stark mad, and singing aloud to himself with a crown upon his head which he had made of straw, and nettles, and other wild weeds that he had picked up in the corn-fields. By the advice of the physicians, Cordelia, though earnestly desirous of seeing her father, was prevailed upon to put off the meeting, till by sleep and the operation of herbs which they gave him, he should be restored to greater composure. By the aid of these skilful physicians, to whom Cordelia promised all her gold and jewels for the recovery of the old king, Lear was soon in a condition to see his daughter.

A tender sight it was to see the meeting between this father and daughter; to see the struggles between the joy of this poor old king at beholding again his once darling child, and the shame at receiving such filial kindness from her whom he had cast off for so small a fault in his displeasure; both these passions struggling with the remains of his malady, which in his half-crazed brain sometimes made him that he scarce remembered where he was, or who it was that so kindly kissed him and spoke to him; and then he would beg the standers-by not to laugh at him, if he were mistaken in thinking this lady to be his daughter Cordelia! And then to see him fall on his knees to beg pardon of his child; and she, good lady, kneeling all the while to ask a

blessing of him, and telling him that it did not become him
to kneel, but it was her duty, for she was his child, his true
and very child Cordial! And she kissed him (as she said) to
kiss away all her sisters' unkindness, and said that they
might be ashamed of
themselves, to turn their
old kind father with
his white beard out
into the cold air,

when her enemy's dog, though it had bit her (as she prettily expressed it), should have stayed by her fire such a night as that, and warmed himself. And she told her father how she had come from France with purpose to bring him assistance; and he said that she must forget and forgive, for he was old and foolish, and did not know what he did, but that to be sure she had great cause not to love him, but her sisters had none. And Cordelia said that she had no cause, no more than they had.

So we will leave this old king in the protection of his dutiful and loving child, where, by the help of sleep and medicine, she and her physicians at length succeeded in winding up the untuned and jarring senses which the cruelty of his other daughters had so violently shaken. Let us return to say a word or two about those cruel daughters.

These monsters of ingratitude, who had been so false to their old father, could not be expected to prove more faithful to their own husbands. They soon grew tired of paying even the appearance of duty and affection, and in an open way showed they had fixed their loves upon another. It happened that the object of their guilty loves was the same. It was Edmund, a natural son of the late earl of Gloucester, who by his treacheries had succeeded in disinheriting his brother Edgar, the lawful heir, from his earldom, and by his wicked practices was now earl himself; a wicked man, and a fit object for the love of such wicked

creatures as Goneril and Regan. It falling out about this time that the duke of Cornwall, Regan's husband, died, Regan immediately declared her intention of wedding this earl of Gloucester, which rousing the jealousy of her sister, to whom as well as to Regan this wicked earl had at sundry times professed love, Goneril found means to make away with her sister by poison; but being detected in her practices, and imprisoned by her husband, the duke of Albany, for this deed, and for her guilty passion for the earl which had come to his ears, she, in a fit of disappointed love and rage, shortly put an end to her own life. Thus' the justice of Heaven at last overtook these wicked daughters.

While the eyes of all men were upon this event, admiring the justice displayed in their deserved deaths, the same eyes were suddenly taken off from this sight to admire at the mysterious ways of the same power in the melancholy fate of the young and virtuous daughter, the lady Cordelia, whose good deeds did seem to deserve a more fortunate conclusion: but it is an awful truth, that innocence and piety are not always successful in this world. The forces which Goneril and Regan had sent out under the command of the bad earl of Gloucester were victorious, and Cordelia, by the practices of this wicked earl, who did not like that any should stand between him and the throne, ended her life in prison. Thus, Heaven took this innocent lady to itself in her young years, after showing her to the world an illustrious example of filial duty. Lear did not long survive this kind child.

Before he died, the good earl of Kent, who had still attended his old master's steps from the first of his daughters' ill usage to this sad period of his decay, tried to make him understand that it was he who had followed him under the name of Caius; but Lear's care-crazed brain at that time could not comprehend how that could be, or how Kent and Caius could be the same person: so Kent thought it needless to trouble him with explanations at such a time; and Lear soon after expiring, this faithful servant to the king, between age and grief for his old master's vexations, soon followed him to the grave.

How the judgment of Heaven overtook the bad earl of Gloucester, whose treasons were discovered, and himself slain in single combat with his brother, the lawful earl; and how Goneril's husband, the duke of Albany, who was innocent of the death of Cordelia, and had never encouraged his lady in her wicked proceedings against her father, ascended the throne of Britain after the death of Lear, is needless here to narrate; Lear and his Three Daughters being dead, whose adventures alone concern our story.

V.

MUCH ADO ABOUT
NOTHING

There lived in the palace at Messina two ladies, whose names were Hero and Beatrice. Hero was the daughter, and Beatrice the niece, of Leonato, the governor of Messina.

Beatrice was of a lively temper, and loved to divert her cousin Hero, who was of a more serious disposition, with her sprightly sallies. Whatever was going forward was sure to make matter of mirth for the light-hearted Beatrice.

At the time the history of these ladies commences some young men of high rank in the army, as they were passing through Messina on their return from a war that was just ended, in which they had distinguished themselves by their great bravery, came to visit Leonato. Among these were Don Pedro, the prince of Arragon; and his friend Claudio, who was a lord of Florence; and with them came the wild and witty Benedick, and he was a lord of Padua.

These strangers had been at Messina before, and the hospitable governor introduced them to his daughter and

his niece as their old friends and acquaintance.

Benedick, the moment he entered the room, began a lively conversation with Leonato and the prince. Beatrice, who liked not to be left out of any discourse, interrupted Benedick with saying: 'I wonder that you will still be talking, signior Benedick: nobody marks you.' Benedick was just such another rattle-brain as Beatrice, yet he was not pleased at this free salutation; he thought it did not become a well-bred lady to be so flippant with her tongue; and he remembered, when he was last at Messina, that Beatrice used to select him to make her merry jests upon. And as there is no one who so little likes to be made a jest of as those who are apt to take the same liberty themselves, so it was with Benedick and Beatrice; these two sharp wits never met in former times but a perfect war of raillery was kept up between them, and they always parted mutually displeased with each other. Therefore when Beatrice stopped him in the middle of his discourse with telling him nobody marked what he was saying, Benedick, affecting not to have observed before that she was present, said: 'What, my dear lady Disdain, are you yet living?' And now war broke out afresh between them, and a long jangling argument ensued, during which Beatrice, although she knew he had so well approved his valour in the late war, said that she would eat all he had killed there: and observing the prince take delight in Benedick's conversation, she called trim 'the prince's jester.' This sarcasm sunk deeper into the mind of Benedick than all Beatrice had said before. The hint she gave him that he was a coward, by saying she would eat all he had killed, he did not regard, knowing himself to be a brave man; but there is nothing that great wits so much dread as the imputation of buffoonery, because the charge comes sometimes a little too near the truth: therefore Benedick perfectly hated Beatrice when she called him 'the prince's jester.'

The modest lady Hero was silent before the noble guests; and while Claudio was attentively observing the improvement which time had made in her beauty, and was contemplating the exquisite graces of her fine figure (for she was an admirable young lady), the prince was highly amused with listening to the humorous dialogue between Benedick and Beatrice; and he said in a whisper to Leonato: 'This is a pleasant-spirited young lady. She were an excellent wife for Benedick.' Leonato replied to this suggestion: 'O, my lord, my lord, if they were but a week married, they would talk themselves mad.' But though Leonato thought they would make a discordant pair, the prince did not give up the idea of matching these two keen wits together.

When the prince returned with Claudio from the palace, he found that the marriage he had devised between Benedick and Beatrice was not the only one projected in

that good company, for Claudio spoke in such terms of Hero, as made the prince guess at what was passing in his heart; and he liked it well, and he said to Claudio: 'Do you affect Hero?' To this question Claudio replied: 'O my lord, when I was last at Messina, I looked upon her with a soldier's eye, that liked, but had no leisure for loving; but now, in this happy time of peace, thoughts of war have left their places vacant in my mind, and in their room come thronging soft and delicate thoughts, all prompting me how fair young Hero is, reminding me that I liked her before I went to the wars.' Claudio's confession of his love for Hero so wrought upon the prince, that he lost no time in soliciting the consent of Leonato to accept of Claudio for a son-in-law. Leonato agreed to this proposal, and the prince found no great difficulty in persuading the gentle Hero herself to listen to the suit of the noble Claudio, who was a lord of rare endowments, and highly accomplished, and Claudio, assisted by his kind prince, soon prevailed upon Leonato to fix an early day for the celebration of his marriage with Hero.

Claudio was to wait but a few days before he was to be married to his fair lady; yet he complained of the interval being tedious, as indeed most young men are impatient when they are waiting for the accomplishment of any event they have set their hearts upon: the prince, therefore, to make the time seem short to him, proposed as a kind of merry pastime that they should invent some artful scheme to make Benedick and Beatrice fall in love with each other. Claudio entered with great satisfaction into this whim of the prince, and Leonato promised them his assistance, and even Hero said she would do any modest office to help her cousin to a good husband.

The device the prince invented was, that the gentlemen should make Benedick believe that Beatrice was in love with him, and that Hero should make Beatrice believe that Benedick was in love with her.

The prince, Leonato, and Claudio began their operations first: and watching upon an opportunity when Benedick was quietly seated reading in an arbour, the prince and his assistants took their station among the trees behind the arbour, so near that Benedick could not choose but hear all they said; and after some careless talk the prince said: 'Come hither, Leonato. What was it you told me the other day that your niece Beatrice was in love with signior Benedick? I did never think that lady would have loved any man.' 'No, nor I neither, my lord.' Answered Leonato.

'It is most wonderful that she should so dote on Benedick, whom she in all outward behaviour seemed ever to dislike.' Claudio confirmed all this with saying that Hero had told him Beatrice was so in love with Benedick, that she would certainly die of grief, if he could not be brought to love her; which Leonato and Claudio seemed to

agree was impossible, he having always been such a railer against all fair ladies, and in particular against Beatrice.

The prince affected to hearken to all this with great compassion for Beatrice, and he said: 'It were good that Benedick were told of this.' 'To what end?' said Claudio; 'he would but make sport of it, and torment the poor lady worse.' 'And if he should,' said the prince, 'it were a good deed to hang him; for Beatrice is an excellent sweet lady, and exceeding wise in everything but in loving Benedick.' Then the prince motioned to his companions that they should walk on, and leave Benedick to meditate upon what he had overheard.

Benedick had been listening with great eagerness to this conversation; and he said to himself when he heard Beatrice loved him: 'Is it possible? Sits the wind in that corner?' And when they were gone, he began to reason in this manner with himself: 'This can be no trick! they were very serious, and they have the truth from Hero, and seem to pity the lady. Love me! Why it must be requited! I did never think to marry. But when I said I should die a bachelor, I did not think I should live to be married. They say the lady is virtuous and fair. She is so. And wise in everything but loving me. Why, that is no great argument of her folly. But here comes Beatrice. By this day, she is a fair lady. I do spy some marks of love in her.' Beatrice now approached him, and said with her usual tartness:

'Against my will I am sent to bid you come in to dinner.' Benedick, who never felt himself disposed to speak so politely to her before, replied: 'Fair Beatrice, I thank you for your pains' : and when Beatrice, after two or three more rude speeches, left him, Benedick thought he observed a concealed meaning of kindness under the uncivil words she uttered, and he said aloud: 'If I do not take pity on her, I am a villain. If I do not love her, I am a Jew. I will go get her picture.'

The gentleman being thus caught in the net they had spread for him, it was now Hero's turn to play her part with Beatrice; and for this purpose she sent for Ursula and Margaret, two gentlewomen who attended upon her, and she said to Margaret: 'Good Margaret, run to the parlour; there you will kind my cousin Beatrice talking with the prince and Claudio. Whisper in her ear, that I and Ursula are walking in the orchard, and that our discourse is all of her. Bid her steal into that pleasant arbour, where honeysuckles, ripened by the sun, like ungrateful minions, forbid the sun to enter.' This arbour, into which Hero desired Margaret to entice Beatrice, was the very same pleasant arbour where Benedick had so lately been an attentive listener.

'I will make her come, I warrant, presently,' said Margaret.

Hero, then taking Ursula with her into the orchard,

said to her: 'Now, Ursula, when Beatrice comes, we will walk up and down this alley, and our talk must be only of Benedick, and when I name him, let it be your part to praise him more than ever man did merit. My talk to you must be how Benedick is in love with Beatrice. Now begin; for look where Beatrice like a lapwing runs close by the ground, to hear our conference.' They then began; Hero saying, as if in answer to something which Ursula had said:

'No, truly, Ursula. She is too disdainful; her spirits are as coy as wild birds of the rock.' 'But are you sure,' said Ursula, 'that Benedick loves Beatrice so entirely?' Hero replied: 'So says the prince, and my lord Claudio, and they entreated me to acquaint her with it; but I persuaded them, if they loved Benedick, never to let Beatrice know of it.'

'Certainly,' replied Ursula, 'it were not good she knew his love, lest she made sport of it.' 'Why, to say truth,' said Hero, 'I never yet saw a man, how wise soever, or noble, young, or rarely featured, but she would dispraise him.' 'Sure, sure, such carping is not commendable,' said Ursula. 'No,' replied Hero, 'but who dare tell her so? If I should speak, she would mock me into air.' 'O! you wrong your cousin,' said Ursula: 'she cannot be so much without true judgment, as to refuse so rare a gentleman as signior Benedick.' 'He hath an excellent good name,' said Hero: 'indeed, he is the first man in Italy, always excepting my dear Claudio.' And now, Hero

giving her attendant a hint that it was time to change the discourse, Ursula said: 'And when are you to be married, madam?' Hero then told her, that she was to be married to Claudio the next day, and desired she would go in with her, and look at some new attire, as she wished to consult with her on what she would wear on the morrow. Beatrice, who had been listening with breathless eagerness to this dialogue, when they went away, exclaimed:

'What fire is in mine ears? Can this be true? Farewell, contempt and scorn, and maiden pride, adieu! Benedick, love on! I will requite you, taming my wild heart to your loving hand.'

It must have been a pleasant sight to see these old enemies converted into new and loving friends, and to behold their first meeting after being cheated into mutual liking by the merry artifice of the good-humoured prince. But a sad reverse in the fortunes of Hero must now be thought of. The morrow, which was to have been her wedding-day, brought sorrow on the heart of Hero and her good father Leonato.

The prince had a half-brother, who came from the wars along with him to

Messina. This brother (his name was Don John) was a melancholy, discontented man, whose spirits seemed to labour in the contriving of villanies. He hated the prince his brother, and he hated Claudio, because he was the prince's friend, and determined to prevent Claudio's marriage with Hero, only for the malicious pleasure of making Claudio and the prince unhappy; for he knew the prince had set his heart upon this marriage, almost as much as Claudio himself; and to effect this wicked purpose, he employed one Borachio, a man as bad as himself, whom he encouraged with the offer of a great reward. This Borachio paid his court to Margaret, Hero's attendant; and Don John, knowing this, prevailed upon him to make Margaret promise to talk with him from her lady's chamber window that night, after Hero was asleep, and also to dress herself in Hero's clothes, the better to deceive Claudio into the belief that it was Hero; for that was the end he meant to compass by this wicked plot.

Don John then went to the prince and Claudio, and told them that Hero was an imprudent lady, and that she talked with men from her chamber window at midnight. Now this was the evening before the wedding, and he offered to take them that night, where they should themselves hear Hero discoursing with a man from her window; and they consented to go along with him, and Claudio said: 'If I see anything to-night why I should not

marry her, to-morrow in the congregation, where I
intended to wed her, there will I shame her.' The prince
also said: 'And as I assisted you to obtain her, I will join
with you to disgrace her.'

When Don John brought them near Hero's chamber
that night, they saw Borachio standing under the window,
and they saw Margaret looking out of Hero's window, and
heard her talking with Borachio: and Margaret being
dressed in the same clothes they had seen Hero wear, the
prince and Claudio believed it was the lady Hero herself.

Nothing could equal the anger of Claudio, when he
had made (as he thought) this discovery. All his love for the
innocent Hero was at once converted into hatred, and he
resolved to expose her in the church, as he had said he
would, the next day; and the prince agreed to this, thinking
no punishment could be too severe for the naughty lady,
who talked with a man from her window the very night
before she was going to be married to the noble Claudio.

The next day, when they were all met to celebrate the
marriage, and Claudio and Hero were standing before the
priest, and the priest, or friar, as he was called, was
proceeding to pronounce the marriage ceremony, Claudio,
in the most passionate language, proclaimed the guilt of
the blameless Hero, who, amazed at the strange words he
uttered, said meekly: 'Is my lord well, that he does speak
so wide?'

Leonato, in the utmost horror, said to the prince: 'My lord, why speak not you?' 'What should I speak?' said the prince; 'I stand dishonoured, that have gone about to link my dear friend to an unworthy woman. Leonato, upon my honour, myself, my brother, and this grieved Claudio, did see and hear her last night at midnight talk with a man at her chamber window.'

Benedick, in astonishment at what he heard, said: 'This looks not like a nuptial.'

'True, O God!' replied the heart-struck Hero; and then this hapless lady sunk down in a fainting fit, to all appearance dead. The prince and Claudio left the church, without staying to see if Hero would recover, or at all regarding the distress into which they had thrown Leonato. So hard-hearted had their anger made them.

Benedick remained, and assisted Beatrice to recover Hero from her swoon, saying: 'How does the lady?'

'Dead, I think,' replied Beatrice in great agony, for she loved her cousin; and knowing her virtuous principles, she believed nothing of what she had heard spoken against her. Not so the poor old father; he believed the story of his child's shame, and it was piteous to hear him lamenting over her, as she lay like one dead before him, wishing she might never more open her eyes.

But the ancient friar was a wise man, and full of observation on human nature, and he had attentively

marked the lady's countenance when she heard herself accused, and noted a thousand blushing shames to start into her face, and then he saw an angel-like whiteness bear away those blushes, and in her eye he saw a fire that did belie the error that the prince did speak against her maiden truth, and he said to the sorrowing father: 'Call me a fool; trust not my reading, nor my observation; trust not my age, my reverence, nor my calling, if this sweet lady lie not guiltless here under some biting error.'

When Hero had recovered from the swoon into which she had fallen, the friar said to her: 'Lady, what man is he you are accused of?' Hero replied: 'They know that do accuse me; I know of none' : then turning to Leonato, she said: 'O my father, if you can prove that any man has ever conversed with me at hours unmeet, or that I yesternight changed words with any creature, refuse me, hate me, torture me to death.'

'There is,' said the friar, 'some strange misunderstanding in the prince and Claudio' ; and then he counselled Leonato, that he should report that Hero was dead; and he said that the death-like swoon in which they had left Hero would make this easy of belief; and he also advised him that he should put on mourning, and erect a monument for her, and do all rites that appertain to a burial. 'What shall become of this?' said Leonato; 'What will this do?' The friar replied: 'This report of her death shall change slander into pity: that is some good; but that is not all the good I hope for. When Claudio shall hear she died upon hearing his words, the idea of her life shall sweetly creep into his imagination. Then shall he mourn, if ever love had interest in his heart, and wish that he had not so accused her; yea, though he thought his accusation true.'

Benedick now said: 'Leonato, let the friar advise you; and though you know how well I love the prince and Claudio, yet on my honour I will not reveal this secret to them.'

Leonato, thus persuaded, yielded; and he said sorrowfully: 'I am so grieved, that the smallest twine may lead me.' The kind friar then led Leonato and Hero away to comfort and console them, and Beatrice and Benedick remained alone; and this was the meeting from which their friends, who contrived the merry plot against them, expected so much diversion; those friends who were now overwhelmed with affliction, and from whose minds all thoughts of merriment seemed for ever banished.

Benedick was the first who spoke, and he said: 'Lady Beatrice, have you wept all this while?' 'Yea, and I will weep a while longer,' said Beatrice. 'Surely,' said Benedick, 'I do believe your fair cousin is wronged.'

'Ah!' said Beatrice, 'how much might that man deserve of me who would right her!' Benedick then said:

'Is there any way to show such friendship? I do love nothing in the world so well as you: is not that strange?'

'It were as possible,' said Beatrice, 'for me to say I loved nothing in the world so well as you; but believe me not, and yet I lie not. I confess nothing, nor I deny nothing. I am sorry for my cousin.' 'By my sword,' said Benedick, 'you love me, and I protest I love you. Come, bid me do anything for you.' 'Kill Claudio,' said Beatrice. 'Ha! not for the wide world,' said Benedick; for he loved his friend Claudio, and he believed he had been imposed upon. 'Is not Claudio a villain, that has slandered, scorned, and dishonoured my cousin?' said Beatrice: 'O that I were a man!' 'Hear me, Beatrice!' said Benedick. But Beatrice would hear nothing in Claudio's defence; and she continued to urge on Benedick to revenge her cousin's wrongs: and she said: 'Talk with a man out of the window; a proper saying! Sweet Hero! she is wronged; she is slandered; she is undone. O that I were a man for Claudio's sake! or that I had any friend, who would be a man for my sake! but valour is melted into courtesies and compliments. I cannot be a man with wishing, therefore I will die a woman with grieving.' 'Tarry, good Beatrice,' said Benedick; 'by this hand I love you.'

'Use it for my love some other way than swearing by it,' said Beatrice. 'Think you on your soul that Claudio has wronged Hero?' asked Benedick. 'Yea,' answered

Beatrice; 'as sure as I have a thought, or a soul.'

'Enough,' said Benedick; 'I am engaged; I will challenge him. I will kiss your hand, and so leave you. By tints hand, Claudio shall render me a dear account! As you hear from me, so think of me. Go, comfort your cousin.'

While Beatrice was thus powerfully pleading with Benedick, and working his gallant temper by the spirit of her angry words, to engage in the cause of Hero, and fight even with his dear friend Claudio, Leonato was challenging the prince and Claudio to answer with their swords the injury they had done his child, who, he affirmed, had died for grief. But they respected his age and his sorrow, and they said: 'Nay, do not quarrel with us, good old man.' And now came Benedick, and he also challenged Claudio to answer with his sword the injury he had done to Hero; and Claudio and the prince said to each other: 'Beatrice has set him on to do this.' Claudio nevertheless must have accepted this challenge of Benedick, had not the justice of Heaven at the moment brought to pass a better proof of the innocence of Hero than the uncertain fortune of a duel.

While the prince and Claudio were yet talking of the challenge of Benedick, a magistrate brought Borachio as a prisoner before the prince. Borachio had been overheard talking with one of his companions of the mischief he had been employed by Don John to do.

Borachio made a full confession to the prince in Claudio's hearing, that it was Margaret dressed in her lady's clothes that he had talked with from the window, whom they had mistaken for the lady Hero herself; and no doubt continued on the minds of Claudio and the prince of the innocence of Hero. If a suspicion had remained it must have been removed by the flight of Don John, who, funding his villanies were detected, fled from Messina to avoid the just anger of his brother.

The heart of Claudio was sorely grieved when he found he had falsely accused Hero, who, he thought, died upon hearing his cruel words; and the memory of his beloved Hero's image came over him, in the rare semblance that he loved it first; and the prince asking him if what he heard did not run like iron through his soul, he answered, that he felt as if he had taken poison while Borachio was speaking.

And the repentant Claudio implored forgiveness of the old man Leonato for the injury he had done his child; and promised, that whatever penance Leonato would lay upon him for his fault in believing the false accusation against his betrothed wife, for her dear sake he would endure it.

The penance Leonato enjoined him was, to marry the next morning a cousin of Hero's, who, he said, was now his heir, and in person very like Hero. Claudio, regarding the solemn promise he made to Leonato, said, he would marry this unknown lady, even though she were an Ethiop: but his heart was very sorrowful, and he passed that night in tears, and in remorseful grief, at the tomb which Leonato had erected for Hero.

When the morning came, the prince accompanied Claudio to the church, where the good friar, and Leonato and his niece, were already assembled, to celebrate a second nuptial; and Leonato presented to Claudio his promised bride; and she wore a mask, that Claudio might not discover her face. And Claudio said to the lady in the mask: 'Give me your hand, before this holy friar; I am your husband, if you will marry me.' 'And when I lived I was your other wife,' said this unknown lady; and, taking off her mask, she proved to be no niece (as was pretended), but Leonato's very daughter, the lady Hero herself. We may be sure that this proved a most agreeable surprise to Claudio, who thought her dead, so that he could scarcely for joy believe his eyes; and the prince, who was equally amazed at what he saw, exclaimed: 'Is not this Hero, Hero that was dead?' Leonato replied: 'She died, my lord, but while her slander lived.' The friar promised them an explanation of this seeming miracle, after the ceremony was ended; and was proceeding to marry them, when he was interrupted by Benedick, who desired to be married at the same time to Beatrice. Beatrice making some demur to

this match, and Benedick challenging her with her love for him, which he had learned from Hero, a pleasant explanation took place; and they found they had both been tricked into a belief of love, which had never existed, and had become lovers in truth by the power of a false jest: but the affection, which a merry invention had cheated them into, was grown too powerful to be shaken by a serious explanation; and since Benedick proposed to marry, he was resolved to think nothing to the purpose that the world could say against it; and he merrily kept up the jest, and swore to Beatrice, that he took her but for pity, and because he heard she was dying of love for him; and Beatrice protested, that she yielded but upon great persuasion, and partly to save his life, for she heard he was in a consumption. So these two mad wits were reconciled, and made a match of it, after Claudio and Hero were married; and to complete the history, Don John, the contriver of the villainy, was taken in his flight, and brought back to Messina; and a brave punishment it was to this gloomy, discontented man, to see the joy and feastings which, by the disappointment of his plots, took place in the palace in Messina.

VI.

HAMLET, PRINCE OF DENMARK

Gertrude, queen of Denmark, becoming a widow by the sudden death of King Hamlet, in less than two months after his death married his brother Claudius, which was noted by all people at the time for a strange act of indiscretion, or unfeelingness, or worse: for this Claudius did no ways resemble her late husband in the qualities of his person or his mind, but was as contemptible in outward appearance, as he was base and unworthy in disposition; and suspicions did not fail to arise in the minds of some, that he had privately made away with his brother, the late king, with the view of marrying his widow, and ascending the throne of Denmark, to the exclusion of young Hamlet, the son of the buried king, and lawful successor to the throne.

But upon no one did this unadvised action of the queen make such impression as upon this young prince, who loved and venerated the memory of his dead father

almost to idolatry, and being of a nice sense of honour, and a most exquisite practicer of propriety himself, did sorely take to heart this unworthy conduct of his mother Gertrude: insomuch that, between grief for his father's death and shame for his mother's marriage, this young prince was overclouded with a deep melancholy, and lost all his mirth and all his good looks; all his customary pleasure in books forsook him, his princely exercises and sports, proper to his youth, were no longer acceptable; he grew weary of the world, which seemed to him an unweeded garden, where all the wholesome flowers were choked up, and nothing but weeds could thrive. Not that the prospect of exclusion from the throne, his lawful inheritance, weighed so much upon his spirits, though that to a young and high-minded prince was a bitter wound and a sore indignity; but what so galled him, and took away all his cheerful spirits, was, that his mother had shown herself so forgetful to his father's memory; and such a father! who had been to her so loving and so gentle a husband! and then she always Appeared as loving and obedient a wife to him, and would hang upon him as if her affection grew to him: and now within two months, or as it seemed to young Hamlet, less than two months, she had married again, married his uncle, her dear husband's brother, in itself a highly improper and unlawful marriage, from the nearness of relationship, but made much more so by the indecent

haste with which it was concluded, and the unkingly character of the man whom she had chosen to be the partner of her throne and bed. This it was, which more than the loss of ten kingdoms, dashed the spirits and brought a cloud over the mind of this honourable young prince.

In vain was all that his mother Gertrude or the king could do to contrive to divert him; he still appeared in court in a suit of deep black, as mourning for the king his father's death, which mode of dress he had never laid aside, not even in compliment to his mother upon the day she was married, nor could he be brought to join in any of the festivities or rejoicings of that (as appeared to him) disgraceful day.

What mostly troubled him was an uncertainty about the manner of his father's death. It was given out by Claudius that a serpent had stung him; but young Hamlet had shrewd suspicions that Claudius himself was the serpent; in plain English, that he had murdered him for his crown, and that the serpent who stung his father did now sit on the throne.

How far he was right in this conjecture, and what he ought to think of his mother, how far she was privy to this murder, and whether by her consent or knowledge, or without, it came to pass, were the doubts which continually harassed and distracted him.

A rumour had reached the ear of young Hamlet, that an apparition, exactly resembling the dead king his father, had been seen by the soldiers upon watch, on the platform before the palace at midnight, for two or three nights successively. The figure came constantly clad in the same suit of armour, from head to foot, which the dead king was known to have worn: and they who saw it (Hamlet's bosom friend Horatio was one) agreed in their testimony as to the time and manner of its appearance: that it came just as the clock struck twelve; that it looked pale, with a face more of sorrow than of anger; that its beard was grisly, and the colour a sable silvered, as they had seen it in his lifetime: that it made no answer when they spoke to it; yet once they thought it lifted up its head, and addressed itself to motion, as if it were about to speak; but in that moment the morning cock crew, and it shrunk in haste away, and vanished out of their sight.

The young prince, strangely amazed at their relation, which was too consistent and agreeing with itself to disbelieve, concluded that it was his father's ghost which they had seen, and determined to take his watch with the soldiers that night, that he might have a chance of seeing it; for he reasoned with himself, that such an appearance did not come for nothing, but that the ghost had something to impart, and though it had been silent hitherto, yet it would speak to him. And he waited with impatience for the coming of night.

When night came he took his stand with Horatio, and Marcellus, one of the guard, upon the platform, where this apparition was accustomed to walk: and it being a cold night, and the air unusually raw and nipping, Hamlet and Horatio and their companion fell into some talk about the coldness of the night, which was suddenly broken off by Horatio announcing that the ghost was coming.

At the sight of his father's spirit, Hamlet was struck with a sudden surprise and fear. He at first called upon the angels and heavenly ministers to defend them, for he knew not whether it were a good spirit or bad; whether it came for good or evil: but he gradually assumed more courage; and his father (as it seemed to him) looked upon him so piteously, and as it were desiring to have conversation with him, and did in all respects appear so like himself as he was when he lived, that Hamlet could not help addressing him: he called him by his name, Hamlet, King, Father! and conjured him that he would tell the reason why he had left his grave, where they had seen him quietly bestowed, to come again and visit the earth and the moonlight: and besought him that he would let them know if there was anything which they could do to give peace to his spirit. And the ghost beckoned to Hamlet, that he should go with him to some more removed place, where they might be alone; and Horatio and Marcellus would have dissuaded the

young prince from following it, for they feared lest it should be some evil spirit, who would tempt him to the neighbouring sea, or to the top of some dreadful cliff, and there put on some horrible shape which might deprive the prince of his reason. But their counsels and entreaties could not alter Hamlet's determination, who cared too little about life to fear the losing of it; and as to his soul, he said, what could the spirit do to that, being a thing immortal as itself? And he felt as hardy as a lion, and bursting from them, who did all they could to hold him, he followed whithersoever the spirit led him.

And when they were alone together, the spirit broke silence, and told him that he was the ghost of Hamlet, his father, who had been cruelly murdered, and he told the manner of it; that it was done by his own brother Claudius, Hamlet's uncle, as Hamlet had already but too much suspected, for the hope of succeeding to his bed and crown. That as he was sleeping in his garden, his custom always in the afternoon, his treasonous brother stole upon him in his sleep, and poured the juice of poisonous henbane into his ears, which has such an antipathy to the life of man, that swift as quicksilver it courses through all the veins of the body, baking up the blood, and spreading a crustlike leprosy all over the skin: thus sleeping, by a brother's hand he was cut off at once from his crown, his queen, and his life: and he adjured Hamlet, if he did ever

his dear father love that he would revenge his foul murder. And the ghost lamented to his son, that his mother should so fall off from virtue, as to prove false to the wedded love of her first husband, and to marry his murderer, but he cautioned Hamlet, howsoever he proceeded in his revenge against his wicked uncle, by no means to act any violence against the person of his mother, but to leave her to heaven, and to the stings and thorns of conscience. And Hamlet promised to observe the ghost's direction in all things, and the ghost vanished.

And when Hamlet was left alone, he took up a solemn resolution, that all he had in his memory, all that he had ever learned by books or observation, should be instantly forgotten by him, and nothing live in his brain but the memory of what the ghost had told him, and enjoined him to do. And Hamlet related the particulars of the conversation which had passed to none but his dear friend Horatio; and he enjoined both to him and Marcellus the strictest secrecy as to what they had seen that night.

The terror which the sight of the ghost had left upon the senses of Hamlet, he being weak and dispirited before, almost unhinged his mind, and drove him beside his reason. And he, fearing that it would continue to have this effect, which might subject him to observation, and set his uncle upon his guard, if he suspected that he was meditating anything against him, or that Hamlet really knew more of his father's death than he professed, took up a strange resolution, from that time to counterfeit as if he were really and truly mad; thinking that he would be less an object of suspicion when his uncle should believe him incapable of any serious project, and that his real perturbation of mind would be best covered and pass concealed under a disguise of pretended lunacy.

From this time Hamlet affected a certain wildness and strangeness in his apparel, his speech, and behaviour, and did so excellently conterfeit the madman, that the king and queen were both deceived, and not thinking his grief for his father's death a sufficient cause to produce such a distemper, for they knew not of the appearance of the ghost, they concluded that his malady was love, and they thought they had found out the object.

Before Hamlet fell into the melancholy way which has been related, he had dearly loved a fair maid called Ophelia, the daughter of Polonius, the king's chief counsellor in affairs of state. He had sent her letters and rings, and made many tenders of his affection to her, and importuned her with love in honourable fashion: and she had given belief to his vows and importunities. But the melancholy which he fell into latterly had made him neglect her, and from the time he conceived the project of counterfeiting madness, he affected to treat her with unkindness, and a sort of rudeness: but she good lady, rather than reproach him with

being false to her, persuaded herself that it was nothing but the disease in his mind, and no settled unkindness, which had made him less observant of her than formerly; and she compared the faculties of his once noble mind and excellent understanding, impaired as they were with the deep melancholy that oppressed him, to sweet bells which in themselves are capable of most exquisite music, but when jangled out of tune, or rudely handled, produce only a harsh and unpleasing sound.

Though the rough business which Hamlet had in hand, the revenging of his father's death upon his murderer, did not suit with the playful state of courtship, or admit of the society of so idle a passion as love now seemed to him, yet it could not hinder but that soft thoughts of his Ophelia would come between, and in one of these moments, when he thought that his treatment of this gentle lady had been unreasonably harsh, he wrote her a letter full of wild starts of passion, and in extravagant terms, such as agreed with his supposed madness, but mixed with some gentle touches of affection, which could not but show to this honoured lady that a deep love for her yet lay at the bottom of his heart. He bade her to doubt the stars were fire, and to doubt that the sun did move, to doubt truth to be a liar, but never to doubt that he loved; with more of such extravagant phrases. This letter Ophelia dutifully showed to her father, and the old man thought himself bound to communicate it to the king and queen, who from that time supposed that the true cause of Hamlet's madness was love. And the queen wished that the good beauties of Ophelia might be the happy cause of his wildness, for so she hoped that her virtues might happily restore him to his accustomed way again, to both their honours.

But Hamlet's malady lay deeper than she supposed, or than could be so cured. His father's ghost, which he had seen, still haunted his imagination, and the sacred injunction to revenge his murder gave him no rest till it was accomplished. Every hour of delay seemed to him a sin, and a violation of his father's commands. Yet how to compass the death of the king, surrounded as he constantly was with his guards, was no easy matter. Or if it had been, the presence of the queen, Hamlet's mother, who was generally with the king, was a restraint upon his purpose, which he could not break through. Besides, the very circumstance that the usurper was his mother's husband filled him with some remorse, and still blunted the edge of his purpose. The mere act of putting a fellow-creature to death was in itself odious and terrible to a disposition naturally so gentle as Hamlet's was. His very melancholy, and the dejection of spirits he had so long been in, produced an irresoluteness and wavering of purpose which kept him from proceeding to extremities. Moreover, he could not help having some scruples upon his mind,

whether the spirit which he had seen was indeed his father, or whether it might not be the devil, who he had heard has power to take any form he pleases, and who might have assumed his father's shape only to take advantage of his weakness and his melancholy, to drive him to the doing of so desperate an act as murder. And he determined that he would have more certain grounds to go upon than a vision, or apparition, which might be a delusion.

While he was in this irresolute mind there came to the court certain players, in whom Hamlet formerly used to take delight, and particularly to hear one of them speak a tragical speech, describing the death of old Priam, King of Troy, with the grief of Hecuba his queen. Hamlet welcomed his old friends, the players, and remembering how that speech had formerly given him pleasure, requested the player to repeat it; which he did in so lively a manner, setting forth the cruel murder of the feeble old king, with the destruction of his people and city by fire, and the mad grief of the old queen, running barefoot up and down the palace, with a poor clout upon that head where a crown had been, and with nothing but a blanket upon her loins, snatched up in haste, where she had worn a royal robe; that not only it drew tears from all that stood by, who thought they saw the real scene, so lively was it represented, but even the player himself delivered it with a broken voice and real tears. This put Hamlet upon thinking, if that player could so work himself up to passion by a mere fictitious speech, to weep for one that he had never seen, for Hecuba, that had been dead so many hundred years, how dull was he, who having a read motive and cue for passion, a real king and a dear father murdered, was yet so little moved, that his revenge all this while had seemed to have slept in dull and muddy forgetfulness! and while he meditated on actors and acting, and the powerful effects which a good play, represented to the life, has upon the spectator, he remembered the instance of some murderer, who seeing a murder on the stage, was by the mere force of the scene and resemblance of circumstances so affected, that on the spot he confessed the crime which he had committed. And he determined that these players should play something like the murder of his father before his uncle, and he would watch narrowly what effect it might have upon him, and from his looks he would be able to gather with more certainty if he were the murderer or not. To this effect he ordered a play to be prepared, to the representation of which he invited the king and queen.

The story of the play was of a murder done in Vienna upon a duke. The duke's name was Gonzago, his wife Baptista. The play showed how one Lucianus, a near relation to the duke, poisoned him in his garden for his estate, and how the murderer in a short time after got the love of Gonzago's wife.

At the representation of this play, the king, who did not know the trap which was laid for him, was present, with his queen and the whole court: Hamlet sitting attentively near him to observe his looks. The play began with a conversation between Gonzago and his wife, in which the lady made many protestations of love, and of never marrying a second husband, if she should outlive Gonzago; wishing she might be accursed if she ever took a second husband, and adding that no woman did so, but those wicked women who kill their first husbands. Hamlet observed the king his uncle change colour at this expression, and that it was as bad as wormwood both to him and to the queen. But when Lucianus, according to the story, came to poison Gonzago sleeping in the garden, the strong resemblance which it bore to his own wicked act upon the late king, his brother, whom he had poisoned in his garden, so struck upon the conscience of this usurper, that he was unable to sit out the rest of the play, but on a sudden calling for lights to his chamber, and affecting or partly feeling a sudden sickness, he abruptly left the theatre. The king being departed, the play was given over. Now Hamlet had seen enough to be satisfied that the words of the ghost were true, and no illusion; and in a fit of gaiety, like that which comes over a man who suddenly has some great doubt or scruple resolved, he swore to Horatio, that he would take the ghost's word for a thousand pounds. But

before he could make up his resolution as to what measures of revenge he should take, now he was certainly informed that his uncle was his father's murderer, he was sent for by the queen his mother, to a private conference in her closet.

It was by desire of the king that the queen sent for Hamlet, that she might signify to her son how much his late behaviour had displeased them both, and the king, wishing to know all that passed at that conference, and thinking that the too partial report of a mother might let slip some part of Hamlet's words, which it might much import the king to know, Polonius, the old counsellor of state, was ordered to plant himself behind the hangings in the queen's closet, where he might unseen hear all that passed. This artifice was particularly adapted to the disposition of Polonius, who was a man grown old in crooked maxims and policies of state, and delighted to get at the knowledge of matters in an indirect and cunning way.

Hamlet being come to his mother, she began to tax him in the roundest way with his actions and behaviour, and she told him that he had given great offence to his father, meaning the king, his uncle, whom, because he had married her, she called Hamlet's father. Hamlet, sorely indignant that she should give so dear and honoured a name as father seemed to him, to a wretch who was indeed no better than the murderer of his true father, with some

sharpness replied: 'Mother, you have much offended my father.' The queen said that was but an idle answer. 'As good as the question deserved,' said Hamlet. The queen asked him if he had forgotten who it was he was speaking to? 'Alas!' replied Hamlet, 'I wish I could forget. You are the queen, your husband's brother's wife; and you are my mother: I wish you were not what you are.' 'Nay, then,' said the queen, 'if you show me so little respect, I will set those to you that can speak,' and was going to send the king or Polonius to him. But Hamlet would not let her go, now he had her alone, till he had tried if his words could not bring her to some sense of her wicked life; and, taking her by the wrist, he held her fast, and made her sit down. She, affrighted at his earnest manner, and fearful lest in his lunacy he should do her a mischief, cried out; and a voice was heard from behind the hangings: 'Help, help, the queen!' which Hamlet hearing, and verily thinking that it was the king himself there concealed, he drew his sword and stabbed at the place where the voice came from, as he would have stabbed a rat that ran there, till the voice ceasing, he concluded the person to be dead. But when he dragged for the body, it was not the king, but Polonius, the old officious counsellor, that had planted himself as a spy behind the hangings. 'Oh me!' exclaimed the queen, 'what a rash and bloody deed have you done!' 'A bloody deed, mother,' replied Hamlet, 'but not so bad

as yours, who killed a king, and married his brother.'
Hamlet had gone too far to leave off here. He was now in
the humour to speak plainly to his mother, and he pursued
it. And though the faults of parents are to be tenderly
treated by their children, yet in the case of great crimes the
son may have leave to speak even to his own mother with
some harshness, so as that harshness is meant for her good,
and to turn her from her wicked ways, and not done for the
purpose of upbraiding. And now this virtuous prince did in
moving terms represent to the queen the heinousness of
her offence, in being so forgetful of the dead king, his
father, as in so short a space of time to marry with his
brother and reputed murderer: such an act as, after the
vows which she had sworn to her first husband was enough
to make all vows of women suspected, and all virtue to be
accounted hypocrisy, wedding contracts to be less than
gamesters' oaths, and religion to be a mockery and a
mere form of words. He said she had done such a deed,
that the heavens blushed at it, and the earth was sick of her
because of it. And he showed her two pictures, the one of
the late king, her first husband, and the other of the
present king, her second husband, and he bade her mark
the difference; what a grace was on the brow of his father,
how like a god he looked! the curls of Apollo, the forehead
of Jupiter, the eye of Mars, and a posture like to Mercury
newly alighted on some heaven-kissing hill! this man, he

said, had been her husband. And then he showed her
whom she had got in his stead: how like a blight or a
mildew he looked, for so he had blasted his wholesome
brother. And the queen was sore ashamed that he should
so turn her eyes inward upon her soul, which she now saw
so black and deformed. And he asked her how she could
continue to live with this man, and be a wife to him, who
had murdered her first husband, and got the crown by as
false means as a thief--and just as he spoke, the ghost of
his father, such as he was in his lifetime, and such as he had
lately seen it, entered the room, and Hamlet, in great terror,
asked what it would have; and the ghost said that it came to
remind him of the revenge he had promised, which Hamlet
seemed to have forgot; and the ghost bade him speak to his
mother, for the grief and terror she was in would else kill
her. It then vanished, and was seen by none but Hamlet,
neither could he by pointing to where it stood, or by any
description, make his mother perceive it; who was terribly
frightened all this while to hear him conversing, as it
seemed to her, with nothing; and she imputed it to the
disorder of his mind. But Hamlet begged her not to flatter
her wicked soul in such a manner as to think that it was his
madness, and not her own offences, which had brought his
father's spirit again on the earth. And he bade her feel his
pulse, how temperately it beat, not like a madman's. And he
begged of her with tears, to confess herself to heaven for

what was past, and for the future to avoid the company of the king, and be no more as a wife to him: and when she should show herself a mother to him, by respecting his father's memory, he would ask a blessing of her as a son. And she promising to observe his directions, the conference ended.

And now Hamlet was at leisure to consider who it was that in his unfortunate rashness he had killed: and when he came to see that it was Polonius, the father of the lady Ophelia, whom he so dearly loved, he drew apart the dead body, and, his spirits being now a little quieter, he wept for what he had done.

The unfortunate death of Polonius gave the king a presence for sending Hamlet out of the kingdom. He would willingly have put him to death, fearing him as dangerous; but he dreaded the people, who loved Hamlet, and the queen who, with all her faults, doted upon the prince, her son. So this subtle king, under presence of providing for Hamlet's safety, that he might not be called to account for Polonius' death, caused him to be conveyed on board a ship bound for England, under the care of two courtiers, by whom he despatched letters to the English court, which in that time was in subjection and paid tribute to Denmark, requiring for special reasons there pretended, that Hamlet should be put to death as soon as he landed on English ground. Hamlet, suspecting some treachery, in the

night-time secretly got at the letters, and skilfully erasing his own name, he in the stead of it put in the names of those two courtiers, who had the charge of him, to be put to death: then sealing up the letters, he put them into their place again. Soon after the ship was attacked by pirates, and a sea-fight commenced; in the course of which Hamlet, desirous to show his valour, with sword in hand singly boarded the enemy's vessel; while his own ship, in a cowardly manner, bore away, and leaving him to his fate, the two courtiers made the best of their way to England, charged with those letters the sense of which Hamlet had altered to their own deserved destruction.

The pirates, who had the prince in their power, showed themselves gentle enemies; and knowing whom they had got prisoner, in the hope that the prince might do them a good turn at court in recompense for any favour they might show him, they set Hamlet on shore at the nearest port in Denmark. From that place Hamlet wrote to the king, acquainting him with the strange chance which had brought him back to his own country, and saying that on the next day he should present himself before his majesty. When he got home, a sad spectacle offered itself the first thing to his eyes.

This was the funeral of the young and beautiful Ophelia, his once dear mistress. The wits of this young lady had begun to turn ever since her poor father's death. That he should die a violent death, and by the hands of the prince whom she loved, so affected this tender young maid, that in a little time she grew perfectly distracted, and would go about giving flowers away to the ladies of the court, and saying that they were for her father's burial, singing songs about love and about death, and sometimes such as had no meaning at all, as if she had no memory of what happened to her. There was a willow which grew slanting over a brook, and reflected its leaves on the stream. To this brook she came one day when she was unwatched, with garlands she had been making, mixed up of daisies and nettles, flowers and weeds together, and clambering up to hang her garland upon the boughs of the willow, a bough broke, and precipitated this fair young maid, garland, and all that she had gathered, into the water, where her clothes bore her up for a while, during which she chanted scraps of old tunes, like one insensible to her own distress, or as if she were a creature natural to that element: but long it was not before her garments, heavy with the wet, pulled her in from her melodious singing to a muddy and miserable death. It was the funeral of this fair maid which her brother Laertes was celebrating, the king and queen and whole court being present, when Hamlet arrived. He knew not what all this show imported, but stood on one side, not inclining to interrupt the ceremony. He saw the flowers strewed upon her grave, as the custom was in maiden burials, which the

queen herself threw in; and as she threw them she said:
'Sweets to the sweet! I thought to have decked thy bride-bed, sweet maid, not to have strewed thy grave. Thou shouldst have been my Hamlet's wife.' And he heard her brother wish that violets might spring from her grave: and he saw him leap into the grave all frantic with grief, and bid the attendants pile mountains of earth upon him, that he might be buried with her. And Hamlet's love for this fair maid came back to him, and he could not bear that a brother should show so much transport of grief, for he thought that he loved Ophelia better than forty thousand brothers. Then discovering himself, he leaped into the grave where Laertes was, all as frantic or more frantic than he, and Laertes knowing him to be Hamlet, who had been the cause of his father's and his sister's death, grappled him by the throat as an enemy, till the attendants parted them: and Hamlet, after the funeral, excused his hasty act in throwing himself into the grave as if to brave Laertes; but he said he could not bear that any one should seem to outgo him in grief for the death of the fair Ophelia. And for the time these two noble youths seemed reconciled.

But out of the grief and anger of Laertes for the death of his father and Ophelia, the king, Hamlet's wicked uncle, contrived destruction for Hamlet. He set on Laertes, under cover of peace and reconciliation, to challenge Hamlet to a friendly trial of skill at fencing, which Hamlet accepting, a day was appointed to try the match. At this match all the court was present, and Laertes, by direction of the king, prepared a poisoned weapon. Upon this match great wagers were laid by the courtiers, as both Hamlet and Laertes were known to excel at this sword play; and Hamlet taking up the foils chose one, not at all suspecting the treachery of Laertes, or being careful to examine Laertes' weapon, who, instead of a foil or blunted sword, which the laws of fencing require, made use of one with a point, and poisoned. At first Laertes did but play with Hamlet, and suffered him to gain some advantages, which the dissembling king magnified and extolled beyond measure, drinking to Hamlet's success, and wagering rich bets upon the issue: but after a few passes, Laertes growing warm made a deadly thrust at Hamlet with his poisoned weapon, and gave him a mortal blow. Hamlet incensed, but not knowing the whole of the treachery, in the scuffle exchanged his own innocent weapon for Laertes' deadly one, and with a thrust of Laertes' own sword repaid Laertes home, who was thus justly caught in his own treachery. In this instant the queen shrieked out that she was poisoned. She had inadvertently drunk out of a bowl which the king had prepared for Hamlet, in case, that being warm in fencing, he should call for drink: into this the treacherous king had infused a deadly poison, to make sure of Hamlet, if Laertes had failed. He had forgotten to warn

the queen of the bowl, which she drank of, and immediately died, exclaiming with her last breath that she was poisoned. Hamlet, suspecting some treachery, ordered the doors to be shut, while he sought it out. Laertes told him to seek no farther for he was the traitor, and feeling his life go away with the wound which Hamlet had given him, he made confession of the treachery he had used, and now he had fallen a victim to it: and he told Hamlet of the envenomed point, and said that Hamlet had not half an hour to live, for no medicine could cure him; and begging forgiveness of Hamlet, he died, with his last words accusing the king of being the contriver of the mischief. When Hamlet saw his end draw near, there being yet some venom left upon the sword, he suddenly turned upon his false uncle, and thrust the point of it to his heart, fulfilling the promise which he had made to his father's spirit, whose injunction was now accomplished, and his foul murder revenged upon the murderer. Then Hamlet, feeling his breath fail and life departing, turned to his dear friend Horatio, who had been spectator of this fatal tragedy; and with his dying breath requested him that he would live to tell his story to the world (for Horatio had made a motion as if he would slay himself to accompany the prince in death), and Horatio promised that he would make a true report, as one that was privy to all the circumstances. And, thus satisfied, the noble heart of Hamlet cracked; and

Horatio and the bystanders with many tears commended the spirit of this sweet prince to the guardianship of angels. For Hamlet was a loving and a gentle prince, and greatly beloved for his many noble and princelike qualities; and if he had lived, would no doubt have proved a most royal and complete king to Denmark.

國家圖書館出版品預行編目資料

羅密歐與茱麗葉（中英雙語典藏版）/ 威廉·莎士比亞（William
Shakespeare）、蘭姆姊弟（Mary and Charles Lamb）著；楊宛
靜繪；張佩雯譯. -- 二版. -- 臺中市：晨星，2023.04
　　面；　公分. --（愛藏本；116）
中英雙語典藏版
譯自：Tales from Shakespeare
ISBN 978-626-320-379-2（精裝）

873.596　　　　　　　　　　　　　　　　112000833

愛藏本：116

羅密歐與茱麗葉（中英雙語典藏版）
Romeo and Juliet

填寫線上回函，立刻享有
晨星網路書店50元購書金

作　　者｜廉·莎士比亞（William Shakespeare）、
　　　　　蘭姆姊弟（Mary and Charles Lamb）
繪　　者｜楊宛靜
譯　　者｜張佩雯

責任編輯｜呂曉婕
執行編輯｜江品如
封面設計｜鐘文君
美術編輯｜黃偵瑜
文字校潤｜呂昀慶、江品如

創 辦 人｜陳銘民
發 行 所｜晨星出版有限公司
　　　　　407 台中市西屯區工業 30 路 1 號 1 樓
　　　　　TEL：04-23595820　FAX：04-23550581
　　　　　https://star.morningstar.com.tw
　　　　　行政院新聞局局版台業字第 2500 號
法律顧問｜陳思成律師

讀者專線｜TEL：02-23672044 / 04-2359-5819#212
傳真專線｜FAX：02-23635741 / 04-23595493
讀者信箱｜service@morningstar.com.tw
網路書店｜https://www.morningstar.com.tw
郵政劃撥｜15060393　知己圖書股份有限公司

初版日期｜2002 年 09 月 30 日
二版日期｜2023 年 04 月 01 日
　ISBN｜978-626-320-379-2
　定價｜新台幣 280 元

印　　刷｜上好印刷股份有限公司